A Hidden Gem

Scottish Island Escapes

Book 7

MARGARET AMATT

Margaret Amatt x

Cover designed by Margaret Amatt
Map drawn by Margaret Amatt
ISBN: 978-1-914575-86-0
An eBook is also available: 978-1-914575-87-7

LEANNAN
PRESS
INDEPENDENT PUBLISHER

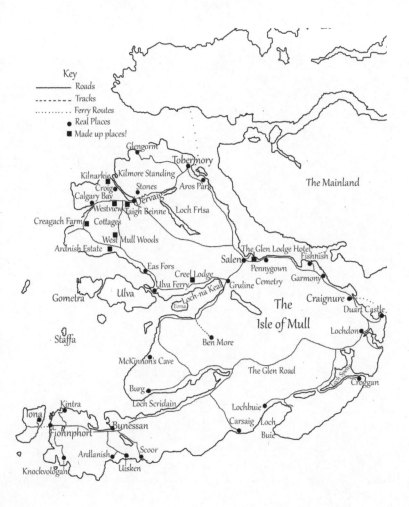

Key

—————— Roads

– – – – – Tracks

· · · · · · · · · Ferry Routes

● Real Places

■ Made up places!

Glengorm

Tobermory

The Mainland

Kilnarkie
Kilmore Standing
Croig
Stones
Aros Park
Calgary Bay
Dervaig
Westview
Taigh Beinne
Loch Frisa
Creagach Farm
Cottages
West Mull Woods
Ardnish Estate
The Glen Lodge Hotel
Eas Fors
Salen
Fishnish
Creel Lodge
Pennygown
Garmony
Ulva Ferry
Cemetry
Loch-na Keal
Gruline
Craignure
Gometra
Ulva
Eorsa
Duart Castle
Staffa
The
Isle of Mull
Lochdon
Ben More
McKinnon's Cave
The Glen Road
Burg
Loch Scridain
Croggan
Kintra
Lochbuie
Iona
Carsaig
Loch
Bunessan
Buie
Fionnphort
Ardlanish
Scoor
Knockvologan
Uisken

For friends who make the world go round.

Prologue

Rebekah

The cart shook on the bumpy track. Wind bit and the rain clung to the fibres of my shawl. I shivered and peered up at the figure shrouded in black, steering the pony deeper into the mist. Where were we going?

Rebekah got out of her car and bit her lip, the mysterious words swirling round her head. She almost pinched herself. The view was like something from a dream, not the cold dreary image the words from her grandmother's old photograph conjured, but a tranquil beach, waves rushing to the shore, a little ferry dotting back and forward to the Isle of Iona just opposite. Bright blue sky sprawled overhead, reminding her of the day she'd walked away from the High Court in Accra rather than the grim visions she'd had since finding that faded old photo. That, along with her grandmother's dying words, had occupied her mind so much she'd almost forgotten to be thankful for being free. Her heart flipped. *I'm free. Free. That's what matters.*

And she was here, in Fionnphort, a tiny village at the south end of the Scottish Isle of Mull, a place she hadn't even heard of a few months ago.

'Hi. Pleased to meet you in person,' said a tall, dark-haired man, adjusting the lapels on his dark blazer and stepping up to meet her, his hand outstretched. 'I'm Calum.'

'Hi, Calum. Rebekah.' She shook his hand. *Hmm, he's younger than he sounded on the phone, my age perhaps, mid-thirties at most.* Her eyes travelled over his shoulder to a small stone building with scaffolding close to the door. The modern roof looked too new; thatching would have suited better. With a slight frown, Rebekah held on to Calum's hand, and her mind wandered. Would it be an enormous coincidence if this croft was *the* croft? Had the girl in the picture lived here? Could the words also belong to this place?

'I'm sorry the croft isn't completely finished,' said Calum, removing his hand from her grip.

'Oh. It's not a problem.' Had he misread her expression? She hadn't meant to look in two minds about the croft but all the mysteries had her mind buzzing. 'I agreed to it.' *I would have agreed to anything to get a house here.* Answers were here, she was certain.

'So, you're in the property business,' he said, unlocking the door. 'Are you going to be working from here or are you on a break?'

'No,' said Rebekah swiftly, adjusting the toothed headband holding back her thick black curls and ducking into the croft. She didn't need a break, she needed to work. Throwing herself into a job would be the quickest way to forget the past year. 'I'm hoping to do some property flipping.' An old school friend had suggested the idea and it might be exactly what she needed. And why not start here in the place that had plagued her thoughts for the last few months?

Calum pushed open a door at the other side of the living area. Rebekah tried to take it all in. Unfinished walls surrounded a compact open-plan kitchen and sitting area. At the far end, French doors opened into a modern garden room. She'd like to look at that but Calum was indicating she should follow him.

'The bedrooms are in the new extension through here,' he said. 'One of them is ready. Jesus!' He jumped back and collided with Rebekah. A loud clattering resonated through the small hallway.

'What happened?'

'Sorry,' he said. 'I think Blair's booby-trapped the place.' Stooping, he picked up a long metal pole and propped it against the wall. 'I'll tell him to make sure stuff like this isn't left lying about.'

Maybe agreeing to live in an unfinished building wasn't the smartest move after all. The finished bedroom looked clean and tidy but the spare room was barely more than a shell. What would it be like trying to work here with some bumbling old builder hanging about, leaving equipment left, right and centre, and getting under her feet?

'Here's Blair now,' said Calum, returning to the main living area. 'I'll have a word in his ear. I don't like the idea of anyone living like this. Property is my business too and this doesn't make me happy.'

'Believe me, I've seen worse,' said Rebekah. Years working for an international aid agency had shown her some dreadful conditions. This old croft was a step up from the conditions the little girl in her dreams had known and far better than the prison cell Rebekah had very nearly landed in.

There was a knock on the door and it opened. A man put his head around and Rebekah's stomach did a one-eighty. He stepped in with a crooked grin, running his hand over an impressive set of blond dreadlocks. Rebekah swallowed. This wasn't the middle-aged man with a string vest and builder's backside she'd imagined. No. The space-time continuum had ruptured and a young Viking warrior

9

had emerged: muscly and broad-shouldered with rugged fair skin and tattoos.

Rebekah sucked in her lower lip as he gazed at her and rubbed his hand over his mouth.

'This is Rebekah,' said Calum.

'Hi.' She couldn't wrench her eyes from the joiner; her heart was doing manic summersaults. Coming face to face with this man every few minutes was going to be so awkward if he had this effect on her heart rate.

'Hi, I'm Blair, the joiner, minion and general dogsbody.' He dusted his palms together before reaching out.

'Pleased to meet you.' Rebekah took his hand; his skin was rough but his handshake warm and friendly.

Here she was shaking hands with a man who was sending her pulse rocketing when that kind of thing was exactly what she was trying to avoid. *I don't need any entanglements, especially with someone who's going to be working here.* Hopefully Blair was happily in a relationship and that would be that; she could focus her mind on the important things. Her eyes strayed to Calum. Was he single too? He seemed like a nice guy with classic good looks – on paper, he was definitely someone she'd like. He gave her a half smile but it didn't have the effect Blair's look was causing.

What was she thinking? She'd come to the end of the earth to work and to find answers in peace and solitude. Complications were not required; she'd had enough of them to last a lifetime. All she wanted was to throw herself into her new idea and solve the mysteries that had burned their way into her soul.

So much had happened to bring her here… to the most unlikely place imaginable. It had all started just after the not guilty verdict, some three months ago in March when she'd been called to her grandmother's deathbed…

Chapter One

Three months earlier

Rebekah

Rebekah glanced around the terminal and darted ahead of a dawdling couple. The automatic doors swished open and she pulled up the collar of her white wool coat, marching towards the baggage reclaim area. The bustle of Heathrow was an easy place to blend in and keep her head down. She wished she had a pair of sunglasses to hide behind. Who did she think she was? A celebrity? *Hardly*. Any fame she'd won over the last year was nothing to shout about. No one here would recognise her, surely.

Ten days after the end of the trial, she still woke up in cold sweats, panicking about how different life could have been if Seth Eastman had got away with his plans and thrown her down in his place. Thank god the Ghanaian justice system had pulled through and he was now serving jail time for embezzlement. She should be celebrating walking free but shame and fear still festered inside. *I didn't do it. I did nothing wrong.* The words played over and over like an affirming message on a Post-it note attached to her forehead. The only mistake she'd made was to trust Seth. His attentions had been nothing but a backup plan to ensure he had a scapegoat in case he got caught; Rebekah had nearly taken the fall.

'Oh god.' She shuddered as she lifted her case from the carousel. How idiotic had she been? Sleeping with her manager had been stupid, she'd known it from the start but she hadn't listened to herself. Nine years of hard work, and for what? That cheat. At least she was free. She clung to that.

CEO Carmen Wells had offered to reinstate Rebekah, but she couldn't face it. The idea of entering that building again made her nauseous. Carmen's words hadn't filled her with confidence; at their last meeting, she'd mentioned it might be too compromising to resume her old job and offered her a new start elsewhere. Rebekah couldn't help feeling Carmen subscribed to the 'no smoke without fire' belief. Maybe she was just being paranoid but she needed to find a new direction and soon.

This London trip presented her with a bona fide excuse not to make any decisions about her future, no matter how sad its true purpose, and it put space between her and Seth Eastman. Behind bars or not, she wanted him far away. She loved Ghana and her life there but change was blowing on the wind.

Keeping her head down, she didn't make eye contact with anyone as she hastened through the airport. If she'd trusted her gut last year, she'd have reported the inconsistencies in the accounts straight away, instead of telling Seth and giving him the chance to cover his tracks and implicate her. It'd been there for her to make the connection but she hadn't. She'd believed his lies.

She grabbed a black coffee and inhaled its deep aroma like it was the breath of life. Caffeine fuelled her existence at the moment. It couldn't be good for her. She hadn't slept more than a few hours at a time for a year, hardly surprising with her gargantuan coffee intake and everything that had happened. Friends and family kept reminding her it was over and she could relax, but it wasn't that easy.

Her heart hurt as she moved along the line of cabs.

'Rosepark Nursing Home in Greenwich, please,' she told the driver. He nipped out and helped load her case in the boot. The streets of London passed by in the pale March sunshine. Familiar buildings came into view and the weight on her chest lifted. The Thames was busy with tour boats as they sped across a bridge.

Soon they were passing the Cutty Sark, the domed Royal Observatory and the cobbled streets of the village Rebekah had such fond memories of. How often she'd come back from boarding school for the holidays and spent hot summers' days walking those streets, browsing the boutiques, eating cake with her grandmother in an on-street café or reading on a picnic blanket stretched out on the green park in front of the National Maritime Museum. Sometimes she'd spent more time watching the passers-by than concentrating on her books.

Daffodils swayed in the garden of the Rosepark Nursing Home, and Rebekah sighed as she collected her case and paid the cabby. The pretty scenery mocked what was happening behind the shiny glass doors. In there, a woman was dying: a woman who'd been so strong, who Rebekah had looked up to. She'd been a pinnacle of strength who knew what she'd wanted in life and got it. In some ways, Rebekah was glad her grandmother hadn't been well enough to learn about the past year's events. How could she have borne the shame through the trial? As a woman from an upstanding family, her grandmother wouldn't have understood. It would have destroyed her to think her granddaughter was in any way connected with criminality – innocent or not.

Dread gnawed at Rebekah as she turned off her mobile and shoved it into the pocket of her coat. The doors to the wide foyer opened, ushering her in.

'Hello.' She stepped up to the reception desk. 'I'm here to visit Elsie Quinn. She's my grandmother.'

'Of course.' The receptionist stood and placed an open book on the shelf in front of Rebekah. 'If you'll sign in, please.'

Rebekah signed and waited for a staff member to pass by, pushing a resident in a wheelchair, before heading into the corridor. She held the handrail, supporting the emotional weight pressing on her. Soft music and indistinct TV noises came from behind closed doors as she walked by.

Rebekah crept into the room, inhaling a waft of strong cleaning fluid. Her mother, Cheryl, glanced up from the bedside, her elegant fingers stroking the wizened old knuckles of Rebekah's grandmother. Rebekah closed the door quietly and took the few short steps across the carpet. She fingered the leather strap of her bag, letting the softness soothe a surge of bitter sadness. A white blanket shrouded the old woman's frail body, barely contrasting her deathly white skin.

A neat flower arrangement sat on the clinical cabinet beside a lamp and a water glass. On the ceiling was a pulley and Rebekah sucked her lips tight between her teeth at the thought of her poor grandmother being hoisted into bed. This was exactly what Elsie Quinn had dreaded all her life: losing her faculties and being locked up – as she referred to it – yet here she was. Rebekah had escaped prison but her grandmother was lodged in a different cell.

'How is she?' she asked, setting her case at the foot of the bed and inching closer.

'As well as can be expected,' said Cheryl. Rebekah leaned over and gave her mother a cursory peck on the cheek before scrutinising her grandmother. Her heart shrank and tears welled as she contemplated the cruelty of old age.

'It's good to see you, darling,' said her mother. 'I just wish things were different.'

'Me too.'

Her grandmother had been there for her through tough times. As an eleven year old, Rebekah had been sent almost five thousand miles from Kumasi to an English boarding school. She raised her fingers to her lips, recalling how she'd bitten the skin beside her nails until it bled, worrying if she would fit in, not knowing what it would be like, wondering how she would survive without the constant care she'd had from their team of servants in her father's home. Her grandmother being close by had been the only thing that had stopped her from having a full-on panic attack when she'd arrived in London those twenty years ago.

'Hello, Grandmother.' Rebekah peered at the old lady. Glassy blue eyes stared back from the paper-like face. Could she hear or see anything?

'She hasn't said much for the last couple of days and when she does, it's hard to make out what she's talking about. Some of it's just nonsense.' Cheryl got to her feet and placed the old lady's skeletal hand back under the covers. She sidled to the window and ran her fingers through her shiny chestnut bob. Her tall, lithe figure and easy elegance was a throwback to her modelling days and, if she wanted to, she could still grace the pages of a magazine in her pink cashmere sweater and white skinny jeans. 'Can you sit with her for a while? I could do with a break. I thought Tim might come round.'

'Yes, of course. How is Uncle Tim?' Rebekah took the seat by the bedside and stared at her grandmother.

'Busy,' said Cheryl, taking out a comb and running it through her sleek bob while examining her reflection in the small mirror. 'Isn't he always?'

'Yes.' Rebekah's answer was robotic; she couldn't tear her attention from her grandmother. The old woman's frail hand contrasted against Rebekah's warm brown skin. Rebekah stroked her grandmother's bony knuckles. How had this happened? How had someone so strong and determined got so weak and lost?

'And, er, how's your father?' asked Cheryl. 'We spoke after the trial, you know...'

Rebekah swallowed. She'd kept her mother up to date with everything via messages and brief phone calls. Now they were face-to-face, she didn't want to meet her mother's eyes or talk about it. 'He's well.' She didn't elaborate. Cheryl asked out of politeness. How could Rebekah tell her that all Peter Yeboah wanted in his life was his wife back? Without her, he'd never be quite himself again. It wasn't something Rebekah felt able to say. Cheryl was happy being divorced and back in London with her friends and family; she'd never go back. She'd made that clear a long time ago.

'Good. Listen, I think I'll go and get a coffee. Do you want anything?' said Cheryl.

'I'll have coffee too, please.' Though she probably shouldn't.

Cheryl gathered her expensive coat and leather bag and Rebekah sat in silence, frowning slightly as she gazed at her grandmother. After a few long minutes, she took off her coat and slung it over the back of the seat. The rest of her outfit comprised a black polo neck and skinny black three-quarter trousers with kitten-heeled boots. *Oh no, I*

16

look dressed for a funeral. Her shoulders slumped a further notch.

'I'm not sure if you can hear me, but it feels awkward being silent,' she said. 'I remember you telling me all sorts of things when I was younger.' She gave a wry smile. Elsie had never forgiven her daughter for marrying a Ghanaian man and, worse, deciding to stay in Ghana rather than return to England. She got her wish sixteen years ago when they'd divorced. Cheryl had come home and never looked back.

'I know you were uncertain about me returning to Ghana after I left university, but I'm glad I did,' Rebekah told her. 'I don't regret it.' No, even with the horror of the past year, she couldn't discount the wonderful schemes and projects she'd been part of. 'I wish I'd been able to spend more time with you.'

Her grandmother twitched and made an odd little noise.

'Are you all right?' Rebekah adjusted her covers, making sure she was warm.

Her grandmother didn't reply but closed her eyes.

'I spent so much time with Nanabaa and Nanabarima,' Rebekah continued. 'They told me lots of stories.' Her father's parents were both gone too and the bonds to the past were about to snap further. So much was lost when an elder died. Once her grandmother was gone, that whole generation of their family would be nothing but memories. 'I've always loved how my parents each have a different heritage. It's given me such insight into people.'

'You don't know anything about me,' her grandmother croaked.

Rebekah blinked rapidly and leaned in closer. The old woman's voice came as a shock.

'Don't I?' Perhaps it was true. She struggled to think if she knew anything beyond her grandmother, grandfather, her mother and uncle Tim. She knew all about her nanabaa and nanabarima. Their stories were the lifeblood of her childhood. She'd scribbled them down and had notes and documents from her father. One day she wanted to organise it and write it properly, so the histories weren't lost for future generations. Though when that day would come, she didn't know. Her mind was too full of other things.

'No.' Elsie coughed and looked like she was trying to sit up but she could barely move.

Rebekah frowned and shook her head. 'Lie still, Grandmother.' She adjusted her blanket again. 'Why don't you tell me now? I'd like to hear.' A rush of sadness flooded her. Why hadn't she asked before? How had the subject never come up? Or had it been avoided?

'My diamond necklace,' croaked Grandmother. 'I told your mother but she didn't listen. I don't know where it is but you need to find it.'

Rebekah tried to follow her grandmother's wandering thoughts. 'It must be in the safe.'

'I want you to have it, it'll suit your beautiful long neck, but it's not mine to give.'

'Isn't it?'

'No.' Her grandmother's eyes closed and Rebekah leaned forward as ice-cold dread trickled over her shoulders. *Is she dead?* Just as Rebekah lifted the old woman's wrist to check for a pulse, she whispered, 'I stole it.'

'Pardon?'

'From my cousin.' Elsie gripped the bedcover with her bony fingers. 'I think she's long dead now.'

'When was this?'

'Years ago. In the war.'

Rebekah slid the chair forward. 'The war?' she repeated.

'I shouldn't have taken it, but I didn't know how valuable it was. I thought I was saving it. She wouldn't ever have cause to wear it. The place was so poor, her clothes were so old.'

'Your cousin?'

'When I met him, your grandfather,' Elsie continued, not heeding Rebekah's interruption, 'he guessed it was valuable.' The old woman gave a little cough, her eyes roaming about unfocused. 'I told him it was a family heirloom, that pleased him. When I had it valued, I couldn't believe it. He wouldn't have married me had it not been for that necklace.'

'Why?'

'Status, child. Why else? He thought if I had money enough to be wearing jewellery like that about every day, then there must be more money.'

'And there wasn't?'

'No. We had money but not as much as that.' Elsie grabbed Rebekah's hand and her tight grip challenged her fragile appearance. 'I should never have taken it. She needed it more than me. She wrote to me years later asking if I'd taken it by accident; she couldn't think where it could have gone. How could I tell her? My husband had it locked in a safe.'

'What did you do?'

'Ignored her letters. I never replied. I'd promised she could visit and I'd introduce her to London once the war was over, but I didn't. I shut her out. I forgot who I was. I've been hiding for over sixty years.'

Rebekah stared at her grandmother. The wrinkled old face was now a top sheet hiding six decades' worth of secrets. 'No, Grandmother. I think you've got mixed up; maybe you should rest.' She meant it, but her pulse was thumping fast. Grandmother needed to wake up in a talkative mood because Rebekah wanted answers. It was just the deluded ramblings of an old forgetful lady, right?

'I was a foolish child and terribly homesick in a foreign place. I regret it now. I want you to have the necklace. You're the one who can put things right.'

'But, Grandmother…'

'Please, do it. The necklace gave me status I didn't deserve and I can't forgive myself for taking it. Use it to do good, my girl.'

'I'll try.'

The old woman's eyes closed, and Rebekah's heart froze.

'Grandmother.' She leaned forward, snatching her wrist.

Too late. Instinct told her Elsie Quinn was dead.

An overwhelming sense of loss barrelled through her. The pain at losing Seth now seemed nothing but a tiny shard of glass from a shattered vase. He'd crushed her by using her as a pawn in his criminality, but Grandmother's confession had ripped the heart from her and an invisible boot had trampled on it. How could a woman with such scruple have been a thief? Utter confusion drowned Rebekah. Who was this body lying before her? The hollow shell that moments ago had contained the beating heart and living soul of her grandmother? How could Rebekah put things right when she didn't know where to start?

Chapter Two

Blair

Blair lowered his head and barged into the wind. Forty-mile-an-hour gusts roared from the wide-open beach, carrying sand up the steep embankment and over the lane. May wasn't usually this stormy but weather here was completely unpredictable.

'Christ,' muttered Blair, drawing his zip right up, using his broad shoulders to thrust forward. Wind was common on the Isle of Mull, and with twenty-six years of life on the island to brag about, Blair had known blustery days, but this was something else. The tide crashed across the flat sand towards a monolith of stone cracked down the middle by an act of god. A god. Thor with Mjölnir, his thunder hammer? Blair smirked at the idea, racing to the end of the lane where it struck the main road. Down the hill was a small harbour and jetty where the ferry took off for Iona. The black and white ship sat at anchor, dipping up and down. No sailings today. This was the village of Fionnphort at its most tempestuous.

Blair strode over the road and into the shop, slamming the door shut on the angry blasts and ran his hands over his head, wiping excess water from his blond dreadlocks. He grabbed a basket and picked up a few bread rolls, ignoring the handmade sandwiches, expensive cheeses, and the rumbling in his stomach. His wages didn't run to anything beyond the basics. He'd crafted a tight physique from forced fasting and a few snatched moments pumping iron, but right now he could murder a bag of fish and chips.

After bundling his purchases into a carrier bag, he braced himself before stepping outside. A chill gust whipped the breath from him. He jogged up the road, his cheeks stinging. His dreads slapped his shoulders as they buffeted around. The croft he was working on was a two-minute walk but with the wind pushing him back, it was like skiing uphill. Ahead on the lane was a stooped and tiny old lady, pulling an old-fashioned tartan shopping trolley. *Poor woman.* One more gust and she'd be bowled over. Her frame was so wispy; *how's she managing to stay upright?* The lane wound in a short path to the tumbledown croft where Blair had downed tools for lunch. Only a few houses remained between it and the road, so wherever the old lady was going, wasn't far. A colossal blast howled across the low hillside, knocking the bristly bushes and the tufty grass flat in its wake. The old woman wobbled, grabbing her clear plastic hood and clinging to it. Blair bolted towards her as the wind sent her trolley flying. The contents scattered across the lane; some tins rolled to the edge and were blown down the bushy verge towards the beach.

'Oh no... No.' She let out a desperate cry, turning her back to the persistent puffs and being shoved forward in its powerful wake. Her words were carried off like butterflies in a hurricane.

'Hey, it's ok.' Blair stepped in front of her, preventing her from being blown off the edge; his broad shoulders shielded her. She froze, blinking rapidly as her gaze ran over him. Blair rubbed the back of his thick neck – he probably looked intimidating with his long hair, unshaven jaw and scruffy clothes.

The woman's thin lips trembled as she stooped towards a bagged loaf of bread on the ground before her. Her fingertips were a hair's breadth from it. 'I've made an awful mess. And, oh dear. I can't bend. The mind is willing but these old bones aren't.'

'Hey, don't worry, I'll get it.' Blair picked up the bread and grabbed the overturned trolley. 'If you hold on to that, I'll get the other things.' He dropped his own bag and picked up the scattered items, packing them in her trolley. She clung to the handle and peered out from under the clear plastic head-covering tied beneath her chin; it flapped wildly. Her wrinkled forehead creased even more as she peered at him. Blair smiled and nipped down the embankment to collect the tins that had rolled away. 'Which one is your house? I'll see you get in ok.'

'Oh, I eh… Are you sure?'

'Of course. I'm working at the croft at the end, so it's on my way.'

'Oh.' She braced herself as another gust roared up from the beach. 'Just along here, the one with the blue door.'

'Do you want me to take that?' He pointed at her trolley.

'I think it's keeping me on the ground,' she said. 'If I let go again, I might take off.'

Blair grinned. 'Yeah, I wondered.'

'It was silly of me to come out,' she shouted over the wind. 'But I've been putting it off for days. I've barely a scrap left in the house.' She hobbled along and Blair stayed his pace, shielding her and keeping in step.

'Yeah, that's not so good. But you're nearly home and no harm done.'

'Just as well you came along.' She blinked, as if she wasn't sure he was real. 'I've never had a rescue like that and I'm eighty-three.'

Blair laughed as they reached the door. 'Well, let's hope you don't need another one. But if you do need anything, just nip along and give me a shout, it's closer than going to the shop and I don't mind.'

'Oh, that's very kind. The lad next door is usually good at helping me get bits and pieces, but this was a bit much, you know what I mean?'

'Sure.'

'He's just a boy, he helps out and I give him a pound to get a sweetie, but it's not fair for him to do the weekly shop.'

'Too right.' Blair couldn't agree more. When he'd been growing up, his family wouldn't have had a weekly shop if he hadn't done it. Not the nicest way to spend his teenage years.

'And what's your name?' she asked.

'Blair.'

'Well, Blair, thank you. I'm Mary.'

'Cool, nice to meet you.' He lifted her trolley into her little hallway and left with a wave.

Only one other white-washed house separated her home from the shabby old croft. If Blair had the cash, he'd love this old place for himself but it didn't seem likely in his lifetime. He just had to get the work done and quickly. Though nothing was ever quick enough for his boss, Calum *everyone-else-is-a-slacker* Matheson.

After scoffing his crappy lunch, he took up his saw and started heaving it back and forward. Cool air hung around the draughty room and the wind whistled under the rickety old door.

An engine rumbled outside and Blair wiped a layer of sweat from his brow with his forearm. Calum's weekly site inspection? *He picks his moments.* Blair scanned around. The place was a tip, covered in sawdust, woodchips, tools, and planks. Work had reached the stage where it had to look a whole lot worse before it got better, and Calum hated that.

'What a wind,' muttered Calum, shouldering the door shut. His piercing eyes scanned the musty stone walls and the carnage on the floor. He rubbed the dark facial hair on his pointy chin.

'Yeah. It's hideous out there,' Blair agreed.

'So, how are you getting on? Still on track?'

Blair dropped his saw and wiped his forehead with the back of his rough hand. 'There's no way.' Honesty was the best policy, even if Calum wouldn't like it. 'I can't see this place being finished in six months, never mind three.' And definitely not one, which was what Calum was hoping for.

'You think? That could be a problem.' Calum pocketed his mobile in his slick blazer pocket. Everything about his smart demeanour was at odds with the mess of the old but 'n' ben-style stone croft.

Blair grimaced and ran his hand across his tattoo-covered biceps. 'Why?'

'I've been chatting to a woman who needs a place to stay for the next six months and her heart's set on Fionnphort. There's nowhere else available for that length of time, so I offered her the croft.'

'What?' He had to be kidding, right? Why would he do something so stupid? 'When is she coming?'

'Next month, so there's a while yet.'

Blair looked away to hide his eyeroll and gritted his teeth. 'There's no way I can finish it in a month.'

'Sorry, mate. This is obviously a big undertaking for one person. I could call in someone else. This is your first big job. I suspect a more experienced joiner would be able to get it done quicker.'

Blair didn't reply but picked up his saw. *Yup, I'm newly qualified, ergo cheap.* Calum's barely veiled threat was clear. *Get this done in the time I want or I'll replace you with someone more competent.*

'Sure,' said Blair, placing the joist on the bench and positioning it with the knee protruding from his ripped jeans. 'But nothing ever moves as quickly as customers want in the building trade. I already waited several months to get in here.' He couldn't conceal the bitter edge to his tone.

'Yeah, that's true,' said Calum. His dark eyebrows knitted together as he peered out an unframed window. A hefty gust howled past and he reeled back. 'But don't worry about being here when she arrives, the woman is cool with the work going on around her.'

'Right. That's all very well, but it's not fit to live in. Where's she gonna be? Sleeping on a floor with no kitchen, no toilet?'

'My plan is to get the essentials in, then you do the rest while she's there.'

Blair let out a sigh. What was the point of arguing? Calum wouldn't change his mind. He never did, even if what he was asking was impossible.

'Thanks, Blair,' said Calum. 'You're a lifesaver. I'll take you for a drink sometime.'

'Sure.' He braced himself. *Seriously?*

Once the work was done and the place transformed into Calum's vision of a studio-style house with an open-plan living and kitchen area, then it would be worth something. Calum could inflate his bank balance some more by renting it to another incomer while islanders like Blair were left slumming it. But no one could live in it just now. It may have a sublime Hebridean location at the island's south end, with views to die for, but it hadn't been built to modern standards or with any guarantees. Still, it was considered a building of historical importance. Blair had listened to several of Calum's rants on the subject. On the one hand, he wanted to keep its character, but the cost was a different matter, not to mention the planning constraints. Just getting its foundations safe had been a trial. Blair's contract had been held up for weeks while he waited to hear from Calum that the foundations were secure. The bills didn't stop however. He'd given up his tiny flat in Tobermory to finance buying a van and was now bunking in a caravan on a nearby farm.

'What's still to be done in here?' Calum asked, looking into the extension.

'Plasterboard, flooring, fitted cupboards, window frames, doors, doorframes, skirting boards...' Should he go on? The list was endless. When added to a state-of-the-art kitchen and bespoke fire centrepiece in the main area, it mounted up.

'Wow.' Calum rubbed his brow and let out a sigh as he returned to the room, closing the door on the extension.

'I thought you'd want quality, not speed,' said Blair. 'I can do everything here but I don't want to build a reputation for sloppy work. If you want things done to your specifications, I need time. If not, feel free to hire someone else. You're the boss.'

Yup, Blair was the minion and didn't he know it. Calum slung his hands into his pockets and frowned at the mess. Blair waited for the blow.

'It's looking good,' said Calum. Blair almost lopped off his finger in shock. 'Just keep it up, and hopefully by the time Rebekah arrives it'll be habitable.'

'Right.' Blair flicked out his dreads, squinting at Calum. Calum couldn't be more than six or seven years older than him but somehow he'd made enough money to buy properties all around the island. *How?* Blair grimaced at the bare stone wall. *If only I knew.*

The croft's rickety door rattled, and Blair grabbed another piece of wood. The afternoon dragged. Blair liked company and working in this cold shell alone was dull. But what could he do about it? If he was after a friend, he had loads. Friends were easy to come by. Other relationships not so much. He snorted. Hardly surprising, he didn't have much to offer long-term.

Darkness closed in as he made his way home, his van swaying in the wind. Would he get a wink of sleep? The caravan might not last the night. Set on the edge of a farm behind Fionnphort, it looked like one heavy blast would topple it. Not far off were a couple more modern static caravans the farmer let to tourists. A basic toilet and shower cubicle, the farmer was forever promising to update, stood between the statics and Blair's caravan. It was like living a hundred years in the past. Visiting a toilet in an outhouse during stormy nights was horrific. How had people survived living on this island for so many centuries?

He braved the toilet block with his torch before setting foot in the caravan, because once he was in, he wasn't coming back out. Showering in the tepid water was even more daring when it felt like the building might collapse at any moment. When he couldn't take any more, he wrapped his hoody around his waist and dashed for the caravan door. Once he'd jammed it shut and grabbed a towel, he put on his little radiator and set the kettle to boil. A stream of messages flashed on his phone screen.

Autumn, Dad, Georgia, Mum, Archie. Blair blew out a breath and skimmed through them. Most of them were funny gifs, or requests to do more work. If he could fit it in, he'd take it. One caught his eye and his heart sank.

MUM: Can you call me? I need you to do something for us.

A sour taste filled his mouth at the word *us* and he braced himself on the worktop. This couldn't mean anything good. His stomach roiled. What had happened this time? He couldn't bring himself to ring her immediately. It wouldn't be a matter of life and death. No. Just a case of what trouble Ryan had got into this time. Right now, Blair didn't have the headspace for his younger brother. He flicked to the next message.

LORELIE: I'm coming over for Easter. Fancy hooking up? X

Blair rolled his eyes, filled his hot-water bottle and dug around the tiny cupboard area, wishing a can of beer would magically appear. Lorelie hadn't been in touch for months. How to reply? *Do I want to see her again?* Maybe he should call his mum and get it over with. Something held him back. Whatever Ryan had done this time, Blair could guarantee if he got involved he'd come out of it a lot poorer and possibly with scars. Not for the first time.

He was everyone's go-to mate, pal, chum and friend – with or without the benefits – and it just wasn't cutting it anymore. Was this his life forever? Holed up in a caravan, working all the daylight hours and then some? And for what? A cold shower, an ancient hot-water bottle and not even a beer to ease the pain? Just the possibility of a hook-up with an old friend and the likelihood his brother had dug himself and their family into trouble – again. What were the bets his next wage packet wouldn't make it to his bank account before it was swallowed up to bail someone out?

Blair flopped onto the narrow bed; several springs dug into his back. The caravan rattled and swayed. Outside, something rusty screeched intermittently as tormented blasts rolled over. Sleep was a long way off. He rubbed his palm over the stag's head tattoo on his upper arm, trying to keep warm. Why had he bothered with it? It would have saved him a lot of money and made more sense if he'd just had *MUG* tattooed on his forehead.

Chapter Three

Rebekah

From the parking area at the front of her mother's Greenwich townhouse, Rebekah watched the flowers in the borders dancing while waiting for the taxi. Cheryl hurried out of the house wearing a lightweight black blazer over her shift dress, her hair pinned back by her large sunglasses, looking like a glamorous forty-something rather than a woman in her mid-fifties.

As if Rebekah's grandmother's last words hadn't opened a big enough can of worms, her funeral had caused another. Just as Rebekah and Cheryl had been ready to leave, a knock had come on the door.

'Should I get it? It must be Tim,' Rebekah had said.

'No, let me.' Cheryl had nipped off and Rebekah had taken a few seconds to compose herself, examining the sleep lines under her eyes in the ornate mirror. A rumbling laugh had echoed from the hall and Rebekah's jaw dropped. 'Daddy?'

Peter Yeboah had arrived unannounced. Rebekah had thrown herself into his embrace. She was tall, but he was taller still and even at sixty-five, he was in good shape.

'You bastard,' Cheryl had said, and Rebekah feared the worst, but Cheryl had grinned as she scanned over his well-fitting black suit. 'You look as handsome as ever. And what the hell are you doing here? Don't you know what day it is?'

'Of course, I do,' he'd said. 'That's why I'm here. I wish to pay my respects to your mother and lend moral support...'

And now he was here, living in the townhouse with Cheryl before he returned to Ghana and everything seemed just a bit too rosy. Rebekah didn't want to interfere, it was their life, but her heart was full of misgivings.

'Right,' said Cheryl. 'Are you sure this is sensible?'

'No,' said Rebekah. 'But I need to do something and this will be an interesting change.'

'I think you should forget all about it and take a break. You're exhausted.'

'No, I'm fine. I just need to get back into a routine and work.'

Cheryl frowned, looking completely unconvinced. 'But after everything that happened last year.'

'Let's not talk about that.'

Cheryl bit her lip. 'Why won't you consider staying in London?'

'I might do that when I come back. I want to try out Chloe's property idea first.'

'But surely there are a lot more properties here?'

Rebekah dismissed the idea. 'I want to try.'

'You've worked so hard to get where you are. I used to think you returned to Ghana to get at me, but I see now it wasn't that. You're passionate about your heritage and you have every right to be. It's not something I care much about but I realise how important it is for you.'

'It is, but that's not the only reason I went back. I had such a privileged upbringing but at the same time, I saw the real poverty in Ghana. I wanted to give something back. I know you and Grandmother would have preferred me to do that from here but I felt I could be more useful in Ghana. I always felt more… accepted there.'

Cheryl put her hand on Rebekah's arm. 'It's not been easy for you. But I knew boarding school would pay off. You made good connections there.'

Rebekah adjusted her neckline. Her mother could justify it, but Rebekah didn't look back fondly on those days. Girls there had always compared and judged each other by who their families were. Rebekah's Ghanaian family were wealthy and rich in heritage but instead of that giving her kudos, classmates had raised eyebrows and traded sideways looks, *who does she think she is?* etched into their faces.

'I've lost touch with most people,' said Rebekah. The ones who hadn't scoffed at her heritage had shrugged it off as invalid because it wasn't British. Rebekah learned not to mention it. She chipped a little bit of herself away to fit in.

'That's a pity,' said Cheryl. 'There would be lots of people who could help you with a job if you wanted to change direction. Or maybe, you know, meet someone.'

'We'll see,' said Rebekah. Cheryl rarely mentioned Rebekah's non-existent love life. No one did. It was a given that Rebekah was married to her career and that was all she cared about, however untrue that might be. Since Seth's deception, the world she'd built after university had caved. His lies had slashed the job security she'd built up and her hopes for a future with him. Who could she trust? Building her career and relationships had taken precious time and she'd wasted so much on that hypocrite. How could she do it again?

Peter strolled out of the house, beaming. 'Well, beautiful girl, you're off on an adventure.'

'I'm working, Daddy, don't forget.'

'Ah, curse work. You need a break. Go and enjoy yourself for a while, let your hair down and have some fun, you've worked hard enough for long enough.'

Rebekah gave him a hug, but she couldn't do what he suggested. She'd never missed a day's work in her life – until the trial.

Once in the cab she rested back her head, recalling the day of her grandmother's funeral, when she'd mentioned what had been bothering her since Elsie died.

'Do either of you know about her diamond necklace? Grandmother mentioned it to me before she died.'

'Oh, that,' Cheryl had said. 'Did she say she stole it from her cousin?'

'Yes. Is it true?'

'No. I don't think she even had a cousin.' Cheryl glanced at her brother, Tim.

He scratched his chin and shook his floppy salt 'n' pepper hair. 'I don't think so. I confess I don't know much about mother's family. She didn't ever mention anyone and our grandparents weren't exactly the type to talk about things like that. Grandfather was a military man and Grandma was tight-lipped.'

'What a mystery,' said Rebekah.

'Not really,' said Cheryl. 'Mother enjoyed reading and watching films. Jewel theft wasn't her style but it's definitely something she'd have enjoyed reading about. Towards the end she told me a few bizarre things that I'm pretty sure were stories she'd read and somehow lifted them into her mind, thinking they were real.'

'Such as?' Rebekah asked.

'I don't recall all of it; it was too nonsensical to be real. The oddest story was the one where she told me she'd been evacuated during World War Two. Apparently, she travelled to Scotland on a train and was bundled onto a steamship and transported to a remote island.' Cheryl sipped her coffee and held back a laugh. 'She said she was picked up by a pony and trap and driven several miles in near darkness in a rainstorm with howling winds. The cart almost fell into a ditch and when they arrived, there wasn't even a proper house; it was a tumbledown shack with no water, electricity, nothing.'

'And how do you know it isn't true?' asked Rebekah.

Tim and Cheryl both laughed. 'She hadn't even been to Scotland,' said Tim.

'Exactly. I once went to Edinburgh on holiday and she told me not to go because she'd heard the Scots were criminals and I'd be mugged as soon as I arrived,' said Cheryl.

'Sounds like the old girl finally cracked,' said Tim. 'I suspect if she'd carried on the story, it would have ended up with her living in a haunted house and the cart driver being the Grim Reaper.' Tim had guffawed at his own joke. 'Mother was such a character.'

Rebekah had half-laughed with them, but when they'd cleared out her grandmother's personal belongings, they'd found an old diary with a photograph of a little girl wrapped in a cloak with a leather case, outside what looked like an old tumbledown stone house. The words on the back were like the start of a story, similar to the one Cheryl had remembered Elsie recounting. Rebekah had read them over and over until she couldn't stop thinking about it.

The cart shook on the bumpy track. Wind bit and the rain clung to the fibres of my shawl. I shivered and peered up at the figure shrouded in black, steering the pony deeper into the mist. Where were we going?

Was that her grandmother? Or someone she'd known? Visions played out of the girl, tossing and tumbling on the cart along a stony path, her face ice cold and raw as the rain bit. Wind howled around. The stranger at her side was silent as the grave, taking her into the night, the destination unknown. And Rebekah was ready to follow in her footsteps.

Chapter Four

Blair

Blair panted as he jogged the last half mile to the caravan. The sun was almost up. Was there any point in showering? What had started as an early morning run had turned into a fencing marathon. Blair had spotted the farmer struggling with a broken gate and had stopped to help. Another gate and two blown over fence panels later, Blair knew a peaceful day was out the window. He was already sweating like mad.

He'd almost talked himself into braving the outhouse when his phone rang. Calum. At this time in the morning? Blair's pulse spiked. Had he made a mistake? His hours had been so crazy of late, he was running on empty. High standards were so important – what if he'd slipped up?

He couldn't afford it. Ryan had been up to his usual tricks and borrowed dodgy money. Their mum was in a right state which wasn't unusual but Blair couldn't bear it. He'd given Ryan the cash, hoping with no conviction this was the last time. He swiped open the call and raised the phone to his ear. 'Hi.'

'Blair, hi, mate. Listen, about the croft.'

Blood pounded in his ears; keeping this job was essential. At sixteen he'd made a mistake, a giant whopper of a mistake which had landed his family in years of debt. Couple that with a wayward brother and they'd never been on an even keel since. He couldn't make it up to his family, no matter what he did. 'Yeah, what about it?' Blair sank his teeth into his bottom lip.

'Rebekah's on her way, she's arriving tomorrow.'

'What? I thought it was next week.'

'Yeah, I muddled the dates. Sorry.'

For fuck's sake. Calum, the most organised man on the planet had muddled dates?

Blair scrapped any plans for a shower. In less than half an hour, he'd be dripping with sweat and likely to stay that way for at least twelve hours. There was so much he still had to do just to get the place habitable.

*

By twelve-thirty, his hands were red raw from sawing, fitting and dismantling scaffolding benches from the bedroom he'd painted first thing – though decorator had never been mentioned in his terms, Calum was desperate and he'd offered good money. Blair's phone lit up and he flicked it open.

LORELEI: I'm back. Can I call around tonight? Where are you staying?

He dropped the phone on the workbench and shook his head, barely holding back his laugh, and addressed the phone like she was in the room. 'You want me like this?' He glanced at the t-shirt sticking to his torso. At least when he'd been doing bar shifts and living in a flat, he'd been vaguely respectable. Now, he looked like he'd been living rough for months. He practically had.

Taking lunch breaks had become a thing of the past. A packet of crisps and a can of Red Bull had to suffice before he cracked on again. Just after three, his phone rang and he threw aside the saw to see who it was. *Mum.* He closed his eyes and pulled in a breath before answering. He'd been avoiding her messages but it couldn't go on.

'Hey, what's up?'

'My god, Blair. Why aren't you answering my messages?'

'Yeah, sorry.' He ran his fingertips over the ridges of his dreads. A flicker outside the window caught his attention; a car pulled up. Calum. *Great! Just great.* 'I'm really busy, Mum. I'm working all the time and I can't talk. That's my boss just showed up.'

'Blair, we need your help. Don't hang up.'

His heart slumped to his feet at the 'royal we'. This meant only one thing. 'What's he done this time?'

'Why do you say that? You always suspect the worst. Ryan hasn't done anything except try to help. He's been a godsend since he's moved in. Do you know how hard it was for me to leave the island?'

Blair didn't reply. His mum had left less than a year ago to move in with a man she'd been seeing on and off for years. Now they were officially 'off', she turned to Ryan for companionship and Blair knew how sneaky his younger brother could be. He was an expert at turning on the charm as long as it got him exactly what he wanted.

'Well, anyway,' his mum continued. 'The oven packed in. We needed a new one—'

'Oh no. He didn't take out another loan, did he?'

'We had to. We can't eat without an oven.'

'But, Mum!' Blair grabbed a handful of dreads from his ponytail and tugged on it. 'You already owe so much. *He* owes so much! He can't keep doing this.'

'How were we supposed to eat? You know why we don't have money, don't you?'

Oh yes, he knew all right. Since the age of eight, he'd cared for his infirm nan. He and Ryan had lived with her

39

most of the time while their parents worked all hours. He'd watched Ryan get away with murder while he'd had responsibilities piled on him. Responsibilities that had left him so frazzled, he'd made a balls-up and landed the whole family in debt. His cock-up had triggered his mum's depression.

'You have to stop dealing with these dodgy lenders.' Blair turned to see Calum coming in the front door. He moved towards the wall, turning his back to Calum.

'Please, son. You wouldn't want us to starve.'

'Of course I wouldn't. Look, I'll get the money somehow,' he said through gritted teeth. 'Now, I have to go.'

He put the phone down and peered around at Calum.

'Everything ok?' asked Calum. 'Can I help with anything?'

'No, everything's fine,' said Blair. No way was he confiding in his boss. The fewer people who knew, the better. He'd get them through this; they didn't need outside help.

'Good. I came to see how things were getting on. Are we good for tomorrow?' His expression was closed as usual as he looked around. 'Did you manage to paint the room?'

'Yup, and it's as good as I can get it.'

'Ok, I'll take a look.' He'd barely left the room when he returned. 'That looks fine. Rebekah sounds…' He ran his hand over his hair. 'Nice. A good business person. Genuine, you know.'

'Yeah,' said Blair. *And just up your street.* Great! Was this why Calum was so keen to move her in? Blair was going to be stuck here for several months working under the feet of someone Calum had the hots for – in his very Calumish *I don't show my emotions, I'm far too suave* type way. That really made his day. Maybe if he kept up the no-morning-shower trend, he might scare her away.

*

The following day Blair decided his no-shower tactic was probably not his best idea with the new tenant moving in and braved the chilly water in the outhouse, grunting as it hit him and roused him wide awake. Roll on the summer when cold showers were a treat.

Smelling of chilled tea tree and eucalyptus, he jumped in the van and left. Lorelei had rocked up the night before for what must have been his least successful date ever. They'd known each other for a long time, but even her knowledge of his quirks hadn't prepared her for the caravan. She'd taken one look at it and done a runner. He couldn't blame her.

'There's no way I'm doing anything in that,' she'd said. 'It doesn't even look watertight, let alone soundproof.'

His phone rang and the name *Autumn* flashed on the dashboard. Blair hovered before picking up. Autumn was like his new surrogate sister. He could have done with her support growing up when his mum and dad were out working and he was left doing chores for his sick nan. That would have been enough without his behaviourally challenged brother in the mix.

'Hey,' he said, pressing accept when he couldn't ignore the ringing anymore.

'Hi,' said Autumn. 'Are you ok?'

'Sure, why?'

'I just haven't chatted to you for a while.'

'I'm on the way to work,' he said.

'Is the caravan still standing?'

'Barely,' he muttered.

'I wish you'd come and stay with me. I could ask Richard, I'm sure he wouldn't mind.'

Blair gave a little laugh. Autumn had burst into his life the previous year when her mum had started dating his dad. From the off, they'd had a weird feeling like they'd always known each other. She was good craic and a great listener. But she could talk a lot.

'Yeah, Richard will say anything you want. He worships you.' And who could blame him? She was a beautiful human and they were clearly mad about each other. Lucky them. 'But really, I'm fine. You and Richard don't need anyone else hanging around, not when you're planning a wedding. And your house is too far from this job. I like being here, it's just a stone's throw away.'

'I suppose… But what about Ardnish?'

'Er, no,' said Blair. Autumn's enthusiasm was kind. 'I've thought about that already.' He was on excellent terms with the Ardnish Estate owners, but it wasn't possible. 'I can't, not with Dad living on the estate. It's too close.' Living on the same island as his dad was close enough. Any nearer and they risked the old ways kicking in. His dad would ask him to help out with this and that – which he didn't mind – but it would get more and more until it was too much. 'It's still too far away and probably too pricey. Honestly, I'm cool here.'

'I just worry. I haven't seen you for ages.'

Blair smiled. 'Sorry, I'm so busy with work. Calum wants so much done but his timing is unrealistic.'

'I might have a little job for you too.'

'Oh?'

'I won't tell you just now, not when you're so busy. It's not urgent, it'll keep until things cool down.'

'I don't see that happening any time soon, but I'll let you know when it does. Anyway, that's me. I need to go.'

'Ok,' Autumn said. 'Don't be a stranger.'

He pulled up outside the croft, spotting a red car. That must be the new tenant. Calum's 4x4 was there too. He was here already? Maybe he'd stayed overnight. Quick work. Well, Calum was Mr Slick in every department, though Blair didn't have him pegged as a romantic type. He almost laughed. Who was he to talk after last night? He wasn't really complaining. The whole friends with benefits thing was growing old. He didn't really want that. He never had. But women didn't view him as a serious candidate. He got loads of short-term offers and could have hooked up with a different girl every night in the tourist season if he'd wanted. Guys with decent bods and dreadlocks who worked as barmen-cum-joiners were an easy hit. Guys with no spare cash weren't long-term options. So he'd accepted the benefits with Lorelei; she was sweet and hit the spot for a short period, and being honest with himself, it might be the closest to the real thing he'd ever get. Now, he'd successfully blown it with her too.

As he stepped up to the door, he hesitated. Should he go in or knock? His hand hovered over the letterbox. Compromising, he knocked, then put his head around. 'Hey,' he said.

His gaze fell instantly on the woman and all his prejudiced preconceptions of a stuffy, overdressed woman with stilettos and big shoulder pads melted away. This woman was gorgeous. No point in even pretending to deny it. She was tall and elegant, with a long neck and slender limbs. Her well-fitted pink t-shirt and skinny jeans showed off a trim figure and her black curls were piled into a high bun. Perhaps he was drooling; he forced his mouth closed.

In the back of his mind, hiding in a corner behind the caveman, the memory of who she was pushed forward. She was the woman who'd sweet-talked Calum into letting her have this place. From all accounts, she was a ruthless property tycoon and there was every likelihood she would have a serious aversion to men with tattoos, scruffy clothes and no fixed abode.

Blair forced a smile as Calum announced, 'This is Rebekah.'

'Hi,' she said.

'Hi, I'm Blair, the joiner, minion and general dogsbody.' He dusted his palms together before reaching out.

'Pleased to meet you.' Rebekah stretched out her long fingers and Blair shook her hand. Her skin was beautifully soft in his thick, sweaty and calloused palms. He was a philistine next to her.

'Blair's here to work,' said Calum.

'Yeah, thanks for the vote of confidence, Calum,' said Blair.

'Well, just make sure you tidy up. I nearly did my length back there. There was a pole lying in the corridor and I tripped over it.'

Blair covered his mouth, partly annoyed with himself and partly to hide a snigger. He hadn't left it on purpose but… Well, he shouldn't really find it funny. 'Sorry. I thought I'd taken them all out. I must have missed that one.'

'Mind you do next time,' said Calum. 'No slacking and give Rebekah the space she needs.'

'I'll try not to get in your way,' he said, glancing at her before looking back at Calum. 'But I have worked my backside off to get this place habitable.' It was out before he could stop it.

Calum narrowed his eyes. 'I know that, Blair, and I appreciate it. Just take extra care now we've got Rebekah staying here.'

Rebekah smiled and the lights from the unshaded bulbs reflected in her deep brown irises. 'I'm sorry, I've caused so many problems. I really wanted somewhere here and this was the only place I could get for the whole six months. I pressed Calum quite hard.'

'You did,' agreed Calum.

Was that some secret code? If it was, Blair didn't want to know. But he hoped Calum had noted his displeasure. It was no mean feat putting together a kitchen in the main part of the house, a bathroom, and a bedroom in the new section. Plus, he'd almost finished the conservatory, which he hoped would suffice as a living room because he was still working on the main sitting area and the fireplace.

Rebekah gazed around at the rustic interior. The unfitted kitchen at the end of the open-plan main room was straight out of *Scottish Field* magazine, not that he bought it. 'It's fabulous,' said Rebekah. 'You've done an amazing job. Is it just you?'

'Just me.'

'Wow. I feel bad that I've disturbed you.'

'That's what I pay him for,' said Calum.

Blair gave Rebekah a resigned smile and she grinned back with an expression full of warmth that tickled his soul. He could live with working here for several more months. Even if she was a property guzzling mogul, he wouldn't mind just looking at her.

Calum coughed. 'How about I show you around? We could walk to the beach.'

'Fab,' said Rebekah. 'I'll get my coat.'

As soon as she was out of the room, Calum approached Blair and lifted his eyebrows.

'What?' said Blair. Was he meant to interpret that look and reply?

'Nothing.' Calum gave a half shrug, but the corners of his lips tweaked up and, despite him having an irritating poker face most of the time, Blair could almost see words pinging into his eyeballs: *back off, she's mine.*

'No doubt she is,' Blair muttered, heading for the van. There was no chance someone like that would ever be his. No chance at all.

Chapter Five

Rebekah

When the sun hit the beach, warmth filled Rebekah and she regretted bringing a coat. Calum tramped alongside her, looking around. Did it fill him with the same wonder she felt? He must have seen this view umpteen times. His face gave nothing away. She tried not to examine him too obviously, but he was a good-looking guy, tall and slim, with short dark hair and a smattering of stubble – almost a short beard. Something about him said money but with a casual edge; his jacket was smart if not designer, his jeans were well-fitted and his trainer-boots added a sporty touch. His Scottish accent reminded her of a sport's commentator or someone assured in their subject.

Gulls circled overhead, reeling and squawking in the breeze. A family splashed at the water's edge and Rebekah smiled as the children screamed every time a wave rolled over their toes. If her grandmother had come here as a young girl, what must it have felt like? The journey alone must have been terrifying.

'Tell me about your property plans,' said Calum. 'You must have a lot of experience.' He glanced at her and gave a brief smile. A prickle of heat attacked Rebekah's neck, advancing upwards into her cheeks. She was so bad at relationships. Finding a quiet place to block out the noise of life was her aim, but here was a nice man, paying her compliments, walking with her in a beautiful place, and she couldn't deny liking the look of him. But since Seth, nothing had been normal. Being attracted to someone and finding someone trustworthy were completely different things. She had to take care.

'I do have quite a bit of business experience, though in a completely different sector.'

'Property flipping is great,' said Calum. 'I've been doing it myself for years.'

'Yes. That makes me wonder if I'll be treading on your toes. Mull doesn't seem big enough for both of us.' She tightened the band in her hair as the wind grazed her head. Wouldn't it be just the thing to land the ideal property only to find herself in turf wars with a local? She didn't want anything like that.

Her old school friend, Chloe Carmichael, had suggested a method of property flipping she described as 'an unbeatable system'. Rebekah had listened to everything Chloe had suggested; it diverted them from uncomfortable subjects, such as the trial and Seth Eastman.

Chloe had leaned across the table outside the boutique café in Chelsea and said, 'If you see an upcoming area but you can't find any properties, try approaching some elderly residents, you can often persuade them to sell at good prices.'

'Is that ethical?' Rebekah had asked.

'Oh, absolutely.' Chloe had thrown up her hands as though it was obvious. 'They get enough money to downsize, which is usually what they want. We tend to look for ones where the property needs repairs far beyond their means. It's win-win.'

Rebekah wasn't planning on diddling anyone out of property but there was no denying money could be made in the sector.

Calum walked ahead and glanced back as he spoke. 'Maybe we could help each other out.'

'How?'

'Share expertise. You want to focus more on holiday lets, I'm more into long-term lets. I've learned a lot from working on this croft. I've thrown so much money at the place to extend it and upgrade it, it hardly seems worth it. I'm looking to buy land now. I think building from scratch will be a whole lot easier.' His eyes sparkled in the sunlight. Rebekah smiled and held his gaze.

'When I looked online, I didn't quite appreciate that *islands* meant so many different places and all so spread out.'

'Don't worry about that. This is a good base. If you need to visit other islands, I can easily organise a boat. My mum is originally from Tiree, it's a much smaller island. Over that way.' He pointed and Rebekah wasn't sure if she was meant to be able to see it or just the general direction. 'My family are heavily into boats. My father is a skipper. He used to sail over to see my mum before they were married and that's how he learned to drive a boat, or so the story goes.'

'I'll bear that in mind, thank you.'

'No worries. I've got a boat myself, but I rarely have time to go out in her.'

'You sound very busy.'

'There's always something going on.' Calum stepped onto a boulder and rubbed his hands together. 'What made you choose Mull? You were so set on Fionnphort.'

'Oh… Just this.' She gestured at the scenery. But it wasn't really that at all. The same day Rebekah had met Chloe, she'd also removed a package from the family's safety deposit box. After Chloe had left to pick up her children, Rebekah had remained, fingering the strap of her leather bag. When she was sure no one was watching, she'd opened it and extracted a purple velvet box. The hinges clicked as she opened it. She didn't own much jewellery and definitely wasn't an expert, but she'd gasped. Inside was a work of art. She'd gaped at her grandmother's diamond necklace until she realised she probably shouldn't be looking at it on a London street. As she'd been ready to close the box and put it away, she'd plucked at the satin top layer. Expecting it to be stuck fast, she'd almost lost her grip as it slid out. Fingers shaking, she'd lifted the tray holding the necklace and pulled out a tiny slip of yellowed paper. On it, written in old-fashioned writing, were the words:

To my precious Jeannie on our wedding day. Fionnphort, 12th April. All my love, Robert.

The words were now imprinted in her mind. Who were Jeannie and Robert? A desperate desire had woken in Rebekah and she couldn't rest until she uncovered the truth. She'd made it her mission to find the place in the note and here it was. Add it to her grandmother's faded photograph and she seemed to be holding onto pieces of a puzzle she needed to fit together but there were still too many gaps for it to make sense.

'It looked so remote and beautiful in the pictures,' she continued, deciding to skirt the truth. Telling someone she'd just met all her secrets wasn't sensible. The light wind played on her cheeks, and she closed her eyes, breathing in warmth and calm. So much healing potential hung in the air and rose with the sea.

'Yeah, sure is.' Calum ran his hand over his short hair. The silence wasn't awkward but two days weren't enough to get to know him. His befriending her could be a slick cover – just like Seth. This could all be a ploy to lure her into a false sense of security.

With a six-month sabbatical ahead, there would be plenty of time to talk and learn more. They spent some time at the shore admiring the glistening strand of sea between Fionnphort and the holy Isle of Iona, then strolled back towards the croft. The hillside was bumpy and undulating, with the scattered houses fitted in at quirky angles to fill their plots and get the most out of the sea view while keeping their warmth. And there was the croft that was now her home. Despite its half-finished interior, it was ideal. With the added garden room at the end, she couldn't imagine a more perfect spot.

Had Jeannie and Robert lived in any of these homes or was their place long gone? The village had a mix of old and new, but with no clear idea in what period Jeannie and Robert had lived, Rebekah didn't know where to start. If the photograph had been her grandmother and her story was to be believed, then surely the 1940s? But did people live in houses like that in the forties? There was no evidence as to where the photo had been taken. It could have been anywhere.

The croft was nestled at the end of a row of mismatched white houses in the lee of the rocky hillside. It was a quaint, stone-built, one-storey cottage with small windows to the front, looking towards the lane, and the garden room at one end. It could have been the one from the photograph but for all she knew that photo was taken on a different island. The fact the necklace originated here didn't mean it was where her grandmother had been. It just felt like the place to start.

'It's a great location, isn't it?' said Calum.

'Amazing,' she agreed. 'You don't know who used to live in it, do you? I mean long ago, around the Second World War maybe?'

Calum shook his head. 'No idea, sorry. I'm not even sure if that information's kept anywhere. I just buy the houses. Their history isn't my speciality. In fact it can be a thorn in my side. With houses like this it's so hard to get planning permission. I had to make sure the extension wasn't visible from the front but still big enough to make it worthwhile. Then they let me have the garden room at the end without a fuss.' He threw up his hands. 'There's no rhyme or reason to it sometimes.'

They approached the new stone wall that enclosed the croft's small, barren garden. In the middle, Blair, the joiner, was sawing at a workbench; his thick set of blond dreadlocks trailed down his back and his muscular arms worked back and forward.

Rebekah slipped her hand inside her jacket and trailed her finger along her collarbone as she watched him snap the end of a thick beam. She'd never been a huge fan of tattoos but it wasn't enough to repel her eyes. It gave her a reason not to find him attractive, and she needed one, even as feeble as that, because everything else about him set her senses tingling. He was a ridiculously hot guy, and she was going to be stuck with him in the house for the next few months. The calm bubble that had filled her soul since she arrived was deflating and nerves filled the gap.

Calum cleared his throat. 'I hope Blair doesn't get in your way too much.'

Rebekah flapped off his words. 'It's fine. I agreed to it after all.'

They continued up the hill silently and Rebekah ran her teeth over her lower lip.

'I should crack on,' said Calum. 'But don't be a stranger. If you need anything, give me a call and, assuming I have reception, I'll be here.'

'Thank you, that's really kind.'

'No problem. And if you want company anytime or someone to show you around, again, I'm happy to help.' He smiled briefly but his gaze was distant, almost sad. 'There's a nice restaurant on the west side, Am Bàta, if you wanted to join me sometime? I'd hate to think you were stuck here all alone, unless that's what you're after, a bit of solitude, and if that's the case, tell me to shut up and delete my number.'

Rebekah patted his arm and laughed. He glanced at her hand. 'I am here for some peace and quiet if I can fit it in around my work, but I'm not sure I want to be alone all the time, so I won't delete your number just yet. Thank you.'

'Great. Now, I better head. Enjoy the rest of your day.'

'Ok, fab.'

They shook hands and his grip was reassuring, if brief. An invitation to dinner after just two days? That hadn't been in the plans. Neither was meeting a ridiculously hot joiner. For all her trying to distance herself from men, she could be falling into the Seth-trap all over again.

As she opened the gate, she yawned and rubbed her eyes. Her sleep pattern was still all over the place. The longer daylight hours and the pure calm of the place further confused her body and mind. She'd been up since three in the morning and only had about four hours sleep. Curling up in bed right now appealed to her worn-out inner self but that would knock out her evening routine. And it seemed wasteful. There was so much to explore here.

When she entered the croft, Blair sat on the floor surrounded by planks of timber. He flashed a lopsided but attractive grin. Rebekah bit the inside of her cheek and fidgeted. Should she talk to him or just say hi then ignore him? Would he pick up on her coffee habits or sneer if she spent the day in PJs? Did she want to spend her day in PJs in front of him? Did any of it matter?

'It's a bonny day, isn't it?' he said, still piecing together the wood.

'Yes, really lovely.'

'Hopefully, I won't get in your way too much,' he said. 'I did as much of the conservatory as possible because Calum said you'd be working and that should give you a good space.'

'Yes, it's fab. I can work there. What's this you're doing?'

'The fireplace. Calum gave me a photo he found on the internet which he wants me to copy. It's cool but complicated.'

'Oh, that's a shame.'

'It's pretty standard for Calum. He's a man of big ideas.'

'I should leave you in peace then and not disturb you.'

'Not at all. It's your house. I'll get on around you. Just tell me if you need to talk on the phone or whatever because I'll be sawing and hammering and making lots of noise, but if you need quiet, I'll make myself scarce.'

'I agreed to noise in the terms and conditions, so I really don't mind.'

He quirked a grin. 'I should also apologise in advance for the mess that'll be about. There's not a lot I can do about it, though I'll try not to leave anymore trip hazards lying around.'

'Oh yes, Calum thought you'd booby-trapped the place. But it's fine, really. I'm not planning on doing much today, just settling in, so make as much noise and mess as you like.'

'Ha, thanks.' He held her gaze for a moment and dusted off his palms. 'What is it you do?'

Rebekah sucked on her lower lip, considering what to say. 'I was working for an international aid organisation but I'm trialling a new venture for a while.' She glanced at him. She wasn't going back but he didn't need to know anything about it. If the new venture didn't work, she wasn't sure what she was going to do, but she'd do something.

'Sounds intriguing. I thought you might be here for an extended holiday.'

'No. I'm working.' She'd always worked; she needed to. 'I'm considering investing in properties here, but it's early days yet.'

'Yeah, Calum said you were into property.'

'Did he?'

'Yup. Well, if you're looking for a joiner.' He pointed at himself with his thumb and gave her a cheeky smirk. 'Though you should probably wait until I'm done here in case I'm not up to your standards.'

She raised her fingers to her lips, hiding her grin. No doubt he'd measure up. 'I'll be inspecting,' she said.

He looked back at the planks on the floor with a smile. 'What made you choose Fionnphort?' he asked. His cheerful face and twinkly eyes nipped between focusing on his work and her.

What indeed. 'I'm on a bit of a personal pilgrimage,' she said.

'To Iona?'

'No, nothing like that. I'm just doing some research centred around here. It's stuff I can do around work.'

'Really?' Blair sat up straight, his eyes widening. He was knee-weakeningly attractive. Rebekah's heart bounced. 'That sounds interesting. Is it island history?'

'Sort of, I want to find out about people who used to live here.' Rebekah perched on the sofa arm in the garden room, crossed her legs and looked back into the main room at Blair. 'I discovered I might have ancestors from here. It surprised me. My father is Ghanaian and my mother's English, so it didn't seem terribly likely.' She glanced out of the window. 'I'm not even sure it's true.'

'Wow. Intriguing.' Blair rested his large hands on his knees and Rebekah chewed the inside of her lip.

'I suppose it is.'

'What put you onto it?' asked Blair, laying out the wood again. 'I mean, how did you discover the connection?'

'Would you like a coffee?' Rebekah said. 'I need one, then I'll explain.' Perhaps she shouldn't encourage him but fixing one for herself while he sat on the floor seemed mean.

'No thanks, I don't drink it.'

'I wish I was that disciplined.' She breezed past him into the kitchen area and filled the kettle. While it boiled, Blair drilled holes into the timber and Rebekah tried to focus on what she was doing, but his muscle power was much more compelling than crockery.

Cup in hand, she returned to the edge of the sofa, admiring the view of the small ferry gliding slowly towards Iona. 'So, my grandmother made a weird confession just before she died.'

Blair carried on slotting wood together but glanced up and nodded, his expression full of interest. 'Really?' He settled into a position so he was facing her as he worked.

Rebekah explained about the diamond necklace. 'You should see it. It's stunning. I'm thirty-one and in all those years I never suspected anything. My mother and my uncle

Tim know nothing about it. Why didn't they ask? Why didn't I?' The thought drifted like an anchorless ship.

'You can't ask about something you don't know. You weren't to know there was anything strange about the necklace.'

'That's true. Then we found a photograph with a strange note on the back.' She described it to him. 'I took a picture on my phone.' Pulling it out, she swiped through it and showed him.

He squinted at it. 'Definitely looks like it could be somewhere on the island. It would be weird if it was actually this croft, wouldn't it?'

'Very weird and highly unlikely.'

'Stranger things have happened.' He quirked his lopsided grin. 'So, what's your plan? How are you going to solve the mystery?'

'I'm not sure. I thought about Somerset House, but I don't know where to start. All my family research in Ghana was word of mouth: stories passed through generations, names in the family bible and old photographs.' The words streamed from her. It was her voice talking but her thoughts strayed onto a completely different path. *Why am I telling him this?* Who was he? She didn't know him from Adam but here she was spilling her guts to him like he was her best friend. Any private information in the wrong hands could be lethal. She hadn't meant to say so much.

'That's unreal,' he said when she wound up.

Rebekah folded her arms across her chest. She was so exposed to his keen blue eyes; it felt like she'd just taken her top off.

'And none of your family have heard of Jeannie and Robert?'

She shook her head. 'Nope. I checked my grandmother's birth certificate and it's not her parents.

Nobody knows anything about her past. That's what made me choose here. I wanted to see it for myself. If this place was part of her life, even for a short time, I feel I should try to make sense of it.'

'There were some evacuees here. I remember learning about it at school. There's stuff about it in the Tobermory museum. You could check it out.'

'That's a fab idea. Thank you.'

'No probs, you've got me intrigued now too.' He dusted the wood from his jeans and got to his feet. Rebekah's wayward eyes took him all in. With a smile, she blew over her hot coffee; the aroma soothed her and the tension lifted from her shoulders. Despite feeling like she'd bared all, he wasn't sitting in judgement or sneering. Perhaps more terrifyingly, his presence was like warm hands soothing over her.

An hour or so passed in pleasant chat, just how, she wasn't sure. Blair fiddled about with the timber frame for the fireplace and told her about places to visit on the island, the best walks and viewpoints. So much for his intimidating look; he was a puppy dog.

'I'm sorry, I've yapped on,' she said.

'It's fine,' said Blair. 'I'm happy with some company. I've been here for weeks on my own. It's cool to have someone to talk to other than on my phone.'

Instinctively, Rebekah checked her own. 'Calum,' she muttered, reading a message.

CALUM: Hey, great to catch up with you. I'm free all week if you fancy dinner, just let me know. And I mean it, call if you need anything.

She rested the phone on the sofa arm as she considered her reply. Blair kept his head down, concentrating on what looked like a tough corner joint.

What to do? Blair was easy company and she was sure she'd manage to work alongside him for the next month or so. But Calum was a different matter, a more sophisticated, enigmatic matter. She had to tread carefully and make completely damn sure he was genuine before she committed to anything. No one was going to dupe her this time.

Chapter Six

Blair

Blair pulled on the handbrake, whistling as he grabbed his phone and his hoody from the passenger seat of the van. Rebekah's arrival last week had transformed his days; chats and laughs had replaced the monotony of working on his own.

The postie bustled along the road and Blair gave him a cheery wave.

'Morning,' shouted the postie. 'Just one letter for the croft, can I give it to you?'

'Sure,' said Blair. He took the envelope and read the name. *Rebekah Ama Yeboah*. 'I'll give it to her.'

The postie saluted him and hurried back to his van parked at the far end of the lane.

A rancid burning smell overpowered Blair's nostrils as he opened the croft door. He screwed up his face. Rebekah had her back to him in the kitchen area and was scrubbing something at the sink.

'Good morning, Rebekah Ama,' he said, pinching his nose and looking at the envelope again. 'Are you trying to burn the house down?'

'Oh my god.' She turned around, holding out her arms, her apron covered in some highly suspect brown stuff. Her curly high ponytail stood on end like she'd stuck her finger in a socket and a streak of flour ran across her nose. 'I've done something stupid.'

'Er… What?' Blair squinted around tentatively.

'Well…' She lifted a pot scrubber; her yellow rubber gloved fingers poised like she was about to conduct an orchestra. 'As there aren't any supermarkets nearby, I thought I'd try something new.'

'Yes…' said Blair slowly.

'Cooking.'

'Cooking? That's new?'

'It is for me,' said Rebekah. 'Don't get me wrong, I'm the mistress of heating things up and filling a sandwich, but actual cooking… Well, how hard can it be?'

Blair raised his eyebrows. 'Harder than you thought?'

'Bloody right. Look at this.'

Blair sauntered into the kitchen area and scanned over what had been a spanking new kitchen just twelve hours ago. Now it looked like a Primary One class had got hold of the contents of a larder cupboard, thrown it all over the place and attempted to bake the leftovers on the highest oven setting. 'Jesus Christ,' he muttered. 'I'm not Gordon Ramsay but…' He picked up a charred bit of something from a baking tray and held it out. 'Is this a dead rat?'

'Chicken.'

'Seriously? And how many people are you cooking for?'

'I was reading about meal prepping… and well, this is the result.'

'Wow,' said Blair. 'I think I know a couple of dogs who might enjoy it.'

'Oh, shut up.' Rebekah lobbed a dishcloth at him and laughed.

'I'll shut up, just don't expect me to clear up.'

She waved her hands and scanned around, perhaps deciding where to start.

'There's a letter here for you, Miss Bekah Ama.' He passed it to her.

'Bekah Ama? Is that what it says?'

'No, I just like giving people nicknames.'

She set her hands on her hips. 'What's your full name then?'

'Blair Ewan Andrew Robertson.'

'You realise your initials spell bear?' She put her fingers to her lip, pushing back a smile.

'Yeah, yeah, I might have heard that before, you know, once, twice, or a thousand times. My parents insist they didn't notice and it was a fluke because that's both my grandfathers' names.'

'Well, Mr Bear, it could have been worse. You could have been Blair Ewan Edward Robertson.'

Blair chortled. 'Yeah, that fits better.'

'Oh, I don't know.' Rebekah scanned downwards.

Blair pulled his neckline wide and looked at his pale broad chest; the faintest smattering of blond hair covered it. 'Baldy Bear has not enough hair.'

Rebekah grinned, opening her letter.

'And Bekah Ama cooks like bla.'

'Oh, gosh, you're funny.' She scanned through the letter. 'Maybe I should celebrate – that's my first bill.'

'I'll help you by cleaning up some of this mess. Come on.' Blair lifted the cloth Rebekah had lobbed at him and took a dish from the drainer.

'Aw, you're a sweetheart.'

'Blair, Blair, sweet teddy bear,' he muttered, rolling his eyes.

'Aw, you are a sweet teddy bear.' She pushed some more dishes into the water.

'I've never heard the name Ama before,' said Blair. 'Is that Ghanaian?'

'It is, yes. It's traditional for Ghanaian babies to have a Christian name and a day of the week name. I was born on a Saturday and Ama is a Saturday name. My father is Peter Kobi Yeboah, he was born on a Tuesday and Kobi is a Tuesday name.'

'Wow. Doesn't that mean there's a lot of people with the same names?'

'Not really. There's more than one name for each day and different ones for boys and girls. My grandparents in Ghana used to call me Ama, but no one else uses it. It's an Akan tradition but lots of them have been lost. So much has been westernised over the centuries,' said Rebekah, immersing her hands in the soapsuds.

'It's a beautiful name,' said Blair.

'It was one thing my parents agreed on. Life in Ghana wasn't always suited to my mother, she was used to London. You should hear how they met.'

'Tell me.' Blair rested his elbows on the work surface.

'My father's family are very well off; they're descended from Akan clan chiefs who have quite a history in Ghana.'

'That's impressive.'

'You have no idea. Sometimes I can't even believe it. But it's not all rosy. The chiefs weren't always popular and throughout history, they've been caught in awkward places. They've always been better off than most Ghanaian citizens but for a long time, they had no real power and were viewed as the puppets of the white overlords. It doesn't make for comfortable reading.' She sighed.

'Most history is like that, isn't it?' said Blair. 'Like the clearances here.'

'Exactly. It's not tied up with a ribbon, all neat and tidy. It's a mess. But I'm digressing. My father's family are well off – they own a goldmine near Kumasi and in the eighties, my mother was a model.'

'That explains a lot.'

'About what?' Rebekah flushed and Blair poked his tongue into his cheek. He'd jumped right in with his size elevens.

'Well, you're quite good-looking,' he said. 'You know, a bit, I wouldn't want you to get big-headed or anything, but I'd say you're an eight out of ten, maybe nine, pushing nine point five.'

'Oh, stop it, Blair.' She stared into the sink but kept on smiling as she spoke. 'So, my mother was on this photoshoot at the goldmine and who did she meet?'

'Your dad?'

'Yes, and he's, well, quite good-looking too.'

'Some folk have all the luck.'

'Yeah, so, they liked each other, but here's the clincher. My mother was staying in the best hotel in town. Well, she's always liked comfort.'

'Equally as sophisticated as her daughter.'

'A whole lot more, I assure you. So, after a long day shooting, she went for a bath before an important dinner date with the mine owners.'

'Does this get kinky?'

'Like they'd tell me that much detail. Anyway, the door handle broke off the bathroom door, and Mother was stuck.'

'Seriously?'

'Yes. Then, some hours later, she heard someone walk past the window and shouted for help, and can you guess who it was who rescued her?'

'Peter, Peter, went to meet her, broke the door down with his beater.'

'Really?' She flicked water at him and giggled. 'But yes, something like that.'

'What a blossoming romance.'

'It was for a while.'

'Oh?'

'They're divorced now.'

'I know how that feels,' said Blair.

'You're divorced?'

'No. My parents are.'

'I wondered. You don't look old enough to be married never mind divorced.'

'Too right. So, why did they split after such a budding romance?'

'You know how it is,' Rebekah said. 'My mother liked the privileges life with my father brought, you know, mixing with the elite, joining bridge clubs, going for afternoon teas at the British Club, that kind of thing. But people were fickle and some of my mother's new friends liked her position more than her. She was homesick, I guess. I was looked after by servants and I learned so much from them about real life and how hard it was for them. Many rich expats were terribly mean to their servants. My mother wasn't but she was bored. The servants did everything. She didn't have to cook but sometimes good food was hard to come by; the shops could be empty and the best food would be in restaurants.'

'It sounds like the Hebrides not so long ago.'

'It's a good parallel, certainly for the time frame. For my mother, who'd been brought up on high fashion, there weren't a lot of clothing options, you either made your own or went home to shop. I was sent to boarding school in England, and my mother left my father and came back to London. But I couldn't get away, not in my mind. I wanted to do some good, which was why I took the job with Take-

Action.' Her voice trailed off and she stared into the soap bubbles.

'Are you ok?'

'What? Oh... Yes. You know, telling you about my parents just made me think of something.' She stared at the dishes, frowning.

'What?' said Blair. 'Tell me.'

'After my grandmother died, my father came to London for the funeral. My mother often blamed my grandmother for the divorce and maybe part of it was true. My grandmother certainly didn't like my mother being so far away, but at the funeral, my parents were like a courting couple. They were holding hands, leaning on each other and now... Look.' She pulled off her rubber gloves and picked up her phone, swiping through before turning it to Blair. 'That's a picture of them from the weekend. They're on a riverboat on what looks like a romantic date.'

Blair shook his head and laughed. 'They sure look loved up, and yeah, they're a good-looking pair.' His eyes strayed to Rebekah and her gaze met his. She held it for a moment before returning to her phone.

'So, what do you think is going on? Are they getting back together? Or playing out some weird fantasy? Just what?' She held out her palms.

'Who knows?' Blair flipped her an empathetic smile. 'Whatever it is, it definitely won't happen with my parents. I don't see them ever speaking again, let alone getting back together.'

'It's so hard, isn't it? And confusing, no matter how old you are.'

'Yup.'

'I don't feel I can advise them because deep down I want them back together, but they're blinkered if they think just because my grandmother's gone, it means they can pick up from where they left off. It was a long time ago and the old differences are still there.'

'I suppose you just have to leave them to it.' Though Blair knew how hard that was. For years, he'd been the one keeping his family afloat. But Rebekah's parents didn't have money worries, and by the sound of it, they never had, so they were free to follow their hearts and dreams. Lucky them.

Blair yawned and flapped his hand in front of his face. 'Excuse me. I didn't sleep well,' he said.

'Me neither.' Rebekah mirrored his yawn.

He was still working every hour he had, trying to pay off his mum's latest loan. The farmer he lodged with was giving him money off the caravan rent for fixing up his barn and with the long days, he had light to keep going to after ten o'clock. Some days it left his body bashed and bruised and his soul crushed. 'Let your parents be happy even if it's just for a wee while. I'd love it if I could say that about mine.'

'I'm sorry. Don't they put their differences aside even for you?'

'Not really. My dad's making the most of things. He was on the booze for a while, but he's clean now and he's met someone who was in a similar boat, so they're good for each other. My mum, well, she's got some issues, mostly because of my younger brother. He's always been difficult, but we're working through it. Now listen…' He clapped his hands and beamed. Rebekah cocked her head in anticipation. 'How's about Mr Bear gives Miss Bekah Ama some fail-safe recipes and cooking tips? And I mean proper easy things that even a numpty like me can make on a camping stove. Wanna try?'

Rebekah laughed. 'I do. I definitely need the fail-safe numpty recipes before I try anything else.'

'I'll look them out and message them to you. I suppose I better get some work done. It'd just be my luck this'll be the day Calum turns up and finds me drying dishes. This isn't helping my reputation.'

'Aw, but it is helping me. So, thank you.' She clapped his upper arm.

'No bother, just make sure you let Calum know if he bursts in here cracking the whip.' Blair picked up his tools and the timbers he'd laid at the wall. Rebekah followed him out of the kitchen area.

'Tell me about Calum,' she said, fidgeting with the edge of her apron.

'What about him?' A cold weight dropped in Blair's gut. He could guess. Sophisticated women like Rebekah liked wealthy men like Calum.

'I don't know. He's sort of asked me out. I wasn't planning on dating anyone while I was here, but he's also technically my landlord. I just wonder what kind of guy he is. If we don't get on during the date, will he evict me or push up my rent?'

Blair shrugged. He wouldn't put it past Calum to do that kind of thing, but he suspected with Rebekah he'd be way too suave to try something like that. 'Na, I don't think so. Calum's an ok guy. He's business obsessed and always wants a deal which will suit his pocket more than anything else but that's how he got where he is, I suppose.' *And why I'm sitting here doing the hard labour and doling out counselling from my self-contained friendzone.*

'Do you know about any of his previous dates or relationships?'

'Not really. I suppose he sees people now and then, but I don't really know him like that. I've met him in the pub a couple of times and we've played pool but we're not bosom buddies.'

Rebekah kicked off her pumps and padded towards the garden room in her bare feet. 'I guessed that. I just wondered.' She took a seat at the tiny bistro table at the window and opened her laptop. Her eyes stayed on the view for a long time before she finally turned to the screen. Blair carried on piecing together the fireplace, trying to ignore the needle of irritation. Why did women always see him as a sounding board? Did he look like an agony aunt for Christ's sake? How would it be if he asked Rebekah on a date himself? Why not?

Unfortunately, she was so far out of his league she was in a different sport. He was willing to bet his last pound, if he asked her, she wouldn't go running to Calum to ask about *his* history. Which was probably just as well, because Blair's history with women was just as chaotic and jumbled as the kitchen had been half an hour ago.

Chapter Seven

Rebekah

Wearing her new bright red yoga shorts and crop top, Rebekah held her legs up high, balancing on her bottom in the boat pose. The wind-down evening routine wasn't impacting on her sleep yet, but she'd slipped into an early morning routine that boosted her energy from the word go.

Accounts, spreadsheets, databases, budgets, and rotas were like something from another life. From the wall of glass in the garden room, Rebekah watched the early tide flowing out. She stretched out of her pose and breathed deeply. Memories of Seth Eastman's calculating face watching her as she gave evidence were like something from someone else's life. Something she didn't have to think about. She forced the image to shut down. She wasn't sleeping longer but the nightmares had lessened. Now when she woke up, a new world was waiting to be discovered, and she had the energy to look forward to it and face it head on.

After half an hour, she rolled up her mat and boiled the kettle. Green tea would never replace coffee but her ridiculous caffeine intake wasn't helping with her sleep problems. Her laptop was open, ready for some more work on her family history. She might sneak a peek at properties but so far, the hunt was proving frustrating. No matter how often she refreshed her browser, there were no suitable properties on any websites. Other than that, life couldn't be more idyllic.

With her notes spread around the floor and the nearby sofa, she opened her family tree creator programme. This was the first step, collating the information with as much accuracy as she could. Once she'd populated the tree, she would focus on individual stories. It was challenging enough to be enjoyable without being stressful.

About eight-thirty, Blair's van crunched up outside. Rebekah hadn't changed out of her yoga stuff yet but had thrown a loose white beach shirt over the top. Blair wouldn't mind. She'd gone from worrying about him seeing her in PJs to not caring in the space of a few weeks. Things were easy around him and without meaning to, she'd found an unlikely friend in the hunky joiner. Despite the muscle and Viking looks, he was like a cosy jumper she'd owned forever and when she put it on, she was comfortable and at home.

Blair strolled in without knocking; she'd told him not to bother. That way, she didn't have to worry about going for an early walk or being in the shower when he arrived. His head was down and his gaze glued to his phone as he crossed the threshold. His face was care-worn and grim; he furrowed his brow and compressed his lips together.

'Is everything ok?' Rebekah asked.

'What?' He glanced up and, spotting her, shoved his phone into the back pocket of his jeans. 'Yeah, sure.'

Rebekah got to her feet and picked her way through her research notes. *I must look like a gymnast doing an assault course in this outfit.* Blair said nothing but his eyes roved subtly downwards then returned to her face as she passed him. 'I've been cooking,' said Rebekah, 'and voilà, no mess.'

Blair checked towards the kitchen area and nodded. The oven whirred contentedly and a casserole dish of chilli bubbled in the yellow glow.

'That might do a couple of meals,' she said. 'It's not too bad – for me.'

'Well done, it looks great. But jeez, it's hot in here.' He pulled off his hoody and opened the front door. 'Baking ovens and crazy hot weather both send me to the end of my tether.'

Rebekah smirked at his latest nonsense rhyme but her eyes hadn't found his face. They lingered all over his biceps, following the swirling lines of a stag tattoo. And although she wasn't fond of tattoos, she could appreciate the artistry. Her gaze continued its ramble onto his chest; his tight vest was doing a terrible job at hiding his shapely torso. It was on the tip of her tongue to suggest he got a bear tattooed on it when he said. 'Would you like a photo?'

She blinked and closed her mouth. 'Oh, get over yourself.'

He cast his eyes down and smirked, but when he picked up his tools, a shadow fell over his expression again.

'Are you sure you're ok?' Rebekah pressed. Had she offended him with her staring? Maybe she should reel in her eyes a bit. They were prone to wayward gambols when he was about.

'Yeah. Just family stuff. Nothing to worry about.' He let out a sigh. 'Is Calum coming round today?'

'Not right now, why?'

'I thought maybe the cooking was for him.'

'God no. I might poison him. But your recipes are fab. Are they your mum's?'

'No,' he said indignantly. 'My mum's cooking is on a par with yours. I made them up with trial and error. That's how I survive life on a tight budget.'

'Amazing, I didn't expect that.'

'What? A guy who can cook? It's not unheard of.'

'That's so true. Excuse my appalling sexism. Would you like to sample my latest delicacy?'

'You're not worried about poisoning *me*?'

'Oh gosh, I didn't think that through.' She hid her face in her hands. 'Maybe we should start this over again. Why don't you go out and come back in again like you've never been here?'

He cocked his head and pulled a side pout. 'Er, how about I don't. But I'll try the cooking. I may be bad, I may be good, but I never turn up my nose at food.'

'You're funny. You might have to help me make the rice, then we can have the chilli at lunchtime.

'Oh, Bekah Ama,' he sighed. 'You don't even know how to cook rice?'

'Sorry.' She gave an apologetic shrug.

He grinned and she left him to his work. After showering and dressing, she knuckled down to some serious sorting out of her paperwork. Gorgeous cooking smells filled the room as the morning passed, a pleasant surprise from the usual kitchen carnage. Blair dotted in and out, sawing outside and carrying strips of wood back in. Occasionally they chatted but even their silences were companionable.

'That smells ready,' said Blair. 'Or maybe it's just me who's ready to eat it.'

'I'll check it.' Rebekah left her research and pulled on the oven gloves. Heat smacked her face as she opened the oven door. 'I think it's ready. What about the rice?'

'Leave the chilli in the oven on low,' said Blair, 'and I'll talk you through the rice. It's not rocket science, it's easy.'

Margaret Amatt

Twenty minutes later the rice was done. 'It looks edible,' said Rebekah, peering at it.

'Then let's do the taste test.' Blair scrubbed his hands at the sink while Rebekah arranged two plates of chilli and rice. He took his seat, screwed up his face and tasted a bit with an over-the-top expression of panic. His head moved from side to side, then he winked. 'Not bad.' He took another mouthful. 'Actually good. This is the best lunch I've had in weeks. It beats crisps anyway.'

'Really, Blair, is that all you eat?'

'It's all I can afford. This is great. You're a fast learner.'

She watched him wolf it down. He was joking that he could only afford crisps – surely?

'I better not eat too much,' she said. 'Calum's taking me to Am Bàta tonight; he raves about it. Have you ever been?'

Blair's fork froze for a few seconds on the way to his mouth before he shook his head. He swallowed. 'No. So, you and Calum… A date?'

Rebekah's shoulder twitched. 'Where's the harm? He's a nice guy and it seems rude to say no. I don't really have a reason not to go.'

Blair nodded at his plate. 'Cool. Well, I'm sure it'll be great.' He didn't say anything else as he finished his chilli and Rebekah wasn't sure what to say either. Of course, Calum was Blair's boss and they weren't great friends but hopefully, it wouldn't affect the friendship she'd forged with Blair.

*

Am Bàta was a wooden chalet-like building in the shape of a ship's prow. Calum explained the name meant boat in Gaelic. 'I only know because the owner told me,' he said. 'I don't speak Gaelic.'

'Why not?'

'No one really does anymore. My grandparents did, but only occasionally. It's a dying language.'

'That's a shame. It's like that in Ghana; the native Akan languages get overwritten by English.'

'The price of progress,' said Calum, leading Rebecca up the stairs to a mezzanine level with a view over a woodland. For a restaurant named after a boat, it was in a curiously inland spot with no sign of the sea anywhere.

'I'm not sure it's the best kind of progress,' she said, running her fingers through her hair. It had been a while since she'd subjected her curls to the heavy-duty steam straighteners and it was an odd feeling. 'So much history and identity get lost. Do we want a world of clones? I like to think everyone has a rich heritage. Why be ashamed of the miner or the labourer? Their toil and craft built the foundations of the world.'

'A romantic ideal,' said Calum, signalling for the server. 'But I agree. God knows I have a humble background. My mum works in the village shop in Craignure and my dad skippers boats for a living. It's hardly big-time stuff. But I worked hard and I made my money work hard.'

'How did that come about?' asked Rebekah.

Calum pored over the wine menu and swallowed. 'We should order. I'm driving, so just the soft stuff for me, but a bottle of something good for the lady,' he informed the server. 'Do you like red or white?'

'White, please, but just a glass. I don't want a bottle to myself.' Why would he suggest she got a bottle for herself? Did he want to intoxicate her? She rapped the table edge with her fist. *Stop with the paranoia – not all men are like Seth.*

75

'Fair enough.' He sent the server away with the order and steepled his fingers on the table.

'We were talking about how you built your empire,' said Rebekah.

'Oh, yes.' His expression grew more closed than ever. Surely he hadn't used ill-gotten means? Blair thought him an arse, but he always seemed quiet and private. Where had his reputation come from?

'I inherited my first property.' His words were measured like he was telling her the gist of the story but leaving a lot out. 'It was my grandparents' house in Tobermory. Initially, they left it to my dad but he passed it to me. I was in a pivotal place in my life and it was just what I needed. I never looked back.'

'And they don't have any part in the property business?'

Calum shook his head. 'They're not interested in that kind of thing. I make a good living out of it and it's enough to see them right. They keep their jobs because they enjoy them. I've sorted their mortgage so they can enjoy life.'

'That's fab, they must be proud.'

'I hope so.' He gave a brief smile. 'They're good people. They'd have liked more kids but they only had me.'

'I'm an only child too, but my parents chose that.' She tapped the table. 'You know, I'm not sure the property thing will work for me. I can't find anything suitable.'

The server arrived with Rebekah's wine and Calum poured water from the jug into his glass. He clinked hers and the corners of his mouth twitched. 'Slange.'

'Cheers. I thought you didn't speak Gaelic.'

'When the moment calls.' He took a sip. 'Your hair looks great by the way.'

'Oh.' She stroked it again. If steam straighteners had existed when she was at boarding school, it might have saved her a lot of trouble. But would that just have been her living up to someone else's ideals, not being true to herself? 'Thanks,' she said.

Calum set his glass down and leaned forward. 'Have you met your neighbours yet?'

'Not really. I see a woman out hanging up washing sometimes but I haven't been round and she seems to keep herself to herself. I think she has a son.'

'Yeah, she's a tenant of mine and, if truth be told, a bit of a pain in the neck.'

'Why?'

'I bought that house with her in it. It was a condition of sale that I kept the sitting tenant, but I'd really like her out. That house is on a great plot. If I was able to buy up the one beside it, there's room for another two houses in there.'

'Would you get planning permission for that?'

'I think so. I had the garden room and the extension to the croft approved. I'm confident I could have the buildings designed sensitively. I know a good architect.'

'So, why not do it anyway? Can't you just build around her house?'

'I could, but the access is an issue. I'd either have to knock off a bit of the existing house, then extend it out the back, or buy the neighbouring plot too. Now, the first solution, I could do with her in the house, but it's not very nice. I expect you've heard stories from Blair and everyone else about how heartless I am, but I'm not really.'

She hoped that was true and she didn't just have to take his word for it. Sipping her wine, she momentarily lost her train of thought – it was a fabulous vintage. 'Blair told me you were a good guy.'

'Did he? Well… Ok. So, I don't really want to demolish half a house while there are tenants in it. But buying the other property is proving problematic.'

'Oh?'

'An old lady lives in it, you know the type, fluffy hair, looks as sweet as crème brûlée? But she's stubborn as a bulldog. She will not sell. I've offered her more money than she could ever spend in her lifetime. She's got to be eighty at least. She doesn't have any family, so why hang on to the house?'

Rebekah tilted her head. 'Calum.' Her voice came out stern, like she was a teacher about to scold a pupil, and he fiddled with his shirt collar. 'She's probably lived there all her life. You can't expect her to sell up and move out for any money. If she has no family, then presumably all her friends are close by. Gosh, if she's eighty and still living in her own house, that's incredible.'

'Yeah, I know. I know you're right. It just frustrates me.' He lifted the food menu and sighed as he checked it out. 'I hate feeling like I'm missing an opportunity.'

Rebekah read through the choices but her thoughts roamed back to London and the conversation she'd had with Chloe when she'd originally considered the property idea. Chloe had suggested a similar tactic of buying out OAPs. At the time it hadn't seemed ethical, it still didn't, but was there any harm in talking to the old lady? She could gauge the situation.

Or what if Calum was telling her all this so she would do exactly that? Maybe that was his plan and he was just sweet-talking her so she would do his dirty work. She glanced up at him and he smiled. Finally, it reached his eyes, softening his features and making what was already a handsome face more appealing. It didn't make her feel as happy as it should. Her uncertainty climbed up a notch.

'What are you thinking?' he asked.

'How do you mean?'

'You look like someone who's just had a bright idea.'

'Do I? I'm not sure. I don't think I've got what it takes for the property business. It's so different from what I'm used to.'

Calum raised an eyebrow. 'Business strategies can be applied to different industries,' he said, lifting his glass of water and clinking it on her wine glass.

'Maybe.'

But somehow their ideals didn't seem to align.

'It's a lonely business sometimes and not everyone gets it. I guess I don't make myself popular but often that's the case. People get jealous.' He tapped his finger on his glass. 'But I understand it's not for everyone.'

Rebekah tilted her head. He gazed into the distance, looking suddenly lost. 'Hey. I get that it's tough. All business is. I was a financial manager for Take-Action, the international aid organisation. There were tough calls every day, trying to decide who was the most deserving and where the budget should be spent. All I could do was what I believed was right.' She swigged back her wine. She'd always done everything she could to try and make sure everyone got a fair deal, but she'd also trusted that bastard.

'Very wise,' said Calum. 'But you can't do right by everyone all the time and that's a fact of life. Sometimes even when you try to do right, it goes wrong, or you do it in the wrong way. I know that from experience.'

She nodded and held his gaze. 'I absolutely agree. I know that too.'

The concern that he was somehow using her ebbed away and she saw understanding in his eyes. Perhaps he'd made a mistake somewhere too.

'Maybe we…' Calum started, then sipped his water. 'Maybe we're like kindred spirits.'

'Maybe.' It was possible they had similar experiences but Rebekah still wasn't a hundred per cent sure she trusted him or herself.

Chapter Eight

Blair

Blair opened the croft door. The sun was already high in the blue morning sky and only a soft breeze disturbed the high grass around the stone wall. He checked around the open-plan living area but there was no sign of Rebekah. Putting his ear to the extension door, he listened for sounds of the shower running or movement.

'Bekah Ama?' he called in a singsong voice. 'Come out, come out wherever you a-ar.'

No one replied. A nervous tension spread through his veins. Was she still with Calum? Sure, it wasn't a crime but the thought of the two of them together all night made him nauseous. Rebekah's car was there. So what did that mean? Had the smoothy picked her up, intending to keep her? He lived in Tobermory at the other end of the island. It would've been a long drive to drop her off, then go home again – much better if she stayed over. Would Calum be bold enough after a first date? He was audacious enough in business but he didn't give much away about his private life.

'Well, so what if they're still together?' Blair piled up the wood, clanking timbers one on top of the other. 'Let's be real. If I was as rich as him, I'd do the same thing. I guess without any money there's no chance she'd look sideways at me,' he muttered. Though it wasn't exactly true.

He'd seen her sneak a peek at his muscles before. Maybe she liked to ogle a bit of rough, but it ended there. She was way too good for him. Even as a friend with benefits, she was out. He swallowed and rubbed his throat. Christ, no, he couldn't risk that; he fancied her too much to stick to the rules.

Concentrating was impossible. His mind kept wandering. Where was she and what was she doing? He'd barely eaten a thing since their lunch the day before. She wouldn't mind if he ate something, but it felt wrong raiding her fridge when she wasn't there to ask. He raked about in his pockets and found enough change to get something from the shop.

As he nipped along the lane, he heard voices. Mary, the old lady he'd helped with her shopping, was leaning on her fence talking to the woman who lived in the house between her and Rebekah. Blair rarely saw the woman out and about, but occasionally spotted her son running up to the shop.

He waved to Mary and she smiled. 'Oh, hello, Blair. I keep meaning to come along and say hello to the new young lady but my old knees have been playing up.'

'I'm sorry to hear that,' said Blair. 'Are you managing with shopping?'

'Oh, yes. Thank you. Dee here has a wonderful son, who's very good at nipping up to the shop for me.'

Dee pulled a face. 'Aye, Brogan is a good kid, but sometimes I wish he'd study more.'

'What age is he?' asked Blair.

'Twelve.'

'It's a tough age.' Blair could say with all honesty most of his childhood had consisted of tough ages. At twelve, he'd been all but living at his nan's house, going there straight after school and cooking for her, making sure she had everything she needed and trying to get Ryan to do his homework – when he had his own to do too – not exactly the stuff of dreams. Especially when Ryan would come in, dump his school stuff, and head off on his bike. Blair seethed silently at the memory.

'I hear you know Autumn,' said Mary.

'Yeah, she's become like a sister to me.' Blair realised he was scowling and straightened out his forehead. Maybe he loved the idea of having a surrogate sister so much because his real sibling had done nothing but cause trouble. 'How do you know her?'

'She came knocking on my door looking for her mum last year.'

'Did she? She told me a lovely lady in Fionnphort had helped her, but I didn't put two and two together. It was you, was it?'

Mary's fluffy head bobbed with excitement. 'Yes, Dee told her I was the person to ask if you want to find out anything around here. Funny really, I never thought I was a gossip but maybe I am.'

'You've just lived here for a long time,' said Dee. 'And you're very observant.'

'I hope that's it.'

'Did you also know that Autumn found her mum living with my dad?' said Blair.

Mary chuckled. 'I did hear that. It's a funny old world. So many odd coincidences. Autumn is a lovely girl and I'm so pleased she's settled here with that nice man of hers.'

'Yeah, it's cool.' Blair didn't begrudge anyone their happiness but he sometimes wished he could have a slice of it for himself.

'And what's the young lady like?' asked Mary, gesturing her head towards Rebekah's croft. 'I haven't seen her much.'

Dee folded her arms. 'She's been here at least a month now and I've not had so much as a hello.'

A light breeze rustled the bushes in Mary's garden and the bees hummed. Blair rubbed his chin. 'She's actually a great person,' he said. 'She's used to living and working in big cities. It's not that she's snubbing you or anything, it probably just hasn't occurred to her to come and say hello.'

'It's just manners,' said Dee in a low voice.

'I'll say to her,' said Blair. 'Honestly, she's a good person. You'll like her.'

'I quite understand,' said Mary. 'She must be very busy. What does she do?'

Blair frowned. They'd talked about everything and nothing over the past month, but she hadn't given much away about her job. She seemed more interested in her grandmother's mystery, writing up her family history, and Calum. 'I, er, some kind of charity work,' said Blair. 'She works for an international aid company and she's interested in property.'

'Hmm,' said Dee. 'That's a strange combination.'

'I don't know much about it,' said Blair. 'I'll let her tell you. I'm off to the shop. Do either of you need anything?'

'You might pick me up some bread,' said Mary. She ambled back to the house and returned some minutes later, waving a five-pound note. 'Keep the change and get yourself something.'

'I can't do that,' said Blair.

'Of course you can,' said Mary with a smile. 'You're a good boy and it's only a few pennies.'

Good boy? Blair smirked. He hadn't been called that for a while.

'Oh dear,' said Mary. 'I hear my phone. I hope it's not one of those nuisance callers again. Seem to get them all the time at the moment.'

A trickle of fear ran down Blair's neck. 'Best just to hang up,' he said. If he'd followed that advice at sixteen, he could have saved his family years of misery. He'd been the fool who fell for the con. A lifetime wouldn't be long enough to make up the physical debt or the emotional heartache he'd caused.

'Yes, I'll leave it. If it's important, they'll leave a message.'

Blair nipped up to the shop, grabbed a snack and got Mary the bread.

'I only spent one pound ten,' he told her, handing over the loaf and the change. She patted his arm before he returned to the croft. He pushed open the door.

'Hello,' a voice said from the kitchen area.

'Fecking hell, Rebekah.' Blair's hand leapt to his chest. 'Where did you come from?'

'I went for a morning walk. I woke up so early, I decided to go out.'

'You've been walking? I thought you were still with Calum.'

'Really? After one dinner date?'

'Stranger things have happened.'

Rebekah rested a hand on her hip and cocked her head. 'Maybe so, but that was never going to be one of them.'

A crazy atom of hope zipped through Blair for approximately two seconds. Maybe she didn't like Calum after all, but no. It wasn't that. This was a transient thing for her. She was choosing to spend her time wisely. She took the friendly chat during the day with the one most likely to listen – *yours truly*. And for the dates, she chose the one with the money – fair dos.

'He may have money to throw from afa', but is he the man for Bekah Ama?' Blair waggled his eyebrows.

She shook her head and raised her eyes to the ceiling. 'I doubt it. I like him, but I'm not looking for anything long term. I'm done with that.'

'Why?'

'It's complicated but it boils down to me being better on my own. I like company and I'm not against dates but that's it. I don't want anything more serious.'

'And I assume Calum knows that?'

'I'll make sure he does.'

Blair quirked an eyebrow and knuckled down to work. 'Oh, just to let you know, I'm clocking off early this afternoon. I've got an appointment.'

'Are you ill?'

'No, nothing like that. But please don't say anything to Calum. He'll just moan and threaten to cut my pay.'

'I won't say anything.'

'And the woman next door wonders why you haven't been round to see her or Mary, the old lady two doors down.'

Rebekah clapped her hands to her mouth. 'Should I have? Oh no. I've never lived anywhere that people actually do that.'

'Don't worry about it. Take them some home baking and they'll forgive you.'

'Are you serious? Have you seen my baking? It's worse than my cooking.'

'In that case, buy wine.'

*

Blair left at three and drove north for his 'appointment'. Strictly speaking, it was business and he knew Calum wouldn't approve. After a string of messages from his mum panicking about debt collectors at her door, Blair had decided to take a job on the Ardnish Estate.

Blair liked estate owner Archie Crichton-Leith a lot more than he liked Calum. When he'd worked there the previous Christmas overhauling Monarch's Lodge – a stunning house on the grounds – Archie had helped with the work. He hadn't been afraid to get his hands dirty and they'd had some laughs. Not something he got with Calum.

As Blair pulled up outside Monarch's Lodge, a flicker of envy licked his insides. Archie had moved out of the main mansion house and was now living here with his new partner, local artist, Georgia Rose. Blair tugged on the handbrake a little over-zealously as he spied Georgia and Archie in the garden, laughing. Georgia's tousled blonde bob blew about in the wind and Archie slipped his arm around her shoulder. Blair sank back into the rest and closed his eyes to avoid witnessing the scene of domestic bliss. Another empty cavity opened in his chest.

With an effort, he peeled open his eyelids. Georgia and Archie were now hand in hand, walking away towards the end of the long garden. A wall at the end shielded the outdoor space from the sea, some twenty feet below. With a house set on a cliffside promontory like this, you didn't get much more dramatic or romantic. It suited Georgia: sunny, smiley, cheerful and full of nonsense. The perfect foil for sensible Archie, though he was more fun than he let on. The fire of envy flared again. Not because Archie had loads of money but because he'd landed Georgia.

'Ah bugger me,' muttered Blair. He'd always had a soft spot for her, much the same as he did for Rebekah, but of course, Georgia had never seen him as anything other than a friend. 'And fuck it, I can handle it.' He was happy for her. As happy as he was for Autumn, and his dad, and everyone else who'd found their soulmate. He opened the door and banged it shut, loud enough for Georgia and Archie to hear.

They turned around and Georgia waved.

'Hey, Blair,' she called from afar, skipping up to meet him. The sea crashed up against a cliff at the bottom of the garden. Archie pushed his hands into the pockets of his Barbour jacket and followed. His two pointers trotted along beside him.

'Hey,' Blair replied, and accepted Georgia's hug. These were the kind of hugs he could get all around the island from the people he'd befriended over the years.

'Nice to see you again,' said Archie.

'Yeah, it's good to be back.' He'd enjoyed working here. Why hadn't he waited instead of taking on the job with Calum? Archie had promised him more work, but it hadn't come quick enough.

'Sorry it's taken so long. We've been sorting through so much old furniture. Two of the estate cottages are empty now and there's work needing done on both.'

Blair brushed his palms together. 'I'm happy to start it, but I'm contracted to finish the croft at Fionnphort. Maybe I could do this at weekends? It's such a long drive between Fionnphort and here, I couldn't realistically do both in the same day and I've still got another couple of months' work there.'

'Blair, are you mental?' said Georgia. 'You can't do both. I thought you'd finished there.'

'No, it's cool. If I can start at weekends.'

'It'll keep for a couple of months,' said Archie. 'We can spend the time clearing the other cottages. I don't want you killing yourself.'

But he needed the cash and he needed it soon. 'Weekends are fine. Working for you guys is like helping out friends, so it won't feel like work. I can start straight away.'

He caught the look between them and held his breath.

'Blair, I'm not sure,' said Georgia. 'It seems an awful lot to ask.'

'You're not asking, I'm offering.'

'Are you sure?' said Archie. 'How about just Saturday. Let's not push it.'

'Fine, that's cool.' It was a foot in the door and he could always build up the hours later.

'Come on then, I'll show you what needs to be done.' Archie strode off up the track with the dogs following.

'You look worn out,' said Georgia, pulling Blair aside.

'I just had a restless night, but I'm fine. Everything's cool.'

'And what about Mike, I mean your dad? Is he ok?'

'How do you mean?'

'You know Archie lets him have Gardener's Cottage for a low rent because he does loads of work around the estate?'

'Yeah?'

'Has he lost his other job or something? Because a couple of times he's asked Archie for a loan.' Georgia tucked her hair behind her ear. 'You told me before he used to have a drinking problem and I know Vicky did too. You don't think they've gone back to that, do you?'

Blair shrugged but his blood pressure rocketed. He was ninety-eight per cent certain his dad wouldn't go back to drinking. He didn't know Vicky well enough to speak for her though. His dad was smitten but surely he wouldn't be crazy enough to start fuelling her habit again. 'Have you asked Autumn?' Maybe it would be cruel to bring up the subject with her. Autumn had high hopes her mum was clean and would be crushed if Vicky was drinking again. The two of them had just started forging their relationship anew and Blair could only imagine Autumn's pain if he had to break news like that to her.

'No, I haven't. It might be nothing. It just seemed odd.'

'I'll go and see him after this.' If only Georgia knew; this wasn't odd at all. She didn't know his family. Borrowing money left, right and centre was commonplace for them, paying it back quite another matter, and most of it was his fault. If he'd had his wits about him ten years back, his nan wouldn't have become embroiled in a dodgy insurance scam that had ended up with her losing her house and his parents becoming almost bankrupt trying to pay off the loans they'd taken out to cover the debt. A shitstorm of a mess caused by a sixteen year old who couldn't even sort his own life, never mind anyone else's. Why hadn't he concentrated on getting a qualification so he could do a decent job and be of some use?

The semi-detached cottages Archie wanted fixing up were in reasonable condition, much better than Rebekah's croft had been, but there was still a lot to do. Blair noted it down, fidgeting with the cuff of his hoody as Archie showed him around. He was itching to see his dad and find out what the hell was going on.

As soon as he'd collected his van, he drove along the bumpy track to Gardener's Cottage. He'd thought his dad might be at work but as he rounded a bend, he spotted him, loading a cement mixer next to a tumbledown wall close to Gardener's Cottage. Blair stopped the van and jumped out. Mike looked up and dusted off his hands.

'Hi, son,' he said. 'What brings you here?' Mike kept his hair short and neat. Had he dyed it? His dad wasn't fifty yet and seemed, if anything, to be getting younger.

'Just wondered how you're getting on.'

'Very well, thanks. I'm sorting out the walls round the estate.'

Blair sucked his lips between his teeth. Should he jump in directly or wait for Dad to come round to the subject? A subject he'd probably want to avoid. 'Aren't you doing your forestry job anymore?'

'Aye, I am. But it's part-time and we lost a contract a while back, so things are slow.'

'Is that why you borrowed money from Archie?'

Mike frowned. 'Did he tell you about that?'

'No. I heard it from someone else. But it's a bit worrying, Dad.'

'Na, it's ok. We pay very little rent here but it means I do most of the odd jobs for nothing. I get that it's made up by what I'm not paying in rent, but when I miss a pay check from my other job, it leaves us high and dry. Archie said he understood and didn't seem to mind. It was only to tide me over.'

'I'm sure he does understand. He's a nice guy… But did you pay him back?'

'Not yet,' said Mike, shovelling sand into the mixer.

'But you're going to?'

'Sure. He knows I am. Did he send you here? He hasn't mentioned it to me since.'

'No, I told you. He didn't say a thing about it. I'm sure Archie won't come hounding you for it.' If anything, he'd probably write it off, but Blair didn't want to encourage that.

'I'll pay him as soon as I can.'

'And when will that be?'

'Blair, what has got into you?' Mike straightened up and jammed his hands on his hips. 'Why are you getting so shirty? I'm capable of taking care of myself. I'd rather not borrow money but sometimes needs must, as you well know.'

Blair felt the sting. He knew how much they'd had to borrow to bail themselves out after he'd embroiled them in the scam. Even after they'd realised what was going on, there was no way of recovering the money or catching the perpetrators.

'I do. I just… worry. Mum's been borrowing from dodgy lenders again and I panicked that you, or Vicky, might be… you know, drinking again.'

'Well, we're not. We're doing great actually, and I'm not your mum. What's she needing money for this time?'

'Ryan borrowed money to buy a new oven, but it was from some shady characters, as usual.'

'But that's all sorted. I gave him the money for that.'

'You what?' Blair gaped and held up his palms.

'A couple of weeks ago. He called in a right tizz. You know what he gets like. It brings on his asthma. I thought he was going to pass out.'

Blair gritted his teeth and ground a stone into the gravel with his boot. Ryan and his bloody attacks. He'd suffered from asthma as a child but these days the attacks conveniently coincided with him needing cash. 'So, if you paid for that, why does Mum still need money?'

'Search me,' said Mike. 'I don't know why she needed a new oven in the first place. She could have cooked something in one of her three breadmakers, two sandwich toasters or her George Foreman Grill. I've never known anyone who could buy so much worthless junk as your mum.'

Sadly, it was true. Hoarding was a side effect of her depression. Blair had suffered the horror of clearing out his mum's house the previous year. It would have been quicker blitzing it. 'So, is that the real reason you borrowed the money from Archie? To bail out Ryan.'

'Partly. He's my son too, Blair. And he's suffered a lot with his health.'

Here we go again. Blair restrained his eye roll. Didn't Dad know a lot of Ryan's health issues stemmed from his drug habits? Blair's blood boiled when he considered how much they'd forked out for courses and young apprenticeships, trying to keep Ryan on the straight and narrow, while Blair had foregone any kind of further education until he'd landed himself the joinery apprenticeship the year before. 'Right. Ok.'

'Did you drive all the way up here to ask me about that?'

'No, I'm doing some work in the cottages for Archie and Georgia.'

Mike nodded. 'So is that you finished at Fionnphort?'

'Almost,' Blair lied. He couldn't go through this conversation again. He knew he'd be pushing his mind and body to the limit working two physically draining jobs, but he needed the money and he was determined not to follow in the footsteps of his parents or go down the drain like his brother.

Chapter Nine

Rebekah

Brown mixture splattered up the wall, utensils lay everywhere and a cracked egg oozed across the floor. Stooping over, Rebekah wiped it up. Every indicator pointed at the likelihood of her slipping on the egg while carrying a glass bowl, falling, breaking the bowl and several bones in the process. It was that kind of day and it wasn't even five-thirty in the morning. She hadn't lied when she'd told Blair her baking skills were worse than her cooking. Carnage ruled in the croft kitchen.

Sleeping longer than four hours was nothing but an elusive dream, so Rebekah decided these early mornings were the perfect times to attempt some recipes. If this chocolate brownie cake worked out, she was ready to take it round to the neighbours and beg their forgiveness for not having followed island etiquette. If the cake flopped, she had wine chilling in the fridge and a tin of shop-bought shortbread in the cupboard.

She chuckled at what Blair would make of the mess as she placed the tin in the oven, crossed her fingers and set the timer. With a forty-minute wait ahead, she cleaned up the kitchen and went for a shower.

Although she hadn't called on her new neighbours before, a visit to Mary's had been on the cards ever since her date with Calum. He'd sown the seed and now she looked at the cottage with fresh eyes. It appeared, to her untrained eye, to be a post-war house bursting with character – a cute little seaside home and a holidaymaker's dream. Wild ideas formed as Rebekah stood under the hot water gushing from the tropical showerhead. If she befriended Mary, maybe the old lady would grow fond of her, perhaps leave her the cottage? Rebekah smirked at the idea; it was silly. Things like that only happened in films. But thoughts like that were so much more welcome than the terrors of the last year. The magical waters surrounding Mull had washed clean those memories. Rebekah smoothed the lather over her skin; she was like a new woman, and it felt amazing.

The brownie cake was a flop. Almost. It tasted like a gooey chocolate pudding and was delicious straight off a spoon, but as a gift for the neighbours, it wouldn't do. Rebekah slumped on the sofa in the garden room and watched the sea rolling up the sandy bay below. She stifled a yawn as the morning caught up with her. In a few months, she'd miss this view. Uncertainty tainted her thoughts of the future. Her mother wanted her to live in London and while the notion appealed, she missed Kumasi. She also missed work, real work. What she was doing here was diverting but it was going nowhere. She was treading water and couldn't see a clear way out.

The investigations into her grandmother's past had run aground. She'd visited the Tobermory museum as Blair had suggested and while they had been helpful and dug out the records they had on evacuees, Rebekah didn't see any names she recognised. They couldn't confirm where the photo was taken – it did fit the island in the 1940s, but could be any of a number of islands or highland locations as there was nothing to place it more specifically. The idea of her grandmother ever having been here seemed ever crazier the more she saw of the place. The village was remote and, despite a bustle of fishing boats and tourists, there was a sleepiness here. In the past most of the houses would have been stone crofts with thatched roofs and minimal furniture. It wasn't a place suited to her grandmother. If she had been here, it would have been a traumatic change, no wonder she'd never mentioned it when she returned. But Rebekah had no proof it was even her grandmother in the picture. It was too faded to tell with any certainty. Perhaps it was a relative or a friend or just a picture that had inspired a hidden imagination. If she had been here though, why had she stolen the necklace? Was it a deep unhappiness at being so displaced? Rebekah pursed her lips at her green tea. If only she'd asked her grandmother before it was too late.

Her laptop sat open on the little table but Rebekah remained on the sofa, uncertain what to do next. What a flippant existence she had. Writing up her family history notes while living off her savings and the money her father had given her for the trip was great but restless energy bounced around inside her. She closed her eyes. 'Thank you, Universe, for the gift of financial freedom.' So many people weren't as lucky, people she used to help. A pang needled her, like somehow she was failing people. She couldn't help everyone but now she was helping no one, except herself. Time to live, breathe and regroup was permitted, but six months was excessive. Six days should have sufficed. No matter who she kidded, herself included, she'd never come here to work. Not really. Admitting to needing rest somehow constituted failure though and she didn't want that. Seth had brought her low enough, she couldn't sink herself further, her dignity depended on it.

Conscious thought ebbed away.

The clunk of a door handle woke her and she spun around to see Blair coming in with a length of timber.

'You're awake now,' he said.

'Was I asleep?'

'You sure were.'

'What time is it?'

'Nine thirty.'

Rebekah straightened up and rubbed her neck. It was stiff from lying at a funny angle. 'Fab, I've had three hours sleep, that's almost a record for me.'

'Sorry I woke you. I was trying to be quiet but the plank walloped the door.'

'It's fine. I'm calling on the neighbours today, I don't want to be too late.'

'Is that your offering on the worktop?' asked Blair with a smirk.

'Yes. Is there something wrong with it?' She gave him a challenging look.

'Well, it might stick poor Mary's teeth together.' He peered into the tin and screwed up his nose.

'Don't look at it like that. Do the taste test before you judge. But not with your finger, use a spoon.'

He rolled his eyes. 'You posh girls have no sense of fun,' he said, pulling a spoon from a drawer, scooping up a mound of chocolate goo and placing it in his mouth with a ridiculously over the top motion like he was on a cheesy commercial. 'Very seductive.' He groaned in mock ecstasy. 'You should be feeding this to Calum, not a geriatric neighbour.'

'Oh, very funny.'

'If you want to send him over the moon, feed him chocolate off a spoon.'

'For heaven's sake, Blair.' She laughed. 'You and your crazy rhymes. Have you ever considered a career in children's entertainment?'

'Nope.' He loaded up his spoon again. 'Oops, I double dipped, now you can't have any.' He licked it clean. 'Unless you want to share?' With a waggle of his eyebrows, he held it out.

Rebekah sat opposite and leaned forward. Blair grinned and fed her a drop of chocolate. 'Really, Blair,' she said with a giggle, wiping a drip of the mixture from her lip. 'You should get a girlfriend.'

'Who said I didn't have one?'

She racked her brains. Had he told her he did? They'd talked about a lot of things but she was pretty certain he'd mentioned no one special in his life. 'I assumed.'

'Did you? Well, never assume anything,' he said in a teasing voice, still fooling about with the spoon.

'Do tell.' Rebekah folded her arms and leaned on the surface.

'I don't really,' he said, feeding her another spoonful. 'I was seeing someone but… Well, she lives on the mainland, so we don't get together often.'

'You were seeing her and now you're not, but you still get together?'

His snorted laugh sounded more like a grunt. 'Yeah, something like that. It's more of a mutual arrangement kind of thing.'

'Oh, right. Friends with benefits, you mean?' Her knowledgeable tone hid her inner cringe. Sometimes she felt like she'd led a very sheltered life. Friends with benefits was something she'd seen in films and read in books, not something she associated with real people. But here was Blair, as large as life, talking about it like it happened every day. So, that was the kind of man he was. Something inside her fizzled out and died.

'Yup.' He didn't meet her eye and fiddled with the cake.

'I should make a move.' She picked up her phone and checked the messages. 'You can finish that cake, it's too sickly for me.'

'Yum,' he said with a wink.

A message flashed up.

CALUM: Hey, how are you? Do you fancy trying out The Lobster Creel? It's near Fionnphort. I have a business idea. I can't get it out of my head. I wonder if you'd like to work with me on a little project. Let's meet sometime and chat about it. Really enjoyed your company the other night. Speak soon.

Rebekah pulled in a deep breath, taking in the whirlwind of a message. Work together and go on another date. A ringing started in her ears. The clanging sound of alarm bells. The last time she'd worked with someone and dated them at the same time had ended in catastrophe. She wanted to believe Calum wasn't like Seth but in many ways, he was – his determination in business, his love of fine eateries and his ruthless reputation. Could she be objective without running the risk of falling into a trap? She glanced at Blair as he worked his way through the cake. What a shit judge of character she was. A few minutes ago, she'd never have pegged him as someone who'd be ok with a friends-with-benefits arrangement, yet there he was.

She decided to park her worries about Calum and deal with the neighbours first. No need to rush a reply; Calum wouldn't be sitting by his phone waiting for an answer.

Armed with the plan of going to Mary's house first, Rebekah was forced to abandon it straight away. Her neighbour came bounding out of her house as Rebekah was about to walk past.

'Er, hello,' said Rebekah. 'I was just about to come and see you.'

'See me?' said the woman, stroking back her long and somewhat bedraggled hair.

'Yes. I'm your neighbour, Rebekah. I, er, should have called before but I didn't think to. Sorry. Blair said I should. I've got something for you, a belated hello.'

'Oh, there's no need. Well, that's kind but you didn't have to. I wasn't sure if you maybe wanted privacy or I would have put my head round before.'

Rebekah smiled and handed over the bottle of wine. 'No problem.'

'Thanks, this looks good. I'm Dee,' said the woman. 'I've got an appointment shortly, so I can't talk for long, but I'd like to chat sometime.'

'I won't keep you. Hopefully everything's all right.'

'It's the bloody bank. I'm at my wit's end with money. Honestly, people think living here is some kind of picnic. Well, it's horrendous. The price of life is going to break me.'

Rebekah opened and closed her mouth. How to respond to such an unexpected outpouring?

'Sorry. I'm having a bad day. My landlord wants me out of here and he's just punched my rent up again. It's his sneaky way of trying to move me along. It's the same sleazeball who owns your place. Calum Matheson. I'm sick of him. He's an islander born and bred; you'd think he'd have some compassion. Property prices here are sky high already, but there's bugger all I can do about it. Now I have to go to the bank to see if there's anything else they can do for me.'

'Is everything all right?' A gentle voice spoke from the neighbouring garden and both Rebekah and Dee turned around. A tiny woman with a fluffy white hairdo peered over the fence.

'I'm sorry, Mary. I was just ranting. This is Rebekah from the end croft.'

'Hello,' said Rebekah. 'I'm doing the rounds. I should have done this before. I have some shortbread here for you.'

'Oh, how lovely. It's nice to meet you in person. Blair told us you were a wonderful girl.'

'Did he?'

'Yes, indeed. Oh, I do like this kind of shortbread, thank you.'

'I need to go,' said Dee. 'We'll talk again soon.' She jumped in her car and sped off down the lane.

'Poor woman,' said Mary, gripping the stone wall at the front of her cottage. 'She's having a hard time. Split with her husband a while back and she needed a place on the island to stay. She's a nurse and works long hours in the hospital in Craignure. It's a long drive from here, especially in the dark and in bad weather. Well, you've seen the roads. But there's nowhere affordable on the island now. People like Calum Matheson buy up properties and rent them out at extortionate prices, or make them into holiday houses, or worse, use them as second homes so they're lying empty most of the time. Hardworking islanders like Dee can hardly afford to live here. Since Calum bought her property, he's put up the rent every month and she's struggling. But she's so helpful. She and her son Brogan run errands for me and I'm very glad they do.'

How could Calum seriously want to throw out people like this? And she'd given him the impression she was interested, maybe even able to help him. Had these people got wind of her idea and this was their way of letting her know they didn't approve? She couldn't blame them.

'You're lucky to have such wonderful neighbours. I wish I'd come along sooner. I've been so wrapped up in my own business, I haven't really got to know anyone.'

'You've been working hard,' said Mary. 'It's hardly surprising.'

Rebekah bit the inside of her lip. 'Actually, I'm not working at the moment.' She should have admitted it in the first place, not just to her parents or Calum but to herself. There was never much real danger of her getting into property and now was the time to come clean, she didn't want anyone to get the wrong idea about her. Seth had done enough to paint her as the bad guy, she didn't need to do it to herself. The property idea had appealed on a fantasy level but it was an excuse. What she needed was a place to switch off. 'I'm taking some time off to regroup and possibly change career.' For someone who'd rarely missed a day's work before, it was hard admitting she needed a break. She'd given herself a purpose that seemed noble but it was fake. And now, it seemed nothing short of cruel. Saying the words aloud released a knot of tension in her stomach.

'Oh, that sounds very interesting. Now, would you like a cup of tea? I don't keep coffee.'

'I'm a bit of a coffee addict, but I really need to cut down, so tea will do nicely.'

'Wonderful,' said Mary. 'In you come and we can sample this lovely shortbread.'

If Calum was entertaining an idea that somehow Rebekah was going to persuade Mary to move out, he was mistaken. Rebekah was going to fight tooth and nail to make sure the old lady could stay exactly where she was without further threat from anyone.

Chapter Ten

Blair

A fierce wind picked up in the croft garden and Blair's notes whipped out from under the timber he was sawing. 'Oh crap!' he shouted, vaulting the wall and charging along the lane after them. He couldn't afford to lose them. Calum would not be impressed if he had to provide new copies, or if Blair made things up and didn't follow his exacting specs.

Up ahead, Brogan, the kid who lived in the neighbouring house, was trudging towards Blair with a laden carrier bag on his arm. He checked up, realising what was going on, and stuck his foot on one of the papers. He grabbed it, then leapt towards the embankment and stamped on another one before the wind caught it.

'Thanks,' said Blair, snatching up the third sheet. 'That could have been a disaster.'

'No worries,' said Brogan.

'Really, mate, you've possibly saved my skin.' He clasped the papers to his chest.

'Cool.'

'It's the school holidays, isn't it?' said Blair. 'You doing anything nice with your pals?'

'No, just a bit of footie.'

'Where do you play?'

Brogan shrugged. 'On the beach, if anyone's around.'

'Sounds fun. Give me a shout sometime, I'll come and kick with you.'

'Do you play?' Brogan's expression lit up.

'Not a lot,' said Blair. 'But I bet I can put one past you.'

'Bet you can't.' Brogan smirked. 'Who's your favourite player?'

'Dunno,' said Blair. 'I haven't followed it for a while.'

'I like Troy Copeland. You see what happened to him?' Brogan scrunched up his face and mouthed, 'ouch'.

'Is he the one who was in a car crash?'

'Yeah. Broke loads of bones, but I bet he comes back. He's totally the GOAT.'

'The what?' said Blair.

'The greatest of all time. I might go and see one of his matches next season, if he's recovered; my dad said he'd take me.'

'Sounds awesome,' said Blair. 'I better get back to work. And Mary's probably waiting for her shopping. That's cool of you to do that.'

'She pays me,' said Brogan.

'That's generous because she can't have that much spare cash.'

'Actually, she has tons. I've seen it. She has this jar that looks like a bear hugging a beehive and it's totally full of cash.'

Blair ran his hand over his head. 'Does she? That's probably her life savings. Poor Mary. She should put it in the bank.'

Brogan unclipped Mary's gate. 'I guess. Anyway, see ya,' he said.

'Thanks, mate.' Blair tipped him a wave.

'Cool tats, by the way.'

'Thanks.' Blair smirked. 'But don't go getting any until you're old enough.'

'Haha.'

The rogue wind had blown away the clouds, leaving blue skies and warmth. Blair loved it when the island was baked in sunshine; it was like living in the tropics. The icy winter winds were forgotten. Even showering in the cold outhouse wasn't painful. Blair was tempted to work topless, but if Calum turned up he might object, so his vest stayed on. He tugged it out, trying to let the air cool his sweaty chest.

'This weather is perfect.' Rebekah ambled out of the garden room, wearing a pale blue maxi dress, testing the baking concrete with her bare toes. She rarely wore her hair down, but today it spiralled around her shoulders with only a narrow hairband holding it off her face. Blair swallowed; she was the embodiment of perfection. She always looked naturally beautiful but today she was glowing. Even if she'd dressed up for Calum, Blair couldn't care less, he was going to feed his eyes and enjoy.

'You look beautiful,' he said. The words were exactly what he'd been thinking but he hadn't meant them to tumble out. He held his breath.

'Oh.' Rebekah toyed with the strap of her dress and Blair looked away to silently curse his big mouth. 'Thanks. I didn't know it would get so warm here. Thankfully, I brought some sundresses.'

'Yeah, thankfully,' he mumbled, not making eye contact.

'Can you swim here?' asked Rebekah.

'In the sea?'

'Yes. I've swum in the sea in Ghana. It has some beautiful beaches, but is it too cold here?'

'Well, I've never been abroad so I can't compare it with anywhere else,' he said, lifting a plank onto his workbench. 'I've swum here loads of times. It can feel a bit nippy when you first go in, but once you're over that initial shock, it's fine.'

'Fancy going for a paddle later?'

'Me?'

'Why not?'

'What about Calum? He'll flog me if I go paddling when I'm supposed to be here and then kill me if I go to the beach with his girlfriend.'

Rebekah laughed and shook her head. 'I'm not his girlfriend. We've only been on one date. And you're my friend. I don't see Calum as the paddling type or I would ask him.'

'No, I can't see him getting his feet wet. But I can't really leave this.'

'Not even when you clock off?'

Blair pulled his phone from his back pocket and checked the time. 'Yeah, ok. Or actually… Let's go now.'

'I thought you just said—'

'I know, but it won't be as hot later. This way we can use the hot part of the day to cool down and I'll catch up on the work later when it's cooler.'

'Are you sure?'

'Yeah, why not. YOLO and all that.'

Rebekah skipped to the door. 'Fab. I'm going to put on my swimming clothes, see you in a bit.'

'Oh, Jesus Christ,' muttered Blair, rubbing his hand down his face. What had he let himself in for? Rebekah in swimwear.

She reappeared some moments later wearing the same dress and holding a beach bag stuffed with towels. He didn't ask why she hadn't changed. It was better this way, the more body cover, the better.

'Ready?' she said.

He downed tools and shoved the plans under three bricks so there was no chance of them blowing away. 'As I'll ever be.' They nipped down the verge towards the shore. 'Come this way,' said Blair, veering over the stubbly grass plain known as the machair. 'There are always loads of people on this beach. If we go over the hill here, there are some more secluded places and much nicer beaches.'

'Sounds fabulous. Lead on.'

They crested a small hill and carried on along a ridge until they got to the edge. 'Look down there.'

Rebekah stepped forward, shielded her eyes and stared. 'Incredible.'

The sea lapped up emerald green on the white sands in a cove below. 'Hardly anyone comes here.' Blair led the way towards the beach. 'Only locals know about places like this. The tourists rarely venture off the paths.'

'Tell me about life on the island,' said Rebekah, speeding up and overrunning him as they got to a steep decline.

'What do you mean?'

'I'm curious about what Dee and Mary said to me yesterday. It seems like an affluent place on the surface, but is there a lot of poverty here?'

Blair toyed with a strand of his dreads. 'Not lots, but some people struggle. The shops here are pricey. And there's been a tip in the balance since I was young. Most people you meet are incomers. I'm not saying that's all bad, but it leaves big gaps when it comes to housing.'

'Where do you live?'

'Ha.' He let out a bitter laugh. 'I rent a tiny caravan from a local farmer. It's up the back of the village on the road to Knockvologan.'

'Are you serious?'

'Yup.'

'You see, that bothers me. It's not fair on people like you and Dee. People who need to live here but can't afford it or there isn't housing available.'

'It's more and more the norm. My parents weren't well off but they had a nice house: a little bungalow in Croggan. It's a cute out of the way village. Last year, they sold up. They'd been divorced for a while, but they got a pittance for it. Partly my mum's fault and partly my brother's. She's a terrible hoarder and she'd let the house go to the dogs. He's on and off drugs and he's a mess. Once the money was split between my parents, they barely had enough to cover their debts, never mind do anything else. You should see the place now. It's a pretty little holiday cottage that pulls in about eight hundred and fifty quid a week.'

Rebekah frowned and shook her head. 'That doesn't seem right.'

'It's the way of the world just now.'

'Did your parents find homes on the island?'

'My dad did. He rents a place on the Ardnish Estate, but my mum couldn't afford it. She qualified for a council house, but there were none on the island, so she moved to Oban with her boyfriend. She's got another place there now as they've split.'

'I didn't realise you'd had such a hard a life.'

His feet hit the sand and he drew in a deep breath of salty sea air. It was difficult to think of anything negative here. This cove was a hidden gem few people knew about.

'I guess. So, are you ready to swim?' He looked her up and down. Was she planning to wade in fully clothed?

'Almost. You?'

'I'll have to go starkers, I clean forgot my budgie smugglers.'

Rebekah covered her mouth and chuckled. 'Oh, Blair. You do make me laugh.'

He tilted his head. 'You're going to laugh at me naked? That's not very kind.'

'Stop it.' She hid behind her hands, giggling, then peered between her fingers. 'You are joking, aren't you?'

'Maybe.'

'Oh, boy, this is going to be interesting.' She dropped the bag, then laid a towel on the sand. 'I would tell you to look away, but you're about to get an eyeful one way or another.' The tip of her index finger slid under her dress strap and one by one, she skimmed them down.

Blair nearly died; what the hell was she doing? Was she going in au naturel herself? If so, he had to get in the water and fast. He needed to cool off. Before he could grab hold of any lucid thought, she slipped the dress down and stepped out of it, her perfectly trim body bared before him, covered only by a brief orange bikini.

Swimming trunks wouldn't smuggle anything right now. Blair ripped off his vest and headed for the sea.

'Are you wearing them in?' asked Rebekah, pointing to his knee-length ripped denim shorts.

'Well, I'm not really going naked,' he said, hardly looking around. How could he? The sight of her was messing with every synapse; raw desire hurtled through his body.

'Spoilsport.'

He waded in until the water was well above his middle before he turned around. Rebekah wasn't so sure and took tentative steps at the water's edge. She was like a model or someone from *Baywatch*. Far too bloody sexy to be allowed this close to him. *Focus mind, hands off.* Whether she was Calum's girlfriend or not was irrelevant. *She isn't mine!* And she wasn't going to be. Nothing in Blair's life put him within five hundred yards of Rebekah. He'd be worse for her than Spanish flu. After bobbing up and down for a few seconds to accustom his upper body to the temperature, he sucked in as much air as he could, held his nose and sunk beneath the waves.

When he burst up again, Rebekah still hadn't reached him. She teetered closer, her lips pressed together like she was holding her breath and her arms high in the air. 'Are there jellyfish in here?' She kept her eyes down.

'Probably,' said Blair.

'Will they sting?'

'Depends. I've heard they're particularly fond of women in orange bikinis.'

'Oh, stop it.'

'Rebekah's bikini is terribly swish, and especially attractive to jellyfish.'

'Ok, that's it.' She dipped her hand in the water and flicked him.

'Now you've done it,' he said, splashing her back.

'Get off.' She skimmed the top of a wave and sloshed him.

Blair laughed as they fooled around and the sound of Rebekah's giggles tickled him.

'Oh, god.' She stooped over the water, panting. 'I haven't laughed this much in ages. This is better than therapy.'

'Are you ok? You look like you're having an attack.'

'No, really. This is fab.' She held onto her midriff under the crystal-clear water, a beautiful smile shining from her. Her bikini top hid nothing, especially now it was wet.

A desire to pull her close surged through Blair and he took a deep breath, pinched his nose and dropped under the water again. Maybe if he stayed under long enough, his brain would be so addled he wouldn't notice anything attractive about Rebekah.

He popped up and rubbed droplets from his face with his full hands. His wet dreadlocks weighed a ton. Before he'd gathered his thoughts together, something slimy slapped across his face and onto his chest. Rebekah doubled over laughing again as he peered down to see a massive wodge of seaweed stuck to him. 'Did you throw that?' He peeled it off his chest and picked it from his hair. 'So much for quiet and reserved Rebekah,' he said, wading towards her. 'Where have you left her?'

Rebekah couldn't speak for laughing.

'Looks like you need to cool off,' said Blair. He waded up beside her and lifted the legs from under her. 'Oh, Bekah Ama, brave as can be, I'm gonna dunk you right in the sea.'

'No,' she shrieked, water dripping off her. Her bikini was so skimpy there was barely any point in it. One wrench with his teeth and he could pull it off, and Christ, he wanted to. 'Put me down.'

'My pleasure,' said Blair. She grabbed hold of him, screwing up her face. Was it a laugh or a silent scream? Maddening lust slammed through his system. He let go, but in the split second she hit the water, he caught her again and held her tight.

'Oh my god, stop,' she panted. 'Don't drop me.'

He laughed as she clung to him. 'No? How about we wait for a passing jellyfish? Or would you prefer a crab? There are some big ones around here.'

'Oh, god, I hope you're joking.' She wrapped her arms around his neck and hugged him; tears of laughter misted her eyes.

Jesus fecking Christ. This was going to kill him. Holding her dripping wet body close to his chest while she giggled in his ear was the most painfully delirious thing that had ever happened to him.

'Oh, Blair, I'm sorry.' She gathered herself with some slow breaths; they landed just below his ear. He twitched and almost dropped her.

'What are you sorry for? Covering me with seaweed?' He set her down gently and staggered back. He had to. If she got any closer... If he did. Jeez, he couldn't think straight, he just had to put distance between them.

'Kind of... No, not really.' She winked. 'I'm sorry I lost it. I don't know what came over me.'

'It's called fun.'

'Yes, exactly. That's something my life has been missing for a long time.' The sea bobbed around her, its surface sparkling.

'Mine too,' said Blair.

'Really? You seem like a fun kind of guy to me.'

'I like a laugh, yeah. But you know.' He shrugged.

'Sorry for asking, and feel free to tell me to keep my nose out, but are you in some kind of trouble... Financially?'

He picked at the seaweed in his hair and sighed.

'I only wonder because you work so many hours and from what you said about the caravan.'

'You know...' He swallowed. 'When I said my parents used the money from their house sale to pay off debts.'

'Yes.'

'Some of them were my brother's debts, but most of them were mine.'

'What?' A pained expression eclipsed her beautiful smile.

'I made mistakes growing up.'

'Everyone does.'

'Yeah, but mine led to my nan being defrauded out of thousands of pounds and losing her house. My parents have been in debt ever since – we never got the money back.'

'Oh no.'

'Yup. I was her carer. I was supposed to look after her, but I did the opposite. I broke our family. I took a call from a bogus insurance company when I was sixteen. I believed it was real and my nan was in trouble. She looked to me for guidance, so she thought I must be right. Ugh.' He rubbed his face. 'It was such a mess. She lost all her savings and my parents were left trying to bail her out. We were all sucked into the trap, thanks to my idiocy. Now, I help when I can. It's the least I can do. So, yeah. I guess that could be seen as trouble.'

'Oh, Blair.' Rebekah waded closer and wrapped her arms around him again. The danger returned, doubled, trebled, as he closed his arms around her and placed his rough hands on her beautifully smooth back. She was wonderful. Her hold dispersed all the worries and pain in his body. He dipped his head so their cheeks brushed together while her fingertips played along his shoulder blades. Their wet bodies stuck firmly together in a perfect embrace. He would keep her here forever, cherish her every second if he could, but she wasn't for him. 'You're not to blame. You were just a child. It's your parents' job to look after you not the other way around. I'm so sorry this happened.'

'I'm ok,' he said, giving her a stoic pat. 'It's my reality and I deal with it. I don't want you feeling sorry for me or anything like that. Ok?' He pulled back and stared at her.

'Ok,' she said with a small smile.

'I mean it. If you ever show me pity, I really will dunk you in here.'

Her wide grin cracked her face again and she flung up her hands. 'Ok, ok, I understand.'

'Good… Now, I have something for you.'

Her eyes widened and she took a step back. What was she expecting? From under the water, he laid his hands on a giant, slippery piece of kelp, pulled it out and dropped it on Rebekah's back.

'A jellyfish, just for you.'

They could probably hear her screams back in the village.

Chapter Eleven

Rebekah

Rebekah ran along the ridge above the beach with Blair. The breeze was negligible and the baking sun had dried them as soon as they were out of the water. It was hard to look at him in the same way as before after hearing his dire situation. She'd always suspected he wasn't well off but now her chest ached for him. Naturally, he didn't want to be pitied, he was too tough for that, but it was hard for her not to want to come up with all sorts of helpful solutions. Would he see that as pity? Or interference?

When they got back to the croft, Rebekah made herself scarce. Blair had work to catch up on. She positioned her laptop at the window in the garden room where she could glance up from her writing and catch a glimpse of those muscles in action. He was too damn hot. Their fooling around in the water had woken dormant feelings. When they'd been close, she could have shut her eyes, forgotten the outside world and lost herself with Blair. He was like something from a fantasy. A man she could only have in her dreams.

With a second date with Calum looming, he was the one she should be thinking about. But this was different. Talking about business with Calum was interesting, and they were companionable together, but the raw emotion Blair kindled inside her was a force to be reckoned with.

Why did he have to be a man whose relationships consisted of friends with benefits? Rebekah classed him as a friend now… But what about the benefits?

She rested her chin on her knuckles, elbows on the table edge. What if she'd taken their afternoon fun further? There had been a moment, brief but there, when the urge to kiss him had scorched her. Could she steal a piece of the benefits Blair was happy to offer others? He would do it for her too, wouldn't he? Maybe it was exactly what she needed – a no strings attached fling for the next few months.

Only she couldn't guarantee her heart obeying the no-strings rule. Already threads had snaked out of it, weaving their way into Blair's concerns. It would be hard enough to say goodbye to *friend* Blair in a few months. If they made it any bigger, how could she let it go?

She'd agreed to no pity, but one thing she couldn't allow was for him to starve. He wouldn't appreciate her giving him money or even buying him food, but she'd thought of a subtler and mutually beneficial arrangement. She left it a couple of days in the hope he wouldn't suspect her motives were directly related to his confession.

'Blair,' she said, eyeing him from the kitchen area. 'Could you help me with something?'

'Sure.' He dusted his palms on his jeans. 'What is it?'

'Not now. Later. When you're finished here, would you give me a hand with a recipe?'

'Yeah, no probs.'

'Fab. Even your numpty-proof ones are too advanced for me.'

'Rubbish,' he said. 'You just need practice, but I don't mind helping out. I've been cooking since I was a kid. I had to cook for my nan. She had angina and was bedridden a lot of the time.'

Rebekah stepped out of the kitchen area and patted his arm. 'And your brother didn't help?'

'Don't be silly. Ryan had better stuff to do, like going out on his bike and getting smashed.'

'You're one of the good guys, you know that? A lot of people appreciate you.' She rubbed his arm and didn't want to let go. Making a physical connection with him satisfied a tiny part of the growing urge inside.

'Do they? Sometimes it feels like the opposite – like I'll never be good enough. Ryan gets away with everything. He always has. He's never worked a day in his life but the way my parents talk about him, you'd think the sun shines out his arse – pardon my French.'

'Pardoned.'

'It drives me demented.' Blair ran his hands over his head and Rebekah was forced to snap the bond. 'I work every hour under the sun, send my mum money every few days, usually to cover Ryan's latest debts, and yet what do I hear when she calls? Only how great he is for doing something utterly insignificant like emptying the bin once a year.'

Rebekah cocked her head with a clenched half-smile. 'That's awful, and I don't agree with it, but it seems to me your mum feels she has to praise these silly things because there's precious little else to say about him. I suspect when she's talking to other people she tells them all about you.'

Blair huffed. 'How did we get onto this? Aren't you meant to be working?'

He'd succeeded in closing the subject and Rebekah didn't push it. All the plans she'd made before she came here didn't feel important any more. She'd given up on properties. Even the necklace and the photo, while they intrigued her, weren't gnawing at her in the same way they'd done in London. Maybe her parents had been right

117

and she needed a break to recover and heal. And if that was the case, the best therapy was coming from the man in front of her. Somehow just being able to talk to him calmed her in a way nothing else had ever done.

'Work can wait.' There were three little words she never thought she'd say. 'There's cooking to be done.'

'And what are you planning this time?'

'I like the idea of lasagne.'

'It takes a while, so I can show you before I go.'

'How about, you take a break, we can fix it up and put it on to cook, so when you clock off we can eat together? It's not fair if I eat it all myself.'

'Oh, Bekah Ama.' He raised his eyes to the ceiling. 'I know what you're doing and it's verging close to pity.'

'Bullshit,' she said. 'It's not pity to force you to eat one of my dinners.'

He pulled a sad face and said, 'Poor wee Blair is getting thinner; he won't turn down Rebekah's dinner.'

'You are honestly crazy,' she said with a smirk.

'You think I don't know that?' He grinned and returned to work.

Rebekah set an alarm and went back to typing up the stories of her Ghanaian grandparents. 'My great-grandfather,' she told Blair, 'was instrumental in bringing about Ashanti independence in 1926, then Nanabarima, that's my grandfather, was involved in Ghanaian independence in the fifties.' She was chatting to him again. She couldn't help it. He invited confidence just by being around.

'Wow,' said Blair. 'You have quite a history.'

'It's overwhelming sometimes,' she said. 'I used to be wary of telling people this kind of thing. Girls at boarding school weren't kind. They poo-pooed my heritage.'

118

'Pah,' said Blair. 'People like that aren't worth it. They're jealous and ignorant. Your stories are amazing. What an awesome history to have.'

'We all have interesting histories, Blair. Your family must have been survivors. Their names might not be in the history books but their legacy lives in the land and in you.'

'You say beautiful things,' he said.

'Do I? I just wish I could find out more about the other side of my family. It's still a mystery, but then, I haven't really done much investigating yet.'

'I'd like to help but I'm pretty tied up here and there's not much I can do.'

'I just don't feel like I have the energy. All I want to do is chill, then I feel guilty that I should be working.'

'You don't have to work every waking hour. Some chill time is permitted.'

She raised her eyebrow. 'Says the man who's constantly working.'

'Yeah, well, don't do as I do and all that. Now, go chill and don't worry, I doubt the work police are going to come rapping on the door looking for you. Though they might come for me if I keep talking to you.'

Later in the afternoon, the alarm went off and Blair downed tools to talk her through the recipe. He stepped up behind her and pointed to the list of ingredients. Heat radiated from him, sending tingles of excitement zinging through her veins. As he leaned in to read something, his breath landed on her bare shoulder. She sucked in her lower lip and slipped her hand around her neck, stroking the nape and trying to concentrate.

The front door burst open and Calum strode in. Rebekah spun around and her hand leapt to her chest. Did he think it was ok not to bother knocking? She sensed Blair backing off.

'What's going on?' Calum said to Blair.

'He's helping me with a recipe,' said Rebekah.

'Not on my time,' said Calum. He frowned and clenched his fists.

'Five minutes, Calum,' Blair muttered. 'And I'll make it up at the end of the day. Don't stress, you'll get your full pound of flesh off me.'

'Yeah, ok. Sorry, I'm just pissed off.'

'What's the problem?' Rebekah folded her arms and gave him a challenging look, which she laced with a smile. 'I wasn't expecting you.'

He rubbed his pale forehead like he was trying to stave off a migraine. 'Sorry, yeah. I shouldn't have barged in. I've had a shit day. I came to talk to Dee. I just thought I'd call in and see if you wanted to go to The Lobster Creel this evening.'

'I, er, not tonight, no.'

'Sorry, I know it's taken me an age to get back to you. It's been manic the last few weeks. I've not had a spare second to come down.' He pulled out his phone and checked it.

Rebekah looked up to see Blair slinking by and returning to his workbench. 'I knew you were busy.' Not so long ago, she'd been the same. She'd been a liability when it came to meeting up with people. How often would a meeting come up and she'd have to cancel on friends? Seth was the same. It was partly why she'd liked him. They'd understood each other's lives and the problems of dating with a tough job. Calum's similarity to Seth increased, along with Rebekah's unease.

'The sooner I can get rid of that woman next door, the better. Listen, how about I hang around here and eat with you if we can't go out?'

Rebekah opened her mouth; Blair had his back to her but his shoulders dropped. 'I'm having some guests round from the village, so this isn't a great night for it. I'd be happy to go to The Lobster Creel another time though.'

'Ok, right, that's fine.' Calum checked his phone again. 'Actually, it'll have to be that. I need to go and sort out something else.' He shook his head at the screen. 'And stick to the woodwork, Blair,' he said as he slipped out the door.

Blair flipped him the middle finger as soon as he was out. 'You didn't have to cancel on my account.'

'I already said you could eat here tonight. If I told him the truth, he'd probably sack you and throw me out. I'm not sure what to make of him sometimes and you two don't seem to get on too well.'

'Understatement of the century.'

'Exactly. So best to keep the two of you apart.'

The meeting with Calum hadn't been perfect but the lasagne was. Rebekah credited the success to Blair. She could only imagine the disaster if he hadn't been there.

'There's enough to feed an army,' she said as she cleared her plate. 'Do you want to take some and freeze it?'

'Yeah, great idea, but I don't have a freezer.'

'Oh, sorry.'

'Why not take some round to Mary, she'll appreciate it.'

'That's a fab idea.'

After Blair had left, looking even more ridiculously fit than ever thanks to a proper feed, Rebekah grabbed her sandals and took the Tupperware box of lasagne to Mary's house. She knocked on the blue door and waited.

Mary's fluffy head poked around and her face lit up. 'Oh, it's you. What a lovely surprise. Do you want to come in?'

'If you don't mind. I made some lasagne – with Blair's help – and there's far too much of it. I wondered if you'd like some. It's easy to reheat.'

'Oh, that sounds marvellous. Thank you. Blair can cook, can he?' She led the way into her little kitchen. 'If you could just leave it there.'

'Yes, Blair's a fab cook. He's teaching me because I'm terrible. I never learned growing up.'

'I do like Blair a lot, he's a very helpful young man and always busy. I see him working all day long.'

'Yes, he does work hard.'

'And how are you getting on?'

'Fabulously, thanks. I feel like extending my stay.'

'Oh, that would be lovely. Blair said you worked for a charity. Is that what you used to do or what you'd like to do?'

'I used to. I thought maybe coming here would help me find a new direction.' Why had she ever tried to convince herself that plans which included evicting an old lady from her house and making it a holiday let were a good idea? She took a seat in the cosy living room. Forcing someone from their home for her own financial gain wasn't her. It was selfish and unethical. No one could ever force her down that path, and for her to have considered walking down it freely was insane.

'This is a haven for people to soul-search, but it's not for everyone. Some people find it too harsh.'

'Yes. I imagine winters here can be tough.'

'They are. And things have changed. When I was a girl, we lived a very simple life. It wasn't for everyone and a lot of people left. But we lived and worked with the seasons and you got to appreciate the island because it can be scary. I've seen all sorts, triumphs and tragedies.' She stared into the middle distance as though recalling some of these precious and heartbreaking moments. Rebekah thought of her grandmother. Mary must have lived through similar times.

'Yes. Progress is good when it improves lives but it isn't always positive.' Should she ask about her grandmother? Though she wasn't sure exactly what the question should be.

'Exactly,' said Mary and the moment was lost. 'Look at what Calum is doing to your croft, for instance. It's going to be lovely but who'll be able to afford it? I don't mean any insult to you; I can see you've worked hard and earned your money, but what about islanders like Dee?'

'And Blair,' said Rebekah quietly. Mary didn't hear.

'Poor Dee. Her rent is so high, she can't afford to pay it. She wants to take Calum to court but she doesn't have the money to do that either. She's in a terrible state. If she's evicted, where will she go? She's a nurse, we need her, but there just aren't enough houses.'

'You're right. It's really unfair and I don't see a ready solution.'

'Dee told me last week, it's her fortieth birthday soon and all she wants is something nice for herself. She deserves a treat, but every penny she has goes straight into Calum's pockets.'

Rebekah drew in a breath. So far she'd got on fine with Calum but annoyance needled her more and more. It was time someone stood up to him.

Chapter Twelve

Blair

Blair spent his second Saturday in a row at Ardnish. He hadn't fallen apart yet – not from work anyway. But his heart was in tatters. Just thinking about Rebekah and Calum made his stomach squirm. Rain hurtled into the window and the view was non-existent thanks to a squall blowing across the sea to the front of the cottages. Dreich weather had extinguished the tropical days of the past week.

'Boo!'

Blair spun around to see Georgia. She flicked down an umbrella and bounced into the room wearing a bright yellow jacket.

'Hey,' said Blair.

'How's it going?' She perched on the unfinished windowsill and crossed her legs.

'All good. I'm almost finished at the croft, so I'll be able to spend more time here.' The main living area at the croft was complete. Even Calum had been pleased by the fireplace. Blair still had the fittings in the extension to sort out and a hollow ache ballooned in his chest when he thought about the ever-looming completion date. He couldn't control the Rebekah and Calum situation but at least when he was there, he could see her, talk to her and enjoy her company.

'There'll be no working weekends when you're here full time,' said Georgia, waggling her index finger. 'This is quite ridiculous, Blair. Archie will give you money if you need it.'

'No, Georgia. I'm not a charity case. I can work for it.'

'Yes, Blair, but not if it's at the expense of your health.'

'Yeah, I know, but I'm fine, ok?'

She held up her hands. 'Ok. I don't want to argue. I just worry. You've been a good friend to us.'

He barely hid his snort. *Yup, that's me, always the friend.*

'Seriously, Blair. We appreciate it.'

The word 'we' grated on him almost as much as when his mum used it about her and Ryan, though Georgia couldn't know that. Last Christmas, he'd watched her fall head over heels for Archie. Hopefully Archie knew how lucky he was. Blair rubbed his forehead. Why was he thinking like this? Archie was his friend.

'I know,' he said, pleased his tone had come out level. 'Is everything working out for you and Archie?'

'Definitely. He's amazing. I love the pants off him.'

'Yeah, I bet you do.'

'And has Autumn told you about what we're planning?'

'I haven't seen Autumn for a while, but she mentioned something about a job for me.'

'We're opening a shop. She's making candles and soap and I'm going to sell paintings and photos.'

'Wow. Where?'

'Here… But we need someone to build it.'

'Do you mean me?'

Georgia laughed. 'I do.'

'What kind of thing do you mean? Like a summerhouse type thing?'

'Kind of. But very bespoke. I want it to look like an upturned boat. In fact, if we can get an upturned boat and convert it, that would be even better.'

'You are bloody mental.' He shook his head.

'I know.' She grinned and turned to nosy out the window. An engine idled outside.

'Is that Archie?' asked Blair.

'It's your dad, I think.' Georgia peered through the misty window. 'Yeh, it's him with Vicky... Ooh, and Autumn.' She jumped to her feet and ran to the door.

Blair heard squeals of delight as the friends reunited and he downed tools to see what the fuss was about.

'Blair.' Autumn grabbed him around the neck and hugged him, her auburn curls tumbling down her back as he patted her.

'Hey.'

His focus strayed to Vicky. Autumn's mum had been skeletal and old before her years, when Blair had first met her. Now, she looked impressively youthful. Her eyes were bright and her skin glowed. Seeing her hand in hand with his dad gave him that familiar stomach clench. He was pleased for them but, at the same time, he couldn't quite reconcile himself to it. Somewhere their family nucleus had been blasted apart and Blair couldn't see a way that didn't make it his fault. He was quick to blame Ryan but he couldn't ignore his own part in it.

'Hi, son,' said Mike. 'Listen, it's good you're both here because we want to tell you something.'

'Oh yeah?' said Blair. Autumn looked at him with wide eyes, a mix of expectancy and fear. He knew exactly how she felt. His heart was pounding too.

'We're engaged,' said Mike.

'Oh, wow,' said Georgia, clapping her hands. 'That's amazing. Congratulations.'

'Well, it's official, sis.' Blair winked at Autumn.

'Aw yay, my baby brother.' She grinned and hugged her mum.

Blair patted Mike on the shoulder. 'Nice going, Dad.'

'You'll be my best man, won't you?'

'Sure,' said Blair, deciding not to ask about Ryan. He wouldn't make that an issue and snuff out their happiness with a mention of his younger brother.

'It won't be until next year,' said Vicky. 'We're planning this properly, and I don't want to jump in before you, darling.'

Autumn beamed. She was also planning a wedding.

'I want a beautiful dress and a cake,' said Vicky. 'I was young and pregnant the first time around. So, I felt fat and sick. This time, it'll be perfect.'

'My fault, I guess,' Autumn muttered in Blair's ear.

'You can have whatever you want,' said Mike, putting his arm around Vicky's shoulder and kissing her forehead. Blair forced himself not to look away, but a little man with a hammer chapped on his brain saying, *how are they going to finance this?*

*

Blair got back in his car with his brain in a jumble. He threw his head back onto the rest and closed his eyes. Dad was moving on and that was great but weddings were pricy. Blair had seen some of his friends taking out loans for over fifteen grand to pay for that one day. With this being a second wedding for his dad and Vicky, they might tone it down but from Vicky's words that sounded unlikely.

Before he started the engine, the pile of notes he'd made about the Ardnish cottages caught his eye on the passenger seat. A manila folder was underneath them. He frowned and pulled it out. As he opened it, some loose sheets slipped out along with photos. He smiled, recognising a young Rebekah. She had to be the cutest kid ever in her summer dresses with her hair tied in two curly puffs. Blair's heart swelled. He wanted a child one day to shower with love and laughter. Picture after picture showed Rebekah's joyous face; she looked to be either dancing or singing in all of them. Her parents were in a few and an older couple. Blair flipped the photo over and read a Post-it note on the back in Rebekah's handwriting. *Nanabaa and Nanabarima in the garden of the old house in Kumasi (ask Daddy the name of it).*

He must have lifted the file with his own things. Rebekah had a habit of leaving her notes lying all over the place – so did he. Perhaps she needed it. He could drop it in before returning home in case she was looking for it. As he drove towards Fionnphort, the shining, happy pictures of Rebekah as a child flashed through his mind. Somewhere there were similar photos of him and Ryan. He recalled one where they were dressed in tight shorts and stripy t-shirts, standing with fishing nets on the shore at Croggan. There had been times they were happy but a mountain of resentment squashed the good memories to dust fragments and Blair couldn't find a way to retrieve them.

Going to see Rebekah was the perfect diversion because he had no desire to sit in the caravan and mull over the cost of his dad's wedding for the rest of the night. She didn't know he was coming but if he was lucky, she'd let him come in for a chat. He could even cadge some food.

He knocked on the door and waited. Normally he would just go in, but at the weekend, it felt wrong. He bounced on his toes. Maybe she'd gone out. Eventually, the door opened and Blair's jaw dropped. Rebekah, dressed in a body-hugging black dress and heels, gripped the door handle and frowned. 'Oh, hi,' she said. 'I wasn't expecting you.' Gems sparkled at her wrist, and around her neck was a stunning necklace; gold vines swirled and entwined around gleaming diamond droplets, each one shapely and shiny. A beaded band held her gorgeous curls off her forehead and she blinked with long lashes. Words failed Blair and he stared like he'd lost his wits. He was used to wanting things and knowing they were out of his price range, but the yearning in his gut was way beyond all that.

'Wow,' he said, at last, slowly dragging his hand over his mouth. 'You look freaking awesome. Just stunning. Your dress, your hair, everything.'

'Oh… Thanks.' She ran her fingertips over her curls and her teeth nipped her glossy lower lip. Blair would have given anything to lean in and kiss her. The devil could have his worthless soul if he could have just one kiss. 'I wasn't sure if I should straighten it.'

'No need. You look great.' He couldn't drag his gaze anywhere else. She smiled and traced her nail along a gold vine. Blair didn't dare ask what the occasion was as he stepped inside. 'Is this the famous necklace?'

She nodded. 'Maybe I shouldn't wear it. I never had it valued. It just doesn't seem right having it shut up in a box.'

'No,' he said. His fingers twitched, desperate to take hold of her. 'It's gorgeous and perfect on you. You're perfect for it. You're just so beautiful.'

With a little cough, she looked away. Blair screwed his eyes shut, then opened them again. He was making a right fool of himself but he was only telling the truth. 'And you're a charmer, Blair the bear Robertson. What are you doing here anyway? You didn't come just to shower me with compliments, did you?'

'I, er, no. I... I brought this back. I think it's one of your family research files. I must have picked it up with my notes yesterday. I wasn't sure if you'd need it or not.'

'Oh, thank you.'

'Sorry, are you going out?' As the words slipped out, the acidic burn in his chest told him he wouldn't like the answer.

'Yes. I'm going to The Lobster Creel with Calum.'

Of course she was. 'Great, well, I hope it's good.'

'Listen, Blair. Come here a minute. I want to ask you something before I go.'

He followed her to the kitchen area, wishing a magic machine would drop down from the ceiling and clad him in a full-dress kilt with a sporran stuffed with cash so he could stick out his arm and whisk her off to wherever she wanted. But no, he was still just Blair in a dusty hoody and ripped jeans who couldn't afford a glass of tap water in a restaurant.

'What's up?'

'Are you ok?' asked Rebekah. Her deep brown eyes glittered with concern. 'You look a bit pale. There's still lasagne in the freezer. You can have some if you want.'

'No.' Blair lifted his palms. 'I'm good. Nothing to worry about. What do you want to ask me?'

'Well, I'm going to talk to Calum about the rent situation for Dee this evening.'

'You're brave.'

'I can't just sit here and pretend it's not happening. I have to speak up. But tell me, is there any help for islanders already, a housing agency or anything like that?'

Blair turned a strand of his dreads in his hand. 'There's a community trust that helps locals with lots of things.'

'Right, I'll look that up. I have an idea and I'd like you to help me.'

'Me?' He stopped twisting his hair and frowned.

'Yes. I don't have time to explain it all now, but I'll need your skills. Paid, of course. But first I have to sort out Dee's rent.' She patted the file Blair had handed her and placed it on the shiny worktop. 'Thanks for bringing this round. You're such a sweetheart, you really are.' Her gaze found him again and for a second, Blair was lost in the depth of her eyes. Then she swept her arm around his neck and planted a kiss on his cheek. Blair froze, holding his breath, hoping the moment would last forever. 'I'm so glad we met.'

'Yeah, me too.' He swallowed, resting his palm on her back for a second before taking a step back. 'But I'm covered in dust, so don't get too close. It'll ruin your dress.' Yes, best they kept their distance.

'Ok.'

'Anyway...' He pressed his lips together. 'I had better get going. Have a great night.'

'Thank you.'

She was still at the door when he drove off. Desire nibbled him from the inside. Calum's car turned into the lane as Blair pulled out. What he wouldn't give to be in Calum's shoes right now. He was about to turn towards home when he spotted Mary hobbling up from the harbour. He rolled down the window.

'Are you ok?' he asked. The soothing sound of the waves carried up from the beach below, along with the cries of gulls.

'I'm very well, thank you. I haven't been out for a while so I thought I'd take a little walk. Have you been to see Rebekah?'

'I was just handing something in. She's going out.' Blair couldn't help the bitterness in his tone.

'She seems like a nice young lady. I still haven't seen inside the croft yet.'

'I'll say to her. I'm sure she'd love to have you round.'

'Ah, you're a nice young man. You'd make a lovely couple.'

Blair rolled his hand over the back of his head. 'That's never going to happen.'

'Forgive me, but I've got to the age where I've forgotten the complications of youth. I just see two nice people and fancy all sorts of things, but maybe you don't like her... or not in that way.'

'I do like her, in every way. She's amazing, but that's the problem. I'm a sad loser who lives in a caravan. I don't have anything to give.'

'Oh, dear. You're not a loser. Look at all the things you can do. There are other things besides money.'

'Yeah, I know that. But she's not here forever. I am. I'm stuck here. I can't afford to do anything else.'

Mary tapped the window edge, looking thoughtful. 'I know the feeling. I've been here a long time. I've hardly ever left the island. Life is a strange thing. One minute you're a child running carefree on the beach, the next you can hardly make it to the shop and back without collapsing. Everything in between becomes a bit of a blur. I'm not sure how I'm in my eighties. I always meant to do things that didn't happen. I didn't get married. I didn't have children. I used to teach in a school and I saw all the children grow up and have children of their own. I like being around young people and seeing the world through their eyes, but none of them belong to me. Once I'm gone, that's it.'

Blair tilted his head to the side. 'You've touched a lot of people. That's what you'll leave behind. They might not be your biological children or grandchildren but it doesn't make what you did for them any less important.'

'You're a kind man, and wise in your own way.' She patted his arm.

'Not really. I had a nan who I looked after for years. She's gone now and I'm ashamed to say I don't miss her as much as I should. I was so young and it was such a bind but now I have so many things I wish I'd asked her.'

Mary nodded quietly.

'You must have a lot of stories about island life,' said Blair. 'Rebekah's interested in the history of some people here. Maybe we could come round some time and you could tell us about what things were like.'

'I'd love to, if my memory serves. What changes I've seen. My cottage used to be a croft similar to her one, well, similar before all the work. A poor and lowly place. In the seventies, my father got money to build a new house. It was a government scheme, I believe. But yes, it was another world back then.'

'I'll ask her to call round next week. I might come with her too.'

'Oh, that sounds marvellous. I'll see if I'm up to baking something.'

'Don't go to any trouble.'

'It's no trouble at all. I love having visitors.' She made her way back towards her cottage with what seemed like a renewed spring in her step. Blair frowned into his rear-view mirror as he remembered Rebekah's quest. Why hadn't he considered it before? If she wanted to find out about life in the past, why not ask someone who actually lived it?

His phone rang as he reached the caravan. *Mum*. Blair let out a sigh, got out of the van and pressed the phone to his ear. 'Hey.'

'Oh my god, Blair, I need your help, right now.'

'What is it?' His blood ran cold.

'It's Ryan.'

Those two words set a fire raging in his chest, and before he could speak, a thousand scenarios rampaged through his brain. When he spoke, he was surprised at how normal his voice sounded. 'What's he done?'

'He got a lift to Glasgow with a friend earlier and the friend's left him there. He can't get back. He's got no money and he's stuck.'

Blair's first thought was: *good, serves the fucker right for being so stupid.* He leaned on the caravan wall and massaged his forehead, soothing back the torrent of what he wanted to say, trying to summon calm though rage seethed in his veins. 'Ok. So, why don't you go and pick him up?' He waited for the excuses.

'I don't have my car anymore.'

Blair facepalmed and let out a silent scream. 'Why?' He guessed it had nothing to do with her and everything to do with Ryan.

'It needed so many repairs. I just couldn't afford to keep it.'

'Right. And why did it need repairs? What happened to it?'

'Oh, just wear and tear. With both Ryan and me using it, it went through a lot.'

Blair's mind was shutting down. Ryan had written off two of his mum's cars already and she was still letting him have free rein with them. 'Ok. So, you want me to do what? Come over on the ferry with my van, drive to Glasgow, pick up Ryan, bring him back to Oban, then come home?'

'Oh, could you, Blair? I'm so worried about him.'

'Do you know how much that'll cost me for ferry tickets and petrol? You'd be cheaper getting on a train and going to meet him.'

'I can't leave Jet that long and he won't like being on a train; he's too hyper.'

And there it was. Jet the dog was lovely, surely a neighbour could let him out and feed him? But Blair knew that wasn't going to happen. 'Well, I won't make the last boat tonight. There's no way. He'll have to wait until tomorrow.'

'Are you sure you can't make it?'

'Quite sure. I might bloody kill myself trying to get there in fifty minutes. I'm sure the least he can do is wait until morning.'

'But it'll mean sleeping rough.'

'I can't do anything about that.'

If sleeping rough for one night was all he had to worry about, then why was he complaining? Blair had just sacrificed his Sunday and eighty odd quid to 'rescue' his brother from his own stupidity once again. He ended the call, closed his eyes and let rip a torrent of expletives. Could someone please just send a hitman and end this now?

Chapter Thirteen

Rebekah

Rebekah tapped her knee and peered out the car window as the squally weather hung over Fionnphort. Calum drove into a parking space outside the restaurant. It was set in what should be a beautiful location just above the village, in a low stone building with a modern wooden extension to the front. The weather was doing a good job of obscuring the splendour.

It shouldn't matter but the fact Calum had talked all the way from the croft to here was grating. The topic wasn't an issue; she wasn't against hearing stories about his work, but he hadn't once said anything about her – her dress, her hair, nothing. The feminist in her said not to care. She hadn't complimented him on his smart charcoal blazer or his figure-hugging black jeans. And maybe she wouldn't be bothered if she hadn't seen Blair's reaction. The admiration in his eyes and the awe in his tone were what every girl dreamed of receiving at least once in her life. No one had ever reacted to her like that. She almost wished he was the one sitting beside her. But this wasn't a Blair type place. He might be a good cook, but she saw him more as a takeaway from the chippy with the lads type. Was she doing him an injustice? Who was she to decide that?

'Well?' said Calum.

Rebekah switched her attention to him and realised he was staring like he'd asked her something. 'What?'

'Are we going in? You look like you're in another world.'

'I'm just tired. My sleep pattern is terrible. I barely get three hours some nights and I've been neglecting my yoga.' Though she wasn't sure it had done anything to help.

'I'm sure there are better ways than yoga.' Calum unclipped his belt and jumped out of the car. Rebekah followed. What did he mean? He stepped up to the door and held it open for her. His expensive aftershave washed over her. Did he think if they slept together, it might help her nightly routine? Until he proved he wasn't another Seth, he was getting nothing from her.

They took seats at their table by the window. The promised view was merely a blur of dull grey. It meant she could focus on Calum without distraction. Physically, he was in good shape. He slipped off his jacket and hung it over the back of his chair. His white shirt clung to well-toned shoulders and arms. He had assets but didn't show them off. That wasn't like Seth. He'd known he was attractive and flaunted it.

Calum glanced at her and his eyes searched hers. 'Wakey, wakey,' he said. 'You're in another world again.'

'You were about to suggest something better for my sleep pattern than yoga.'

'Yoga's ok,' said Calum. 'I've always found t'ai chi more successful, that's all.'

'Oh.' Rebekah fingered the necklace, stifling a laugh. 'I might try that.'

'I can show you some moves sometime. Though god knows when. Things are ridiculously busy just now. It's completely doing my head in.'

'Sounds like we both need some relaxation; me for sleep, you for destressing.'

'Definitely.' His gaze fell on the necklace. 'That's pretty,' he said.

'It's a family heirloom.'

'Looks very valuable.'

'I think it is.' Had it been to the island before? Had Robert and Jeannie sat opposite each other at a little wooden table somewhere nearby? Had he got down on one knee as he'd offered her the necklace as his wedding gift? How well off must he have been to have afforded such a gift? Now Rebekah had seen more of the island, the puzzle got bigger. The majority of islanders in the past weren't well off. A niggle of worry bloomed in Rebekah's chest. Had Robert stolen the necklace himself? Perhaps he'd got it through underhand means in the first place. Then there was the mystery of Grandmother's cousin. Who was she and how had she come by the necklace? Rebekah hadn't pushed enough to find out. Some day soon she would ask Mary. Not everyone of Mary's age was as closed about the past as her grandmother had been. Mary seemed a more open soul, though what could she actually know? She would have been a child herself, she wouldn't have known about jewel thefts or anything like that.

'This place has great food,' said Calum, and Rebekah blinked, bumping back to the present.

'I was reading about it.' She opened the menu and glanced through it. Calum launched into a story about the owners and Rebekah listened with one ear, but her mind wandered again, not to the necklace but the subject of Dee's rent. If she was going to say something, the sooner the better. She placed the menu down. 'You know the trouble you were having with Dee?' she said when Calum paused to take a drink.

'Yeah? Has she been complaining about me?'

'Quite a bit, yes.'

'Bitch,' he muttered. 'She's trying to take me to court.'

'I know, Calum.' Rebekah tapped the stem of her wineglass. 'But don't you see why?'

He frowned and scratched the short tufts of hair at his forehead but didn't answer.

'You've pushed the rent up so high she can't afford to live. We're not talking about some millionaire's daughter who can afford it.' *Like me.* She narrowed her eyes at him. 'Taking liberties with people from my background goes with the territory, although it's not right.'

'Have I taken any liberties with you?'

'No, you've been a gentleman. And that's how you should be with Dee. She's a hardworking nurse. God forbid, one day you or someone in your family needs her care and she's too tired to do her job properly because she's had to take on extra work to pay the extortionate rent. And don't say she can go elsewhere because that's the point, she can't. There are no affordable properties on the island. In fact, there is hardly any property for sale at all and everything that comes up is bought by people like you and sold as holiday homes or second houses.'

Calum leaned back in his chair, folded his arms and gaped. 'Well, this is a change of heart.'

'Not really.'

'It is. The last time we spoke, you were all for buying up property yourself.'

'It was never a serious plan.' Rebekah sighed and ran her fingertips across her forehead. 'I just wanted a change of direction, and I picked something I thought would give me purpose. But I was wrong. My business is people not property. And these people are not faceless tenants who can be turned out. They're human beings with lives and families, struggling to get by. This island is beautiful but it's also harsh when you're not well off. It's pricey buying from little shops or taking long ferry trips to the mainland to get to the supermarket. The fuel costs more and you can't be without a car. If your landlord starts bumping up your rent every month, it gets worse.'

'Ok, ok.' Calum put his head in his hands for the count of three, then glanced up. 'I hear you. You're not the first person to complain about me and you won't be the last.'

'I'm not really surprised.' She tried to keep her expression neutral but fire was burning inside her. Calum on the other hand had regained his cool and leaned back, steepling his fingers on the table.

'You're possibly the first person who's had the guts to say it to my face though.'

'I don't want to fight. I know you work hard and that this is your business. But can't you do it with a bit more' – she held out her hands – 'compassion?'

He let out a long slow sigh. 'Yeah, maybe. Maybe you're right. I've lost track of things. I like action, I like doing things and having new projects. I guess I got frustrated with Dee because my mind was already building new houses.'

'New houses you might not even get planning permission for.'

'True. All true. I'm sorry.' He held up his hands. 'I'll think about things. I might have to reassess the Fionnphort project. I'll talk to Dee and put her rent back down.'

'You will?' Rebekah eyed him, willing him to flinch or make some outward sign he was telling the truth, but his expression barely changed except for the briefest smile. Could she trust him? Or was he just saying this to shut her up?

'Well, yes.'

'Just like that?' This felt too easy.

'Yes. I said I would, ok? Everything's getting to me just now. I need to stop stressing.'

Rebekah couldn't hide her astonishment but it made her smile. She stretched out her hand and placed it on top of his. This more humble, vulnerable side to him was unexpected. 'Thank you.'

He frowned at her hand. 'No. Thank you,' he said, letting out a sigh. 'You've dragged me back to earth. I've been running on empty for weeks. It's time to refocus on what's important and what's not. The Fionnphort project was a pie in the sky dream. Planning permission is getting more and more complicated – it's probably better I ditch it before I go crazy thinking about it.'

'Exactly. I honestly think you're doing the right thing.'

'Yeah. Listen, let's not talk shop anymore. Let's shove all this to the side and enjoy our dinner.' He slipped his hand out from under hers and lifted the menu.

*

Calum dropped Rebekah off after eleven. Darkness loomed purply grey with swathes of thick clouds. The light of Scottish summer nights was a phenomenon Rebekah hadn't seen anywhere before. Although it was late and the weather was gloomy, enough light remained to see everything. 'How magical,' she said, gazing around in awe.

'So, um…' Calum busied himself at the wheel and an unspoken pressure to kiss him goodbye or invite him in weighed on Rebekah. She fidgeted with her bag. Calum seemed lost for words too. Apart from property and some brief tales about sailing, he hadn't said much all evening. Despite having spoken to him on so many occasions, she still didn't feel like she knew the real man. Something more lurked behind his closed expression and she wasn't sure she would ever get it out of him.

'I, er… Thanks for tonight,' she said. 'I'll call you… Soon.' She gave his knee a quick pat. Their eyes locked and he took a deep breath. It looked like he was holding it.

'Yeah,' he said. 'I'll talk to you soon.'

She smiled and jumped out of the car, glancing back briefly to wave to him as she unlocked her door. After she stepped inside, she heard the engine start up and retreat down the lane. She breathed slowly. Ok, that was an awkward end to an awkward night. But she'd said her piece and that part at least was ok.

Settling was impossible with Calum and the rent playing around in her mind. She tossed off her shoes and changed into her PJs and slippers. For twenty minutes, she flicked through the channels on the tiny TV, smirking when she realised it was the first time she'd even switched it on, but it was no use. Her brain was full of jumping crickets, leaping around and presenting her with ideas and images she couldn't catch or process, and they definitely didn't want to go to bed.

Without thinking about the time, she thumbed out a message to Blair.

REBEKAH: I know tomorrow is your day of rest, but if you're free can you come round? X

She returned to the bedroom and attended to the pile of clothes she'd flung off when she came in, then stowed the necklace safely away in its purple box, the mystery still unsolved. She'd just got back from brushing her teeth when her phone lit up and vibrated on her covers.

Blair was calling.

'Hello?'

'Hi,' he said. 'Are you ok?'

'Yes, I'm fine.'

'I just wondered why you were messaging me so late. Why aren't you in bed?'

'Why aren't you?' she countered, jumping under the covers.

'You first,' he said. 'I can't come round tomorrow, so tell me what's up.'

'Oh, right.' Rebekah sagged into the pillows and played with the piped edge of her duvet; her heart shrank a notch.

'Are you and Calum getting married and you want me to build you a house or something?'

The smirk in Blair's voice warmed her. 'Don't be ridiculous. But I did have a bit of success with Calum earlier,' she said, teasing her nail around the corner of the duvet.

'Oh please. TMI. Is he still with you? Are you together?'

'No.' She chuckled. 'I meant I talked some sense into him. He's going to lower Dee's rent.'

'Is he? Well, he can be an ok guy. He's just money and power crazy.'

'You could be right. But listen, let me tell you my idea.'

'Ok.'

'So, there aren't a lot of properties for sale on the island, but there are quite a few plots. How would it be if I bought some of them and we put up some affordable houses for locals? I could set up a scheme where they part rent and part buy, so we still break even. Wages will come out of the budget but essentially it'll be a non-profit organisation.'

Blair didn't answer straight away and when he did, his voice was slow. 'It's an amazing idea, but when you say we, do you mean you and me or you and Calum?'

'I mean you and me. I bring the capital and the know-how; you bring the building skills. But I don't want to make an enemy of Calum. I can see him being bristly about this kind of thing, so if I could get him on board, it would be a win-win.'

'I like the idea in principle, but I doubt you'll get Calum onboard.'

'Leave him to me.'

'This sounds like a long-term venture. Does that mean you're staying a bit longer?'

Was she imagining the tone of hope in his voice?

'I might,' she said, glancing at the purple box on the dresser. 'Does that please you?'

'Of course,' he said. 'What man wouldn't be pleased by the promise of more free dinners?'

'Oh, get to bed.'

'Bekah Ama, it's time for bed; rest aside your pretty head. In the morning you'll be wed, to Calum Matheson dressed in red.'

'Oh, stop it. You get worse.'

The sound of his rumbling chuckle made her laugh too. 'So, what are you up to tomorrow?'

'Don't ask,' he muttered.

'That doesn't sound good. Tell me, come on.'

He paused, then sighed. 'I have to go to Glasgow and rescue my brother.'

'You what?' Rebekah's mouth dropped open as he explained. 'Oh, Blair. You really are too kind. Why don't you tell them enough's enough?'

'I can't. I'd never forgive myself if something happened. My mum would be devastated and I couldn't live with myself. So, I have to.'

'How about I take you?'

'No,' said Blair. 'I don't want you getting involved. It's bad enough as it is. My family are... Well, rough. You're too good for that.'

'Blair,' she said sternly. 'I need to go to Glasgow anyway, and—' She cut through his grunt of objection. 'It's not just because you're going. I have a list of things I can't get here but I've been putting it off. Let's be kind to the environment and make this one trip instead of two.'

'I appreciate what you're doing, but really... They're an embarrassment.'

'I won't judge you on them. I already know what you're like. That's the reason I want to come with you. You're a good guy and you help everyone. I'd like to help you... and I won't take no for an answer.'

Chapter Fourteen

Blair

Blair got out of his van in the car park at Fionnphort and yawned; his phone call to Rebekah had gone on into the early hours. She was waiting in her red car and he had a sudden desire to run to her and crumple in her arms. The knowledge she cared enough about him to do this outweighed the shrivelling sensation in his heart when he considered what she would make of his family.

Despite having sat up as late as him, Rebekah looked fresh as a daisy. Birds twittered on a rooftop and a lone gull let off a prolonged eerie squawk, tearing through the calm early morning air. The wind blew tattered clouds across the pale blue sky. Rebekah smiled as Blair approached her car and let himself in the passenger door.

'Morning,' she said, a little too brightly for that time of day.

'Morning,' said Blair, strapping himself in and watching her as she pulled off towards the empty road leading north out of the village. 'I know why you're doing this.' He tapped his knee and turned his attention to the passing scenery. 'You're bullshitting about this trip to Glasgow because you think I'm one of your charity cases, but I'm not and I already told you I don't want pity. I'm going to pay you for the ferry and the fuel.'

'No, you bloody aren't,' said Rebekah.

'Bloody am,' he muttered.

'No, you're not. Because this has nothing to do with pity or charity. I need to go to Glasgow and if I can help you as well, then I want to because you're my friend. And I like you.' She cast him a little look and he briefly raised his eyes to see it. 'I've never made friends easily. I've always felt the pressure to fit in with people or I've been too busy, but with you it's different. I've never had a friend like you, someone I can talk to and enjoy their company.'

The bubble of contentment fought against a prickle of doubt and shame. Having Rebekah with him meant more than he could express, but when she met his family... 'Ugh.' He groaned and put his head in his hands.

'Am I that bad a friend?' Rebekah asked.

'No,' he said from behind his hands. 'Absolutely not. I'm grateful to have your company but I don't want to drag you into the shithole that is my family.'

'You're not dragging me. I'm walking in with my eyes open. I've seen some rough stuff over the years. I once visited a village in Ghana when we were working with a team of local engineers. While we were there, we found a body in one of the storm drains. It was horrific, but after seeing things like that, your family don't scare me. Whatever they are or whatever they've done won't change my opinion of you.'

He dropped his hands and looked her over. Aside from the beauty he admired every time he saw her, there was a wealth of experience behind her glossy brown eyes. He rubbed his collarbone as his gaze travelled the length of her elegant neck onto the straps of her green vest top and the sheer white cardigan covering her shoulders. 'Thank you,' he said. He wanted to lean over and kiss her cheek right on the spot where a rosy glow had blossomed but restrained himself.

147

'So, would you like to hear some more of my ideas for the housing project?' She glanced out the corner of her eye and pouted hopefully.

'Am I allowed to say no?'

She shook her head with a flat-lipped smile. 'Sadly, no.'

Blair gave a little shrug and released a laugh that shook the remaining tension from him. 'Go on then.'

'So, have you heard of a SIPs construction house?'

'Of course. One where all the elements are made on a site and you get shipped the components? Like a flat-pack house.'

'Exactly that. Could you build one of them?'

'Not on my own. That's a big job.'

'But you have the skill?'

'I could work it out, but I've never done one before.'

'Then we have to get you trained up because you're my project manager.'

Blair laughed. 'Wow, just like that. Don't you want references or anything?'

'I don't need them. I've been watching you work for the last two months.'

Goosebumps erupted up his arms as he imagined her cracking open a can of coke behind a half-drawn curtain and observing him sawing in the garden. His lips twitched. Frankie Valli's lyrics kick-started inside his head: *You're just too good to be true...*

'What's so funny?'

'Nothing.' He shook his head.

She squinted at him; her expression told him she didn't believe him. 'I know Calum isn't always the nicest towards you, but I'd like to involve him in this project too. It's only fair to at least let him know what I'm planning and he's very experienced in property so he could be helpful.'

If she'd emptied a bucket of cold water over his head, it would have had the same effect. He stared out the window. But the feeling didn't last. He had her to himself – for now – and he wanted to enjoy her company.

'Ok, tell me more.'

The journey to the ferry port was the quickest it had ever been. They talked the whole way and she was still talking when they drove on board.

As she got out of the car on the strobe-lit underdeck, Blair's mouth gaped like a lovesick puppy. She could pass for a film star and yet she was so natural. She adjusted the loose white boyfriend cardigan on her shoulders. Her slim legs were encased in white cropped trousers and she bounced on the soles of her white deck shoes. 'It'll be chilly on deck, won't it?' she asked, more to herself than him. Flipping open the boot, she pulled out a navy jacket with a striped lining. After putting it on, she perched her sunglasses on her scalp in front of her high ponytail. 'Ready?'

Blair closed his mouth and smiled. *You are utterly gorgeous.* The words stayed locked in this time, though his expression maybe said it. Rebekah blinked and headed for the stairs to the main deck. They made their way outside and took seats on the highest deck, enjoying the sunshine before the clouds swallowed it. Rebekah huddled closer.

'It's a bit chilly,' she said.

Blair shifted his shoulder and put his arm around her without thinking.

'This is very familiar,' she said, giving him a look.

'Oh, sorry… I just… don't want you to be cold.' His hand slipped but she grabbed it and held it in place.

'I don't mind,' she said. 'It's cosy.'

149

Heat radiated through him, filling his chest. He closed his eyes and drank in the scent of strawberry shampoo as Rebekah's ponytail brushed the side of his forehead.

Like a rolling slideshow, the clouds moved off again and sunshine cracked the sky. Rebekah slipped on her sunglasses. Oban Bay slid into view, its Victorian houses, stately seaside hotels and varied shopfronts curled around. The ferry passed through the opening between the ruined castle of Dunolly and the small island of Kerrera in the bay. High on the hill behind the town was McCaig's Folly, a large Romanesque tower like an amphitheatre. Blair swallowed. His mum lived within walking distance of that. They'd soon be at her door. What would Rebekah think then?

She glanced up and smiled at him, their faces too close. Kissing her would be so easy and so perfect. No. He mustn't even think it. 'We should get back to the car,' he said, his voice low and husky.

'Ok.' She patted her knees and got up. His arm was stiff, having sat with it around her the whole way, but he'd rather that than the starkness of losing her. Wouldn't she come back? Let his dream continue?

Reality hit as they got into the car. The ship's great front opened and the warning lights flashed. Blair pulled out his phone to message his mum.

'Is she coming with us?' asked Rebekah, starting the engine. The official waved them forward.

'No, she has to stay with Jet, but we'll go there first. She won't rest until she's seen me and knows I'm here, not just pretending to go.'

'Would you do something like that?'

'No. But when Ryan's involved…' His hands shot up. 'Stop the world.'

Rebekah grinned but his mum's house would wipe the smile off her face. Blair tapped the seat as he directed her to the street and cringed as they pulled up outside the box shaped block of council houses, all exactly the same and somewhat tired.

'I'll wait here if you like,' said Rebekah.

Blair smirked as he unclipped his seatbelt. 'You're chickening out now?' That was good news.

'No. I thought you might want privacy. I'm more than happy to come.'

Cursing his big mouth, Blair waited until she joined him before opening the gate to the nearest block. His mum lived in a ground-floor flat. A low wire fence skimmed the bleak garden area's outer edge. Blair knocked on his mum's door.

As she opened it, a large black Labrador bounded out, wagging his tail and jumping on Blair. 'Hi, Jet.' Blair rubbed him all over and Jet panted with his long tongue lolling out, wriggling about until he spotted Rebekah. He made a dive for her too and she jumped back with her hands in the air.

'Hey.' Blair caught hold of his collar. 'He's really friendly, just overexcited.'

Rebekah leaned over and patted him. 'I'm not used to dogs.'

'Blair! You're here. Thank god. You're the best.' His mum appeared in the doorway, looking drawn and careworn, and pulled him in for a hug. 'I've had so many messages from Ryan. He's in a terrible state. Sleeping rough like that has been an awful experience. I've been up all night worrying or on the phone to him.' She pulled back, stopped her monologue and gaped. Rebekah straightened up from patting Jet.

'This is Rebekah,' said Blair.

'Oh.' His mum stood stock-still.

'Hi.' Rebekah put out her hand to shake it.

'I'm Lynne,' she said with a frown, taking Rebekah's hand briefly. 'Blair, come in here a minute. I've got something I need you to take to Ryan.'

He gave Rebekah a wonky eye roll and went after his mum, edging past the boxes of stuff everywhere. 'What is it I'm to take?'

'Nothing. I just wanted you in here. Who's she?'

'I told you.'

'Is she your girlfriend?'

'No.' He tugged at the neck of his t-shirt.

'I wish you would get a girlfriend. It's about time. I met Lorelei Smith's sister in town the other day. I put my foot right in it. I thought the two of you were still seeing each other, but oh no, apparently you and her just hook up whenever you feel the need.'

'Mum, for god's sake.'

'So, it's true? Well, I don't think much of that idea.'

Blair gritted his teeth, deciding this wasn't the time to remind his mum that having an affair was how she'd sunk the final dagger into her marriage. He didn't think much of that idea either. 'Right. Are you finished?'

'She looks a bit posh for you. She isn't with the social work or something, is she? We don't need any of that kind of thing. We've had them before and they're useless.'

'No, she isn't.' Blair made his way to the front door. Yes, social intervention had never worked for his family but how could they help people who didn't want to be helped?

'Everything ok?' Rebekah touched Blair softly on the arm after he'd pushed Jet back inside and said his goodbyes.

'Just dandy,' he muttered.

'Hey, pecker up.' She flicked her finger under his chin. 'You'll get your just rewards one day. Remember that.'

'Bekah Ama knows just what to say, to chase the bear's bad moods away.'

She elbowed him. 'Stop your nonsense.'

'Right, now for the long drive.'

On a good day, the drive could take about two and a half hours. The roads were quiet to start with but it was a Sunday in late July. As they approached Loch Lomond, the traffic bottlenecked and crawled around the lochside. Blair savoured the last hours alone in Rebekah's company. They ran her errands before going for Ryan. Maybe it was cruel making him wait but Blair didn't care. It was time Ryan tasted a bit of real-life hardship. When they pulled up at the bus station in Glasgow, Blair spotted his brother straight away and squirmed. 'Oh my god,' he muttered.

Sitting inside a bus shelter was a skinny man with straw-coloured, untidy hair, wearing tight jeans, trainers and a stained navy parka. Blair pulled his eyelids tight shut. *Please, do not let that be vomit.* A paper bag rested on the bench beside him. 'So, that's Ryan.'

Rebekah sucked on her lower lip. 'Ok, I admit, he looks worse than I imagined.'

'I warned you.'

'You did. And I'm not bothered. Not for me anyway.'

Blair unclipped his seatbelt. Ryan hadn't noticed him yet. 'He's sitting there like a drunk. I bet that's booze in that bag. This is the kind of dickhead we're talking about. The kind who spends his last money on drink instead of a ticket home. I just hope he doesn't throw up all over your car.'

Rebekah reached over and rested her hand on Blair's knee. 'It's ok. It'll be fine.'

Blair looked at her hand, then glanced to her face before turning his attention back to the bus stop and shouting, 'Ryan'. Ryan gawped around. When he spied Blair, he toppled off the bench and grabbed his paper bag. Blair got out and shoved his hands in his pockets as he approached Ryan.

'Thank fuck you're here. I thought I was going to die. There's folk with knives and all kind of shit in those underpasses. I had to sleep there, you know. I couldn't though. I didn't dare shut my eyes.'

'Right. Well, you're ok now. Listen.' Blair grabbed his shoulders and held him face to face. 'I got a lift here from a friend of mine. She's a special friend and I don't want you saying anything rude, crass, or disrespectful, do you understand?'

'Aye, aye, whatever. Is she your girlfriend?'

'No, but I mean it, you are to behave. None of your shit. And if you feel sick, speak up, I don't want you throwing up in her car.' Blair let go and grabbed the paper bag. 'You never learn, do you?' He slapped the bag back into Ryan's hands and the bottles clinked. With a shake of his head, Blair opened the backseat of Rebekah's car. 'Rebekah this is Ryan, Ryan, Rebekah.'

'Hi,' said Ryan. 'You must be a kind and beautiful lady doing this for my twat of a brother.'

'Ryan, shut the fuck up,' said Blair.

Rebekah gave him a little wink as he tossed his head onto the rest. 'I'm just helping out a friend,' she said, looking at Ryan in the mirror. Blair expected her to screw up her face at the sight but she didn't. 'You're lucky to have him as a brother.'

'Yeah,' said Ryan. 'I know, he's got me out of a few tough scrapes. That's what big brothers are for, mind.'

'Er, no,' said Blair.

Ryan didn't seem to hear. 'But he's got us into a shedload more trouble than he's got us out of.'

'Shut up,' said Blair, but nothing would stop Ryan from embarking on his favourite tale.

'I don't think so,' said Rebekah.

'Aye, he has,' said Ryan. 'Hasn't he told you how he lost all Nan's money?'

Blair rubbed his forehead, wishing the ground would open. 'Not now, Ryan.'

'He told me,' said Rebekah, flipping Blair a wink. 'But you can't keep blaming him for an innocent mistake he made as a child. He's more than made it up to you and your mum since then.'

'Well, actually,' said Ryan, adopting a snooty voice. 'He hasn't. He's hardly paid back any of it. We've had to do that.'

'Just stop talking,' said Blair.

'A lot of the money your mum has paid back came from Blair in the first place,' said Rebekah calmy.

'Don't try to reason with him.' Blair sighed. 'It's pointless.'

'Ah, whatever,' said Ryan. 'I'm too tired to talk. I need to shut my eyes.'

'And your mouth.' Blair pulled down the sun visor and angled it so he could see Ryan in the vanity mirror. Within minutes, he'd slumped against the window with his mouth open.

'Charmer, isn't he?' whispered Blair.

Rebekah gave him a brief smile. 'You're a kind man, Blair. Don't forget that.'

'I forgot to say, I met Mary last night after I left yours. She's a lovely woman but she's really lonely. I suggested we call round and see her sometime.'

'Yes, fab.'

'And she wants to see the croft.'

'Gosh, I'm so bad at this. Of course, I need to invite her.'

'I had a thought. She's lived in the village for over eighty years. If your grandmother came here, Mary might remember.'

Rebekah ran her finger along her lower lip and frowned, steering one-handed through the busy traffic leaving Glasgow. 'I've been wondering that recently too, but Mary would have been a child herself, so how would she have known what was going on in the village?'

'Fionnphort was tiny. Everybody would have known everyone and if someone was evacuated here, I bet they all talked about it. Mary might have gone to school with her.'

'Why didn't I think of it like that? Let's call round this week.'

Blair smiled. If it wasn't for the unfortunate passenger, this could have been a great day out. Ryan slept all the way back to Oban and Blair was pleased to have the excuse of needing to get on the boat so he didn't have to hang around at his mum's.

He waited long enough to see her fawning over Ryan and checking he wasn't hurt before he realised that was as much thanks as he was going to get.

Rebekah stood outside the car, fiddling with the cuff of her loose cardigan. As he shut the gate, she stepped up, put her arms around him and hugged him. 'Well done,' she said. His palms hovered over her before he settled them on her back. He wanted to hold her so tight he could easily have crushed her. Warmth spilled into his veins.

'Thanks.' The urge to kiss her was overpowering now. Just a peck on the cheek would do. Someone wolf-whistled. Blair let go and turned around.

'Hey,' Ryan shouted from the door. 'Thanks, big bruv. And get right in there, ya beauty.'

Blair sucked in a lungful of air and held it before waving goodbye. Rebekah nipped around to the driver's door, looking like she was about to burst out laughing.

Chapter Fifteen

Rebekah

Rebekah glanced up from her work when Blair turned up on Monday morning. They shared a look that transmitted more than words ever could.

'Everything ok now?' asked Rebekah.

'Perfect.' Blair put his thumbs up. 'Did you sleep well?'

'I had five hours, which is better than usual.'

'Great. I'll be through here most of the day,' he said, pointing to the extension. 'I'll put on the skirting boards and catch up with the snagging.'

If he wanted to regurgitate events and analyse them at some later date, that was fine, but it seemed right now he wanted to steer away from them.

Maybe she was imagining it but it felt like something had shifted in the dynamic of their friendship. Blair had opened a door into his private life and let her walk through. He might be embarrassed by his family, but a balloon of pride swelled inside her at being honoured enough for him to trust in her. She'd helped lots of people in her life but never a friend. Hopefully, his embarrassment wouldn't make him shy away.

Rebekah's business plans fluttered around like leaves in the wind. Before she did anything, she wanted to talk to Calum. The business was part of it, but she wanted to try and make it clear how she felt, though she wasn't sure exactly how to articulate it. How did he feel? Maybe she was being paranoid but she got the impression she didn't cut it for him. Whatever he wanted in a woman, she didn't have it and maybe the same could be said for him. She liked his company but that was it. No burning desire to take things further. No electricity.

She messaged him and was surprised when a reply pinged back straight away. Normally he took hours to get back to her.

CALUM: Can meet for lunch but will need to be Tobermory area. If that suits you, let me know.

As she didn't have any other plans, she agreed. It was a reasonably long way but after the Glasgow trip the previous day, she was up for anything. When she arrived, he was at the railings on the waterfront on his phone. Steam coming from his ears wouldn't have surprised her. His brow was furrowed, his eyebrows drawn together and his usually pale skin, almost red. He looked like a volcano about to erupt. She approached cautiously and smiled.

'Listen, can we wind this up now?' he muttered into his phone, pacing in the opposite direction, scraping back his hair and giving curt answers. She hung back, feeling invisible. He finally ended the call and glowered with a manic glint in his eye, like a matador about to face a charging bull.

'I'm sorry,' he said. 'I'm not sure I can do lunch now. This is fucking ridiculous. Excuse my language.' He checked the time. 'Could we reschedule? I know you've driven all this way, but I need to go and see my property at Gruline and I've no idea how long it'll take me to sort it out.' He let out a huge sigh.

'It's fine. 'It's a beautiful day. I'll just spend the day at the shops and see you another time.' She couldn't mention her venture now – or anything.

'Thanks, that's great.' Calum stared at her for a moment, sucking his lips between his teeth. He moved fractionally and Rebekah thought he might kiss her cheek, but his neck twitched, and he stepped towards his car. 'I'll call you,' he said. 'And I really am sorry. I must seem like a right bastard.'

'Really, it's ok,' she said. But was it? Yes, she could sympathise but it still felt like a let-down.

The gift shops in the village were quaint and intriguing. With the sun splitting the sky, the water in the harbour was bright blue and boats gleamed and sparkled. The yacht masts creaked in the gentle breeze. Rebekah pulled on her sunglasses and made her way in and out of the shops. After she'd exhausted everywhere on the promenade, she drove a winding track to Glengorm Castle, where she'd heard there were more artisan shops and a café.

As she sat outside in the café courtyard beside the converted outbuildings, she sipped coffee and browsed SIP designed houses and land for sale. She emailed some former colleagues about her ideas and even considered discussing them with Chloe. But the old feelings of inadequacy stopped her. Chloe would sneer at a project like this.

The heat in the car was stifling even as the afternoon drew on and there was no sign of the sun dropping. Rebekah returned to Fionnphort with the windows open. Blair's van was still there, even though it was after five.

'You're still here,' she said, dropping her bags by the door.

'Yup. You see me here, you see me there, Blair the bear is everywhere.' He folded his muscly arms and the sun streaming in from the garden room highlighted his stag tattoo.

'You're such a case.'

'Well, now you've seen my family, you know why.'

'No, Blair. Now I've seen your family, I think you're even more amazing than I did before.'

'Ha. Funny.' He quirked his eyebrow. 'Mary came along earlier. She's baked you a cake; she's hoping you'll visit soon.'

'Oh.' Rebekah clapped her hands together. 'Let's grab something to eat and go.'

'Now?'

'Why not? In fact, I'll take her something and we can eat there. She likes getting meals, especially ones you've cooked. She has a soft spot for you.'

Blair grinned. 'What can I say?'

A few moments later, they were at Mary's door with a tray of food and boxes of extra salad and bread.

'What's all this?' asked Mary, beaming as she pulled open the door.

'We're here to chat,' said Blair. 'And Rebekah has food.'

'Mostly cooked by Blair.'

'We're an epic team.'

Rebekah caught him winking at Mary, who gave him a cheery nod in return.

Inside, the house was cool, almost too cool for Rebekah, but she realised it was probably way too hot outside for Mary. The table at the window had a lovely sea view and Mary had started setting it by the time Rebekah had offloaded the bowls from the tray.

Blair moved an extra chair from Mary's bedroom, under her direction, to the table and they squeezed in, ready to feast on the various dishes of pasta, cold meat, cheese, couscous, mixed veg, salad and bread. For a thrown together meal, it looked amazing. Rebekah's chest swelled and she glanced up, ready to smile her appreciation at Blair, and found his blue eyes already locked on her. He blinked and poured some water from a jug.

'Well, this is lovely,' said Mary. 'Such a treat. Not just visitors but food too. And I made a cake, we can have it for dessert. I'm not sure what it tastes like; I haven't made one for such a long time.'

'That's so kind,' said Rebekah.

'Not at all. It's the least I can do. You're wonderfully helpful bringing me these lovely meals.'

'I'll have to show you around the croft one day.'

'I had a little peek inside when I went along today, but I'll wait for you to do the tour. What a change in the place. When I was a girl, all these plots had crofts like that one. Most of them came down and houses like this one were built. It was some government scheme. It seemed such a luxury after the croft.'

Blair nudged Rebekah under the table. 'Rebekah's interested in island history,' he said.

'Yes, I am.'

'Well, what would you like to know about?' asked Mary. 'I remember quite a bit but only about the people on the island. I was never much into politics or anything.'

'Do you know if children were evacuated here during the war?' Rebekah took a sip of water.

'Yes, yes, they were. In fact, we had one in our house.'

Rebekah glanced at Blair. He nodded, urging her to go on. 'What was their name?'

'Elsie Hutton.'

162

'Elsie Hutton?' Rebekah's pulse rate rocketed. That was her grandmother's maiden name. 'She lived with you?' Rebekah's grip tightened on her fork and her shoulders throbbed like they were in a vice.

'Yes. She came here from London.' Mary's eyes glazed over and a shadow spread across her face. She touched her hand to her chest. 'She didn't like it here. We weren't good enough for her.'

Adrenaline coursed through Rebekah's veins, making it hard to concentrate on words or thoughts. The evacuation story was real, which meant the necklace story might be too. A warm touch on her goosebumped arm made her look down. Blair's hand was resting on it. He applied gentle pressure and warmth seeped into her, radiating from him. Rebekah swallowed. 'Did she cause trouble?'

Mary's head bobbed slowly, her expression tinged with sadness. 'She was unhappy. We were the same age and I thought I'd found a friend. We had some good times when she forgot to be grumpy.' Mary bumped into the present with a smile.

'Do you know if she had a cousin here?' Rebekah's heart was doing backflips. Everything had become real.

'Oh, yes. Didn't I say? She was my cousin. Her mother was my father's sister.'

'Your cousin?'

Mary nodded. 'My father and his sister had a big falling out. She didn't want to be associated with anywhere as poor as this. She left as soon as she could and we never heard from her until the war.'

Rebekah couldn't move. Blair's hand was still on her arm and he gently stroked her with the pad of his thumb.

'When children started being evacuated, my aunt decided Elsie should go to family rather than strangers,'

Mary continued. 'My father agreed and thought it might heal the rift. I couldn't wait to have a friend my own age. Everyone in the village was either older or younger, you see. But it didn't work out.' Mary stared at her plate and her lips curled down. 'Elsie made all sorts of promises, but she didn't keep them. She said I could come and visit her after the war and she'd show me around London, but after she left, I never heard from her again.'

Rebekah's throat constricted. She could hardly breathe. 'Mary,' she whispered. 'Elsie was my grandmother.'

Mary's glassy blue eyes widened and flashed with surprise. 'Oh, goodness. Oh, forgive me. I said some terrible things just there. I had no idea. How? Why didn't you say so before?'

'I didn't know.' Rebekah put her hand to her mouth, stifling a painful ache rising from her chest to her throat. 'I had no idea she had any family still living. She didn't talk about it.'

'Then why are you here? This can't be a coincidence.'

'Hey,' said Blair, tightening his grip on Rebekah's wrist. 'This is going to be tough for both of you. Are you both ok?'

Mary's wrinkled brow creased some more as she peered at Rebekah. 'I'd like to hear, yes.'

'I can't leave it here,' said Rebekah.

'What happened to Elsie?' Mary asked.

'She died earlier this year.'

'Oh dear. I'm sorry to hear that.'

'But before she died, she told me she'd done a terrible wrong.'

'And what was that?'

'She stole a very valuable necklace from her cousin. She didn't name the cousin but I assume now that was you.' Rebekah concentrated on the deep heat emitting from Blair's thumb as he gently stroked her, not the pain of the past waiting to break her.

Mary sighed. 'I thought she had. I suspected but I couldn't prove it and she didn't reply to any of my letters.'

'She gave the necklace to me and said it wasn't hers to give. I found a note inside which read *To my precious Jeannie on our wedding day. Fionnphort, 12th April. All my love, Robert.* I didn't know who they were, but I knew I had to come to Fionnphort.'

Tears spilled down Mary's pale, thin cheeks. Blair put his hand over her frail fingers and for a few moments he was a lifeline stretched between Mary and Rebekah, until Rebekah got up, walked around the table and hugged the old woman. 'I am so sorry. My grandmother asked me to put things right. I have the necklace and I'll happily give it back to you, but I can't ever put right the years of hurt.'

Mary shook in Rebekah's arms and her fluffy white head tickled Rebekah's neck.

'I'm sorry,' Mary said after a moment, taking a hanky from inside her sleeve and dabbing her eyes. 'It's not something I've thought about for years. I'd put it to bed as a mystery I'd never get to the bottom of, but here it is solved. Robert and Jeannie were my parents. My mother gave the necklace to me to play with. My father used to get cross about it because it was very valuable. The only valuable thing we had. He saved a couple from a boat wreck when he was a youth. It was a bit hush-hush, but they were somehow related to the Duke of Argyll. They gave him the necklace to thank him. He never had it valued but we suspected it was worth a fair price. I think the couple expected him to sell it but he kept it and gave it to my mother instead.'

Rebekah kissed the top of Mary's head before reclaiming her seat. 'And my grandmother ruined it.'

'She was young and frightened. This place wasn't for her. We slept in a box bed together in the old croft. She was used to grander things. The only grand thing here was that necklace. I knew she loved it. We used to dress up and wear it but never out of the house or garden. I didn't dare in case I lost it. That was why I suspected she'd taken it. Well, I'm glad it's safe and, now I know you, I'm glad it came to you.'

Rebekah shook her head. 'It's yours. I want you to have it back.'

'What would I do with it?' Mary peered at her. 'If you're Elsie's granddaughter, that means we're related. Though I was never any good at working out once removed and all that. I'd like to think if things had gone differently and I'd still had the necklace when I met you, I'd have given it to you anyway. As a great-niece or something like that.'

Before Rebekah could protest further, Blair said, 'That's a lovely thing to do, Mary. This must be a huge shock to you.'

'It is.'

'But you have Rebekah now. The other day, you said there was no one, but now there is.'

'That's very true and we have a lot to catch up on.'

'I'd love that. I really would. I wanted to know about my grandmother but I didn't ask in time. I don't want to waste that chance with you.'

'I can tell you a bit about both of us.'

'I'm going to come round every day,' said Rebekah. 'We have some serious catch-up to play.'

Their appetites returned as they talked through the shock and surprise. Mary was cheerful again as she laid her home-baking on the table.

'This looks impressive,' Rebekah said.

'Not really, it's just gingerbread.'

'You're talking to the woman who spreads cake mix up the wall,' said Blair.

Mary chuckled. 'Dear, dear.' A knock sounded on the front door.

'Should I get that?' said Blair as Mary sliced the gingerbread.

'Please.'

Blair got up to answer the door, and Rebekah sat back, accepting a piece of cake. 'Mary, I can't begin to apologise for all this.'

'All what?'

'My grandmother's behaviour, me turning up like this… all of it. I dread to think how unsettling this is.'

'Nonsense. It's about time I had some drama in my life. I was upset because my mother and father were angry about the necklace. I wish they could know the truth too, but *I* know now and that will do.'

'If you're sure.'

'Very. Now, who's Blair talking to?'

His voice chattered in the hall, and a few moments later, he came in with Brogan from next door.

'Hi,' Brogan said, shuffling his feet and rubbing a red patch on his neck. He was dressed in Bermuda shorts and a baggy t-shirt. 'Mum's wanting me to get some stuff from the shop tomorrow morning. She wonders if you need anything?'

'Oh, that would be kind. I need some flour and it's too heavy for me to carry.' Mary crossed to the mantelpiece and lifted a hefty jar styled like a bear hugging a beehive. She took off the lid and peered inside.

Rebekah exchanged a glance with Blair as Mary pulled out a fiver from a stash inside the jar and handed it to Brogan. After he'd gone, Blair said, 'Shouldn't you keep that in a safer place?'

'It's no use. I can't be up and down to the cash machine all the time. This is easier. And besides, who would steal it?'

Rebekah's cheeks flushed. 'My grandmother.'

'Oh, don't be silly. She was just a child who made a bad choice.'

Blair fiddled with the neck of his t-shirt. 'Look, my nan was diddled out of a lot of money. Just keep that safe and don't ever give your details to anyone you can't trust.'

Mary smiled and peered between Blair and Rebekah. 'I'm so glad the two of you turned up. This has been an eventful evening. Now, who's for tea with their cake? And I even bought coffee if you'd prefer that.' She gave Rebekah a little wink. 'Though I never touch the stuff myself.'

'Coffee it is then,' said Rebekah. 'And I'm very glad that of all the people who could have been my grandmother's estranged cousin that it was the nicest woman on the island.'

Mary beamed as she bustled into the kitchen.

Chapter Sixteen

Blair

Blair leaned his forehead on the caravan wall, only just stopping himself from bashing his skull. He held the phone away from his ear but he could still hear his mum's voice, cracking with terror, pleading and crying. After the somewhat stressful meeting between Mary and Rebekah earlier in the day, he could do without this.

If he thought after the Glasgow episode Ryan would calm down, he couldn't have been more wrong.

'I don't know what to do,' his mum cried. 'What if they come back? We'll be left with nothing.' Debt collectors had come hammering at her door, threatening to remove furniture.

'Tell Ryan to stop borrowing dodgy money,' Blair barked.

'I can't. He's not well. He's just stopped having an asthma attack. I was so close to calling an ambulance. I'll have to take time off to look after him and you know what that means.' She sniffed and sobbed.

No money. Her hours were ad hoc; she didn't get paid unless she turned up.

'Fine. I'll transfer some money tonight but for god's sake spend it on food and don't let Ryan get his hands on it. Ok?'

'Ok, ok. No need to shout.'

'I'm not shouting,' said Blair through gritted teeth. Though inside his head, he was screaming. The farmer had come by the day before, offering him some cash in hand to fix a couple of fences. He'd said he'd try when he had time. Fuck that, he'd have to go and do it now to get enough money to keep himself fed for the week.

The croft was close to completion but the snagging and fiddly jobs took forever. The following afternoon, Blair yawned and rubbed his forehead as he tried to piece together a complex built-in cupboard, designed to fit into a non-standard space between the old part of the croft and the extension. His head hurt and his shoulders ached, he'd been doing this all day. He needed to sleep, or at least rest his brain, but raging thoughts of Ryan and his latest misdeeds buzzed around. No doubt the debt collectors were some dodgy friends of Ryan's. Why did Mum keep sticking up for him?

'Oh, my god, no.' He covered his face and dragged his fingers down his cheeks. After having spent the last three hours on this, he realised he'd laid the slats the wrong way. 'You have got to be kidding me,' he groaned. It was already after five. He wanted to throw himself at the wall. Calum had pulled him from the croft to work on his Gruline property where a chimney pot had slipped. It must have been out of place for a long time and the attic space was ruined. The tenants were furious as all their belongings were damaged. Calum was raging as they were threatening to sue him, and Blair had spent several days stuck in a dark, cramped space trying to sort out and replace rotten beams. He only had a couple of days a week at Fionnphort these days and with Ardnish at the weekends, he was stretched so thin there was nothing left to give.

Rebekah was at Mary's – he'd barely seen her all day. Since discovering they were related, Rebekah wanted to spend time with her. Blair couldn't blame her, but his chest ached. Without her, it was empty and lonely. Groaning, he started the slow process of taking off the slats and turning them the right way up. Time could have stopped altogether. He had no idea how long he'd been working on it when the door clicked and Rebekah came in.

'Why are you still here?' she said.

'I screwed up. I'm fixing my mess,' he said from the floor, leaning inside the odd space to check everything held up. It was the story of his life.

'Blair, you look half dead. Why don't you go home and sleep?' she said as he emerged.

'I need to finish this.'

She leaned on the doorframe between the old and new parts of the house and folded her arms.

'How was your day?' Blair asked, hoping to deflect her. Even if he went home and tried to sleep, he wouldn't. He'd just lie awake festering.

She let out a sigh. 'I love Mary, it's so nice just sitting with her but it makes me sad.'

'Why?'

'Because I want to put things right, things that can't ever be put right.'

'Being there for her is enough. Having company is probably the most important thing at her age.' He stuck his fingers under the cupboard edge and wedged the final slat into place.

'I know, but that bothers me too. What will happen when I go? Who knows if I'll ever be back?'

Blair dusted his hands and frowned. 'I thought you were staying for a while. What happened to the project?'

'Once I've set it up, I can manage it remotely. I won't need to be here.'

'Oh, right.'

Rebekah yawned. 'I'm so tired, but if I go to sleep now, I'll be up by midnight.'

'Let's go for a walk,' said Blair. 'I need some air. My head's pounding.'

'Fabulous idea. Shall we take a picnic?'

He grinned. 'Ah, you have a way of making everything special. I needed a walk to clear my head and Bekah Ama makes a picnic instead.'

She poked him in the chest. 'That's more like my Blair bear.'

If only he was hers. 'We should take jackets, or how about blankets?' he said. 'It can get breezy on summer evenings.'

'Fab, let's do it.'

Rebekah collected things together while Blair rustled up some food, courtesy of Rebekah's fridge. And thank goodness, because he had literally nothing.

He was ready to let the bitterness about Ryan pour from his soul, but the bothersome thoughts drifted away in the gentle breeze as they strolled across the machair and didn't seem important anymore. Blair had shoved on his hoody and carried the large shoppers stuffed with food and blankets. Rebekah looked like a model in denim shorts and a white vest with a chiffon pink overshirt wafting about as she made her way along the barely there path. She'd taken off her shoes and the little white flowers in the greenery were like confetti at her feet.

To their left, it was fully exposed to the sea breeze, while on the right a few hillocks rose and fell. After trekking for about half an hour, they stopped in the lee of a mound, in a concave inlet that afforded some shelter. More little flowers dotted the grass, ruffling in the wind.

'Here's a good spot,' said Blair. 'It's out of the wind a bit.' As he spoke, the clouds rolled away from the sun, leaving some balmy late evening sunshine.

'This is divine,' said Rebekah, spreading a blanket on the ground and wrapping herself in another one. 'I've always wanted to do things like this, but well, it isn't safe for a single woman, or at least I wouldn't feel safe.'

Blair wanted to ask why she was single but he didn't know how to phrase it. How could he without sounding too nosey or overly keen? What would she say if he asked her out? Before the idea could develop, he remembered he couldn't... Where exactly could he take her? What they were doing right now was about the most exciting date he could muster and, even then, he'd had to use her food. He was hardly dating material for someone who liked to be wined and dined at The Lobster Creel.

'Well, don't you worry, just sit near; I'll keep you safe, so don't you fear.'

She shook her head and laughed. 'What is it with you and your poetry?'

'Ah, who knows. It's something I can't help.'

'It's extremely annoying, you know. But funny... and clever.'

'Thanks. I don't think I've ever been called that before.'

'I don't know why not. You're a smart guy. You've just had some hard knocks. Do you want a blanket?' She held up a soft grey fleecy one. 'Or are you a hardy islander?'

'Of course I am,' said Blair. 'But I'll still have a blanket.'

'Because you're a big softy really.' She tossed it to him and he folded it, laid it on the ground and propped himself on it.

'Bon appétit,' he said.

The picnic blanket flapped lightly as they made their way through the bag of food. Blair ate double what Rebekah did, but she didn't draw attention to it, and he couldn't stop himself. He was famished.

'I hope I've done enough to put things right with Mary.'

'You have,' said Blair, ripping up a bread roll.

'I wonder if she'd have been happier not knowing the truth.'

'Maybe straight after the initial shock, but not now. It's cleared up a lot for her.'

Rebekah fussed around, putting the rubbish back in the bags and stashing them out of the way. Then she shuffled closer to Blair, wrapped the blanket around herself and hugged her legs. 'I'm not sure if I've solved any of the problems I set out to or caused a lot more.'

'You haven't caused any.' Blair sat up. 'You're constantly trying to solve problems. You've fixed things with Mary; you're helping Dee and planning to help other islanders with housing problems. Christ, you've helped me with my crazy family and you make sure I get a good dinner almost every night. I know that's why you got me to help you with the cooking. You've no idea how much I appreciate it. So much, I don't know how to say it.' He shrugged and looked away.

'You don't have to. It's the least I can do. It's such a little thing and if it makes any kind of difference, then I'm glad.'

'So, why are you beating yourself up? Everything you're doing is making a world of difference.'

Her dark eyes twinkled. 'I'm just exhausted. I can't think straight. I want to help and I'm glad if I can, I'm just no good at helping myself. I came here partly to figure out what I want to do with my life. I've ended up down lots of random rabbit holes but I'm still not sure where exactly I'm going.'

Blair shuffled closer. Desperation tugged his insides. He needed to hold her and he sensed she needed it too. He placed his arm around her back, resting his palm on her shoulder. 'Close your eyes.'

'Why? What are you going to do?'

'Nothing. Just close your eyes and listen. I'll do it too.'

He let his eyelids fall and felt Rebekah relax. She leaned against him until her warm forehead rested on the crook of his neck. 'Just listen,' he whispered, tightening his grip on her shoulder, desperately trying to follow his own advice. *Just listen. Don't think about how close she is, how she smells like a strawberry field, or how soft her lips might be.*

Waves beat gently below against unseen rocks. A light breeze played on Blair's cheeks and Rebekah pulled even closer. He opened his eyes for a second, then stretched across her.

'What are you doing?' she said.

'Getting this.' Blair grabbed the last blanket and the half-empty bag with his free hand and shoved the bag behind them. Then he took the blanket he rolled up earlier and piled it on top like a pillow. 'Lie back.' He gently lowered himself, keeping his arm out for Rebekah to join him. With barely a second's hesitation, she unfurled her own blanket, lay down beside him and threw the blanket over them both. He laid out the last blanket on top of that one and rested back.

'You're so warm,' she said.

He stared at the ceiling of clear sky beginning to fade as the sun began to descend, then shut his eyes. 'Close your eyes. Listen to the waves. Forget about everything else.'

With Rebekah's warm body snuggled up beside him, Blair breathed deeply. He couldn't afford to buy her fancy gifts and he'd never be in her league, but right now he could give her warmth, shelter and care. She seemed to grow heavier against his upper arm. He kept his face towards the sky for some minutes before opening his eyes and turning towards her. Her soft forehead lolled onto his stubbled chin. She didn't stir or open her eyes. Trying hard not to move too much, Blair caught hold of the picnic blanket's edges and one by one wrapped them across the top, almost mummifying the two of them. Then he rested back. Before he closed his eyes, he looked at Rebekah.

'You're beautiful,' he whispered and placed a tiny kiss on her forehead. 'Sleep sound. You're safe with me.'

Chapter Seventeen

Rebekah

Rebekah opened her eyes; her neck was stiff and her nose was cold. Where was she? After a moment of panic, she realised she was still outside with Blair. It was dark but everything was still discernible in the magical glow of the Hebridean summer's night.

Moving wasn't possible. Blair must have wrapped the picnic blanket tight about them and they were cocooned like caterpillars. Very cosy caterpillars. If she'd known this was going to happen, she'd never have shut her eyes. Not because she mistrusted Blair: the opposite. She knew she was safe with him, but sleeping outside on the ground? That wasn't Rebekah Ama Yeboah. She'd never even been camping.

Yet here she was – under a blanket beneath the stars. Her hand splayed over Blair's heart and she felt it beating steadily against her palm. His bear-like chest rose and fell, and she rested on it, letting the movement filter into her until her breathing synced with his. Her fingers slipped further around him and she clung to him. He was fitter than fit. He didn't seem to make any time for himself but when he did, he must work out.

She hadn't been this close to a man since Seth and even when they were together, they'd never done anything like this. Sex had been very much on his terms and, now she looked back, impersonal and not particularly enjoyable. This kind of intimacy was reserved for dreams and it was so much more than just physical proximity. Rebekah adjusted her neck into a more comfortable position, bringing her closer to Blair's face. It was turned slightly towards her and she rubbed the cold tip of her nose softly along his lip before resting her head on his shoulder.

Blair stirred beside her, moving his arm. 'Hey, are you ok?' he mumbled.

'Fine.' But her gaze was transfixed on his lips. The warmth and cuddling had sent an endorphin high whizzing to her brain. The desire to kiss him scorched her insides. Her frustration with her life was part emotional, part mental and part physical. Kissing him would relieve the pressure. And he was used to this kind of thing; friends with benefits was his jam.

'Blair,' she whispered.

'Hmm.'

'Would it be ok… I mean, could I… Could I kiss you?'

'What?' He gave a little grunt and moved to face her.

'I just feel like kissing you.'

He rolled closer and with only the briefest hesitation whispered, 'Do you? Well… Ok.'

Rebekah trembled as she inched in. Should she just go for it? Then his lips brushed hers and she let out a whimper of joy. Her hand slid up his chest and out of the covers to find his cheek; she followed the movement of his jaw with her fingertips as he kissed her deeper, and her stomach clenched with surprise and excitement. He groaned and pulled her in, rubbing his palms over her back with gentle, assured strokes. For what could have been hours, Rebekah lost herself in deep, long kisses, not caring about anything but the touch and taste of his lips, the pressure of his hands, the heat of his body, the light scratch of stubble on her skin.

A conversation with his soul unfolded. She possessed his lips more daringly than she'd ever done with anyone. He pushed up on his elbow, resting just above her and his mouth searched for hers, chasing her deep, electrifying her with an occasional sweep of his tongue. She basked in his heat, every nerve alive and buzzing. Contentment flooded her whole body in his firm and gentle embrace. He was so good at this.

Waves crashed in the distance, near enough to be present but far enough not to be a danger. Blair gave a low rasp and slipped his hand into her hair, knitting his fingers deep into her curls and keeping her close. The empty cavities in her heart filled with a warm liquid; each caress of his lips was feeding her the elixir of life. When she had to pull away to breathe, he set a series of butterfly kisses on her forehead and her cheeks.

'What brought that on?' he murmured, holding her close. His forehead resting on hers.

'I just... wanted to.'

'I see.'

'Maybe. Listen. I'm sorry if that crossed a line but you're used to this kind of thing, aren't you? The friends with benefits type thing.' God, was she making a mess of this? Her heart was hiccupping and words were tumbling out. This wasn't really what she wanted at all. She wanted it to develop organically and go with it wherever it led. How would it be to throw caution to the wind, pull off her clothes, then slowly remove his? She'd never done anything that insane. Her body ached to do it but her sensible head kicked in. They couldn't. 'We can still be friends, right?'

His elbow dropped and he slumped onto his back with a sigh. 'Well… we're still friends, sure. And yeah, I guess it won't be my first time on benefits either.'

'Ok.' She tried to keep her voice level, like it had been just as casual for her as it seemed to be for him, not the earth-shattering reality it had actually been. 'Can we stay here until it gets light? I mean stay like this?'

'Sure. As long as you like.'

Blair closed his eyes again and Rebekah nestled in his arms. His breathing was ragged. He held her too tightly to be asleep and, although she didn't drift off again, she was too warm and secure to move. They were ok. She hadn't messed up. He still liked her, didn't he? He'd said they could still be friends, but what if she'd ruined everything?

When the light had fully crept up, it was almost five in the morning. Blair moved first, sitting up quicker than Rebekah expected and taking the blankets with him. The cool wind was brutal after sharing his body heat for the last seven hours. Rebekah pulled the blanket around her shoulders and shivered. She kept it as they ran back along the path.

'Are you ok?' asked Blair.

'Cold.'

He stopped and put his arm around her. 'Come on, it's not that far. Once the morning mist clears off, it'll be nice again.'

'I need a long hot shower,' said Rebekah. 'My legs are ready to drop off.'

'Let's jog, that'll warm us up a bit.'

Side by side, they jogged back to Fionnphort. Rebekah had never been so delighted to see the croft.

'Do you want to hang about here?' she asked. 'Obviously, I don't want you to do any work.' She gave Blair a meaningful stare but felt a little strange. A few hours ago, she'd kissed him like there was no tomorrow and it had been the kiss to top all kisses. Now she had to get on calmly with things like nothing had happened. 'Not until you're on the clock officially.'

'Yeah, thanks. That'd be great. Your shower is warmer than mine.'

'We need to get you somewhere nicer to live.'

'Don't worry about it. That's my problem. Now get to the shower before a limb drops off.'

After her shower, she felt more human and only just resisted lighting a fire, knowing it would warm up quickly during the day. Blair had spare clothes stashed in his van and while he showered, Rebekah fixed their hot drinks. She attempted to focus her mind on the minutiae of what she was doing and not let it stray to the bigger picture. But she couldn't let it go. She needed to talk to him and make sure the air was clear.

'Why do you carry spare clothes about with you?' she asked as he came out dressed and patting his dreads with a towel.

'Because I've been soaked, covered in muck, sawdust, you name it. It's safer to be prepared.'

Rebekah held up a finger and smiled. 'You have a wise old head on young shoulders.' And jolly nice shoulders. She fiddled with her chiffon scarf. 'Blair… Last night. Can we talk about it?'

He cast the towel over his arm and ran his hand over the back of his dreadlocks. 'Sure.'

'I hope you didn't get the wrong idea.' It was purely an arrangement, right? The kind of thing he'd done before. Maybe she should have done the same thing herself years ago. There was something so free in the knowledge that she could get the comfort she wanted without the strings. Surely this was perfect.

'I don't think so,' said Blair. 'You were pretty clear.'

'And that's ok? It doesn't change us.'

'Not me,' he said, lifting his mug of cocoa and sipping it.

'Even if we do it again?'

He shrugged. 'Sure. If that's the deal.'

'Fab.' Rebekah cradled her mug tightly to stop her hand shaking. The rich coffee aroma momentarily relieved her. She had to keep the gates in her mind firmly shut to the thoughts besieging her.

'Why don't I get on with work?' said Blair. 'If I start early, I can clock off early.'

Rebekah swallowed her coffee. 'Sounds fab to me.' Sitting at the window, she watched Fionnphort come to life; the ferry started up, the early tour boats left for Staffa. Blair was hammering somewhere, so much so, she almost missed the brief knock on the door before it swung open.

Calum poked his head around and Rebekah got to her feet. A wave of heat hit her face and she wasn't sure why. Something about the knowledge she'd spent the night with Blair – kissed him. And here was Calum. 'Hey,' she said brightly. 'I wasn't expecting you.'

The hammering stopped. Was Blair listening? Would their arrangement still stand if she was seeing Calum in any capacity?

'I'm sorry about the other day,' he said. 'What a carry on with that other property. I might have to pull Blair from here to work on it full time until it's fixed. The tenants are causing me all sorts of grief, otherwise I'd have been here sooner.'

'That's fine.' But her heart felt bruised. She wanted to keep Blair here. Mary had become important to her but even that cut into her time with him.

'So, shall we go somewhere?'

'Today?'

'Why not? We could cross to Iona, get some lunch.'

'I, er, that sounds nice. But I have some work to do.'

'What kind of work?'

She sucked in her lips. Was this the time to tell him? His gaze roved over her expectantly. 'So, I've been thinking...' She spilled the idea about buying land and building affordable property.

Calum folded his arms as he listened. 'Sounds interesting, but I doubt it'll change anything in the long run.'

'But, Calum, that's the point. Things need to change little by little to start making a difference.'

'Tell you what? Why don't we talk about it while we're out?'

With a sigh, Rebekah agreed; her emotions rocked back and forward like the ferry. Maybe the best thing to do would be to cut her losses and run before things got any more complicated.

Chapter Eighteen

Blair

Blair walloped nails into the cupboard with such force there was a real risk he might smash the wood but he didn't care. Mr Slick had talked Rebekah into a day on Iona. No doubt they'd lunch at the hotel, which would knock Blair's picnic into a cocked hat. He wedged some nails between his teeth as he hammered on. What grounds did he have to complain? What was he but a friend? Well, he'd managed a kiss. That kiss. Fuck, it had been the most perfect kiss ever. He'd have kept it going all night and let it develop into so much more, but now he was back on benefits. The concept of sharing Rebekah with Calum made him sick. He'd done this before and never cared if the friends saw other people. But Rebekah was different.

She can't be different, he told himself. He'd agreed. What would happen if he backed out? Would she cut him off as a friend too? Everything was such a mess. He wanted to take the hammer and use it on his own head.

'Hey.' Rebekah peeked around the door and Blair almost whacked his hand in shock.

'Morning, Blair,' said Calum, peering around Rebekah. Blair contemplated knocking out his shiny white teeth – one by one.

'Hi,' he said, barely able to force out the word.

'You nearly done here?' Calum said, marching in and looking around as though he owned the place. Technically he did but making himself so free in Rebekah's home just didn't sit right. 'Next week will be the last week here for now. I need you to get the attic at Gruline sorted out. Those tenants are giving me so much grief.'

'Sure,' said Blair.

'Well, we'll leave you. You'll be able to finish this in peace.'

'Right.'

'Just a minute, Calum,' said Rebekah. 'I need to go to the bathroom.'

Calum wandered back into the living area. Before the door had swung shut, Rebekah tapped Blair on the shoulder, put her index finger to her lips and beckoned him into her room.

Blair put down his tools and followed her. She let him pass into the room and shut the door. 'I don't want you to get the wrong idea,' she said.

'What about?'

'About Calum.' She threw her thumb over her shoulder in the direction of the living room. 'He and I aren't—'

Blair held up his hands. 'You can do what you like.' It hurt to say, but it was self-defence.

'This is hard,' she said quietly. 'I've never been in this kind of relationship before.'

'It's not a relationship, that's the point. You can do what you want with Calum. Just like you could have done if last night never happened.'

Rebekah nodded, compressing her lips between her teeth before releasing a sigh. 'It's still confusing, trying to work things out. I'd like to keep Calum on side, maybe he'll come round to my idea.'

'No chance,' said Blair. 'If it doesn't make him money, he won't care.'

'If I could make him see the benefits.'

Blair shook his head. 'You're fighting a losing battle there. Look, I need to get back to work. If he finds me in here with you, it'll be the death knell for my career.'

'Ok, I'll go. But no matter what happens, I care about you. I like Calum,' she said, 'but not in the same way. I need to keep him sweet.'

'I'm sure you'll find a way,' said Blair.

*

Hours after Rebekah had gone, Blair clomped out into the garden and breathed the salty air. Somewhere across the hazy green channel, she and Calum were spending time together. What were they doing? It felt like a hundred years ago they'd had their picnic and spent the night under the stars but it was only last night. Blair had slept well but no amount of sleep cleared the fatigue.

He checked his messages, skimming over a few wedding ones from his dad. They could chat about the arrangements when he went to Ardnish. Autumn wanted to chat about it too. Then:

MUM: *Thanks for the money. We're still not in the clear. Ryan's had a threatening letter and messages. We're really scared they come knocking again.*

Blair didn't dare check his digital banking app. It was always in the red. There wouldn't be even a penny to give to Mum. What more could he do? He called her but it rang off. He hated the idea of her panicking with only Ryan for company. If his brother would just accept help, proper help. He'd always had issues but since his addiction troubles, he'd been completely unstable. There was no getting through to him.

Blair replied, telling his mum to call him when she could.

Beyond the gate, Brogan shuffled out of his house, dragging his feet.

'Hi,' said Blair. 'You ok?' The kid looked down in the mouth.

'Yeah.' He sighed, then jumped up on the wall and sat on it. 'My mum wants me to get a job but where can I work around here?'

'I remember those days,' said Blair. 'There's not a lot of jobs for the kids. Aren't you a bit young to be working?'

'I just turned thirteen.'

'Yeah, it's tough. You should enjoy being young while you can. Work comes soon enough. I'd still like a game of football sometime. I just wish I could fit it all in.'

'I don't want to start working yet, but we don't have any money to do anything.'

Blair's stomach roiled; he knew exactly how the kid felt and how it never stopped. 'Yeah. I get it.'

'Mum's birthday's coming up and I can't afford to get her anything.'

'She'll understand.' Blair clapped Brogan's shoulder. 'Make her breakfast in bed and do the washing up. She'll appreciate that kind of thing just as much.'

'I guess. Here, I better go. I'm supposed to post this.' He waggled a package.

'Bring the ball out when you come back. I'll kick around with you for twenty minutes while I have my lunchbreak.'

'Cool.' Brogan hopped off the wall. 'You'll never get one past me,' he said and ran off down the lane.

'Don't bet on it,' Blair called after him. He ran his hand over his brow and exhaled slowly. If he could save the kid, he would. Football was a cool diversion but it wouldn't solve anything. If he had a spare twenty quid, he'd give it to Brogan to buy his mum something nice, but he didn't have a spare twenty pence, never mind twenty pounds.

Chapter Nineteen

Rebekah

Ambling around Iona with Calum was peaceful and refreshing. Rebekah tried to enthuse him about the subject of her affordable houses, but he was having none of it. He had a knack for changing the subject, or even more annoyingly, bumping into someone he knew and striking up a long conversation about nothing in particular.

Minutes ticked by as Rebekah smiled and twiddled her thumbs while he passed the time of day, listening to the same stories and gossip from various people in their gardens. The scenery kept her busy. Views of the turquoise sea and silver sands were around every twist of the path. The old abbey was remote and eerie-looking with a string of tourists winding up the path on their pilgrimage. The sea lapped on the shimmering shores.

'And are you his girlfriend?' asked one woman, leaning on her wall and scanning Rebekah from top to toe.

'I, er…'

'No, she isn't,' said Calum.

Rebekah nodded. *Good. At least we're on the same page.*

'She's a friend.' He patted her on the back briefly. 'We're in the same line of work.'

'Just as well,' said the woman, giving Rebekah a wink. 'You don't want to get embroiled with a Matheson – always trouble, eh, Calum?'

'Yeah, whatever.' He grouched and turned away.

'And this one more than most, you've had more women than cooked dinners from what I've heard.'

'That's crap,' said Calum. 'And you're a gossiping old bag who makes up bullshit.'

The woman laughed and picked up her garden fork. 'Well, bugger off back to your money-making. And nice to meet you, Miss. Just keep this one at arm's length.'

They'd walked about a quarter of a mile along the winding shore road away from the woman's garden before Calum spoke. 'She was pulling your leg, you know that, right? I'm not a serial womaniser or anything. God knows I don't have the time. I'm sorry if that's been a problem for you. You'll be leaving soon and things didn't fit together this summer the way I'd hoped. But it's been nice having you about.'

'Thanks.' She glanced at him; he was focusing straight ahead, frowning slightly. A sense of relief flashed through her, but it was tinged with sorrow. Calum was a lonely man but chose to devote his time to work rather than finding a companion. Rebekah's fingertips tingled and she almost reached out and linked arms with him until she reminded herself she was in a big enough pickle with Blair. She didn't need to make things worse.

The wind tickled their faces as they rode the ferry back to Fionnphort. From up on the top deck, the village of little white houses came closer and closer. The croft nestled on the hill behind the beach with Blair's van and Calum's 4x4 parked outside. She was blessed with a home in a stunning place but she wasn't sure how much longer it could last.

On their return, Calum trudged along the lane beside Rebekah, past Mary's house, then Dee's. Since talking to the woman in the garden, he'd had a faraway look and been almost silent.

'Hey.' Rebekah tapped his arm. 'Is everything ok? You don't seem quite yourself.'

'I feel like I've let you down. I imagined taking you out a lot more and getting to know you properly, but I haven't.'

'I understand how busy you are. I used to be exactly the same. Now, I've had a taste of my own medicine. I've enjoyed the times we've been out together. I wasn't looking for a relationship and I'm still not, so we're good.' She winced as she remembered Blair's unequivocal comments about their 'relationship' that morning.

'That being said, you're still the smartest single woman on the island, so until you leave, I'm going to keep my promise and take you out just for the fun of it. No more excuses from me.'

She looked at her feet and smiled. 'Really, Calum, that's kind but please don't worry if you're busy.' Abstract images whirled around her mind. Calum, the one she wanted as a friend, was trying to date her and Blair, the one she had as a friend... Well, he was cool with the arrangement but she wasn't sure she was. A wall of emotion pressed against her like a dam about to burst. If she kept on 'playing' with Blair, she was in real danger of the floodgates opening. How could she contain it?

'I'll call you.' The engine of his 4x4 fired into action and he drove away. A cough behind her alerted her and she turned around.

'Hi,' said Blair. 'He's gone then, has he?'

'Yup.'

'I was going to show him something, but never mind. You ok?'

'Fine.'

'You sure? You look a bit dazed. Don't tell me Calum actually liked your idea?'

191

'No,' she said, opening the garden gate. 'He fobbed me off.'

'I don't want to say I told you so, but…'

'It's just frustrating. I don't know how to make him out. Sometimes he's kind but other times he steamrolls right over me.'

'Well, don't ask me. I've only ever encountered steamroller Calum. I don't associate him with kindness.'

'I can believe it.'

Blair waved to someone over her shoulder. She peered around, hoping to see Mary, but it was Dee and Brogan. They waved and Brogan shuffled into the house.

'How are you?' asked Rebekah.

'Not too bad,' said Dee.

'Is everything ok with the rent?'

Dee squinted around. Had she seen her with Calum? 'Calum put it down again, just not as much as I'd hoped.'

Blair grunted and scraped his toe into the ground.

'It's ok though,' said Dee. 'I just got a bit optimistic. It's my fortieth next week and I was going to have a party and invite folk round, but I can't justify the cost right now.'

'How about I organise something?' said Rebekah. 'You invite some friends – I'll sort the rest.'

'I can't have you doing that,' said Dee. 'It's too much.'

'I'd like to. After I was so awful when I first arrived, let me make it up to you.'

'But—'

'Go on,' said Blair. 'You deserve it. You work hard.'

'Exactly,' said Rebekah. 'I insist. Because even if you say no, we're having the party anyway.'

Dee chortled and shook her head. 'Ok, you got me. I better get Brogan some dinner, but thanks, guys. That's really exciting.'

After she'd gone inside, Blair leaned over and ran his fingers up Rebekah's arm. Goosebumps erupted in its wake. 'You're so kind,' he said. His hand dropped. 'That'll really make her and Brogan happy.'

'I'll need your help.'

'Blair the bear is ready to go, just give the orders, Captain Yeboah.' He raised two fingers to his forehead.

'You get worse,' she said, swatting his arm. 'Well, we'll need food, and how about we rig up a big party sign? Though when I say we, I mean you.'

'I kind of guessed that.' Blair smiled and she held eye contact. She wanted to hug and kiss him, let him know how much she appreciated him, but she wasn't sure if that was allowed even as a friend and it probably broke all the rules of their arrangement, though she didn't even know what they were.

'Hey, it's ok.' He pushed his head slightly forward. 'We're good. You know that, yeah?'

She nodded but looked away, unsure what to do until she was enveloped in a huge bear hug.

'You're such a good person. What happened last night' – he lowered his voice – 'was a lot of fun, but it doesn't change our friendship. This is the problem though, it's hard to know where the lines are. If you want to forget about it, then let's do that. Just act like it didn't happen. It'll be simpler.'

Rebekah snaked her arms around his back. He had a knack for making her feel safe and wanted. 'Yes, it would be simpler.' But something died inside. The part of her that wanted to taste those kisses again. If she locked him back in the friendzone, she'd have to leave him there, for both of their sakes.

Chapter Twenty

Blair

Blair hunched up his knees and wrapped his free arm around them while pressing his phone to his ear. As his mum spoke, he sat adrift in the sea of trestle tables on Rebekah's lawn.

'Listen, Mum, I can't send you any more; I literally have nothing.' Now he was finished at the croft, he couldn't cadge free meals from Rebekah and had to spend his wages on food and essentials. Ryan had gone off again and their mum didn't know where. Her sobs mingled with her words. 'And these awful guys have been around, threatening me.'

'Call the police. Please,' said Blair. 'And don't say you can't. If Ryan gets into trouble with the police, it won't be as bad as these thugs.'

Blair closed his eyes and let out a sigh as his mum cried.

'Please, Mum. I'll try to sort something out.'

A gentle hand landed on his shoulder and he whipped around to see Rebekah.

'Listen, I'll call you back later; I've got stuff to do. Just take care.' He ended the call and looked up into Rebekah's big brown irises.

'Is everything ok?' Her expression was laced with concern and her voice soft.

194

Blair ran his hand over his face. 'Mum's in trouble for a change.'

'If it's really desperate, I'll lend you some money.'

He jumped to his feet and moved across the grass to grab another table. They'd borrowed them from the village hall, but he'd already found a broken one and needed to check them all before fixing them up along with the gazebos for Dee's party. 'No. It's not that. I'll sort it somehow.'

'I really don't mind.'

'Let's get these gazebos up quickly,' he said. 'It looks like rain.'

Rebekah gave him a stern look, and he knew she wasn't ready to change the subject, but he was.

'Ok, let me help,' said Rebekah, pulling open one of the giant canvas bags. 'But really, Blair, of course you want to help your mum and Ryan, but there's a limit; let them fight their own battles and live your own life.'

'I know,' he said, but it wasn't that simple. If he hadn't started it in the first place, then maybe he could cut and run, or not feel so responsible, but it was his fault; he had to put it right, even if it took a lifetime.

Soon, gazebo sides were flapping in the wind and the trestle tables, checked and ready, were laid inside. Blair ferried the food trays from Rebekah's kitchen through the house and outside. It was typical Scottish weather. After weeks of glorious sunshine, the rain arrived just in time for a party.

The tide was in and the sea chopped around, looking angrier than it had for a long time. Its emerald hue had faded to murky grey, matching the clouds above and a squally shower loomed over Iona, rendering the island a blurry mass in the distance.

'So,' said Rebekah, scanning around the garden. Everything was set out ready and happy birthday bunting ran along the gazebo front. 'It looks fab.' She checked her watch. 'People should be here in half an hour. Maybe I should fetch Dee. Are we ready for that?'

'Yeah, I think so. Let's both go. I don't like hanging about.'

Together, they walked through the gate and took the short hop along the lane. Blair knocked on the door.

'Hi,' said Dee, clapping her hands together. 'Is it ready? Can I come round now?'

'It is,' said Rebekah. 'Happy birthday.'

'Oh, I'm so excited about this. I can't thank you enough.' She turned around and shouted. 'Come on, guys! It's time.'

Brogan appeared with a smirk, his cheeks pinker than usual. Had he been sampling his mum's wine? A man, a woman and another boy came into the hall behind him.

'These are my good friends, Ewan and Joanne and their son, Rowan,' said Dee. 'Have you met them?'

'No,' said Rebekah. They came outside and shook hands.

'I know Ewan and Joanne, and hi, Rowan, nice to meet you,' said Blair. 'I used to serve these two every Sunday lunchtime in the bar when I worked in Tobermory.'

'Hi, Blair,' Joanne said, stepping up and hugging him. 'How are you? I haven't seen you since Robyn's wedding. We miss seeing you about. The bar's not the same without you.'

'Yeah. Maybe I should ask for my job back. I always need the money.' He kept his tone jokey but it actually wasn't a bad idea.

'This is brilliant,' said Dee. 'After everything that's happened this year with the rent and all. Joanne gave me the most gorgeous flower arrangement.'

'It is my job,' Joanne said with a smile.

'And would you believe this?' Dee lifted a grey and pink tweed handbag from the table at her door. The bag looked brand new and when she moved it around, Blair saw the tissue paper still inside it. 'Brogan bought me this from the craft shop on Iona. Gorgeous, isn't it? I wasn't expecting anything. Little darling has been saving pocket money from his dad for months.'

'Awesome, kid,' said Ewan, clapping him on the shoulders.

Blair raised his eyebrows at Brogan, whose cheeks turned even redder. After he'd claimed just a week before that he couldn't afford anything, he'd somehow managed to afford that? Blair gave him an appreciative nod. If he'd saved enough to do this and spent it on his mum, that was impressive. Blair had never managed to keep savings longer than a month.

'It's beautiful,' said Rebekah. 'I saw them when I was over with Calum. They're handmade, aren't they?'

'Yup, Harris Tweed and very pricey,' said Dee, giving Brogan a warm smile. 'I honestly didn't expect a thing. He managed to sneak off, get on the ferry himself and buy it.'

'That's lovely,' said Rebekah. 'So thoughtful.'

'Our boys are the best,' said Joanne, pulling Rowan in for a hug. He promptly pushed her off and she laughed.

'You ready to come around?' said Blair. 'Everything's set up and the guests'll be here soon.'

'Yes, let's make a move.'

Soon the garden was packed with people, mingling and talking, zips pulled up to their necks and hoods up, but in good old island fashion, still laughing and having fun.

Rebekah had rigged up some music loud enough for them to enjoy without being intrusive.

'Blair.' She tapped him on the shoulder. 'Come with me a second.'

'What's up?'

Taking his wrist, she pulled him away from the garden, around the house to the back, where it was quiet between the new extension building and the rocky hill behind. His heartrate quickened. What the hell did she want him around here for?

'It's Mary,' she said. 'I'm worried about her.'

'Where is she?'

'She came around late because it was too wet to stand about outside. Anyway, I've put her in the garden room, but she's all upset.'

'Why?'

'She reckons some money has been stolen from that jar of hers. She wanted to put money in her card for Dee, but when she opened the jar, the money wasn't there. So she doesn't have anything to give her. I've offered to go and get cash from the machine in the shop, but she's not keen. Nobody would steal from her, would they? It's not a great place to keep it but isn't it more likely she miscounted or thought there was more than there actually was?'

Blair frowned, his mind working overtime. He pinched the bridge of his nose, trying to force his head round the information. Rebekah stared at him with an odd expression, her teeth sucking on her lower lip, her eyes narrowing. 'You don't think I took it, do you?' He shook his head and frowned.

'I…' Her mouth opened and closed but no words came out. 'Did you?'

'You actually have to ask me that?'

'No, but you just said…'

Blair blew out his cheeks and gaped in disbelief. 'I don't believe this. That's as ridiculous as me accusing you. I mean it runs in your family after all.'

'Please, don't say that. I wouldn't.'

'Exactly. I know that. And I wouldn't either. Ugh.' He threw back his head. 'I'm going to talk to Mary.' He dodged past Rebekah, ignoring her calling after him. How could she think that? He'd never given her reason to believe he was dishonest. Throughout his life, he'd made mistakes, but they were honest ones.

Mary was sitting in the garden room tapping her finger on the edge of a sofa and watching the party proceeding outside.

'Hey,' Blair said, approaching and taking a chair by the window. 'Rebekah told me what happened.'

Mary's wrinkled forehead creased together in a deep frown. 'I've lived here for over eighty years and in all those years, I've hardly known any crime. The only thing that's ever been stolen was my necklace. And now this.'

'Are you sure the money was there? You couldn't have miscounted?'

'I'm sure. I withdraw my pension every week and put it in there so I don't have to make trips to the machine. I've been putting a little something aside for a few weeks now so I could get something nice for Dee. She and her lad are very good to me, you know.'

Blair let out a sigh. 'Was it all gone?'

'No, but only ten pound was left. That's hardly a gift these days.'

'That's more than enough,' he said, but it didn't solve the problem.

Beyond the window, the sounds of laughter rose up and Blair noticed Calum chatting to a couple outside the gazebo. Seriously? He'd decided to show face at Dee's party. Blair didn't see that going well after the trouble he'd caused.

'You don't think,' said Mary, her voice weak. 'Given Rebekah's family history, she wouldn't have taken it, would she?'

'No,' said Blair. 'She'd never do that. She doesn't need money.'

'No. That's true. And she's such a lovely girl. I just can't imagine anyone around here doing something like that.'

'Who knows about it? Has anyone knocked on your door and asked for donations or anything? You haven't taken money out in front of anyone.'

She shook her head. 'Only you and Rebekah, Dee and Brogan, no one else.'

Brogan. The name lodged in Blair's brain and while he wasn't about to jump to conclusions or falsely accuse anyone without evidence, he couldn't help wondering. If he hadn't seen the handbag, it would never have crossed his mind. Maybe even now he was making a connection that wasn't there.

'Do you want to come outside and see Dee blowing out the candles?'

'I suppose I should. I just feel terrible that I have so little to give her.'

'Honestly, Mary. Ten pound is enough. She wouldn't want you to give her anymore. And hopefully, we'll be able to get the money back. Let's wait and see, shall we?'

He helped Mary on with her jacket and led her outside and into the shelter of a gazebo.

'Thank you,' she said as he lowered her onto a bench.

It was almost cake time and he'd promised to help Rebekah with it but, as he ducked out of the gazebo into the rain and a crowd of people, he spotted her carrying the cake with Calum. Calum ordered people out of his way with his business-like voice. Blair's jaw stiffened and he glared.

'You're Blair Robertson, aren't you?' said a man beside him.

'Yup,' said Blair, still watching Rebekah and Calum.

'I know your dad. I hear he's getting married again.'

'Yup.' He must sound like a jammed record player.

'Good on him. How's your mum?'

'She's ok,' he lied. Rebekah and Calum had disappeared inside the gazebo.

'I didn't expect to see Calum Matheson here,' said the man. 'Doesn't strike me as his kind of party.'

'I dunno what he's doing here.' He suspected it had everything to do with Rebekah and nothing to do with Dee. 'Maybe he's come to increase Dee's rent again as a birthday treat.'

'Aye, he's bad for that kind of thing. You should hear Alister Lamond talk about him. We're neighbours, and Christ, some of the stories he tells me.' The man shook his head. 'The Lamonds and the Mathesons have hated each other for years. All Calum's fault. He's always been a bully.'

'I can imagine. I work for him and he's a corner-cutting, penny-pinching bastard. He's out for himself and doesn't care about anyone else.' Blair poured all his bitterness into the words, though he hated himself for it as soon as he opened his mouth. He didn't really mean them but his annoyance with Calum and everything else had peaked with Rebekah's accusation.

A loud ringing sounded from inside the gazebo. The chatter died down and Rebekah spoke, calling for Dee to come forward. Everyone who couldn't get in huddled at the door or at the two crinkled clear plastic sides to watch as Dee puffed on the forty candles atop the three-tiered cake. From his spot near the door, Blair joined in with the chorus of "Happy Birthday". Overcome with embarrassment, Dee flapped away the idea of a speech, saying simply, 'Thanks, everyone, you've made my day; this has been the best birthday ever.'

Blair moved away from the door as people started mingling again but he hadn't got far when someone tapped him on the shoulder.

'Blair, a word to the wise.'

He reeled to see Calum at his side. 'What?'

Calum's eyes were cold. 'It's not a great idea to talk about people when they're in earshot.'

'I don't know what you mean.'

'I overheard you back there. I was inside the gazebo, but I heard how you described me. Penny-pinching, corner-cutting bastard, I believe were the exact words.'

Heat rose up Blair's neck. 'Yeah, ok.'

'I'm sorry, but I can't afford to keep you on if that's the way you feel.'

'Excuse me?'

'You asked me some months ago to give you more time for a project so you wouldn't get a bad name if things went wrong because you were rushed. I gave you that time. And yet you still call me names and god knows what else. How can I trust an employee like that? I can't have you blackening my name everywhere. Ignorant dicks like Alister Lamond and whoever you were talking to do that anyway. I'm neither penny-pinching nor corner-cutting, and technically, I'm not a bastard, though I may as well be in the eyes of half the people on this island. But for your information, I work hard and I value hard work. If you don't like it then lump it. It's time for you and me to part company. You can have this week's wages, then we're done. Don't bother coming to Gruline on Monday. I'll find someone else.'

Calum stalked away and Blair stared after him, clenching his fists, a churning sensation in his gut. He couldn't be sacked. He needed the money and not only that, he needed his reputation. Calum had a lot of influence. If he chose to blacklist Blair, what the hell could he do? Just when he thought things couldn't get worse, his idiocy had struck again. He might be able to help everyone else but he just couldn't help himself.

Chapter Twenty-One

Rebekah

A pile of dirty dishes wobbled on Rebekah's arms as she tottered into the house, hoping none of them smashed as she settled them on the worktop. Once they were safely down, she noticed she wasn't alone. Blair was at the opposite end in the garden room. Her heart ballooned at the sight. He was still here. He hadn't gone. Thank god. She couldn't afford to lose him. Her momentary paranoia that he'd stolen the money and duped her like Seth must have shown on her face and Blair had seen it. He'd known exactly what she'd been thinking, but it was fleeting and if he hadn't drawn attention to it, it would have passed swiftly by. Her trust in him was implicit. The hurt when he'd said thieving ran in her family was fair after what she'd said to him. She'd spent a year trying to prove she wasn't a thief, she didn't want to go down that road again or inflict that pain on anyone else. Especially Blair. Not after everything he'd done for her.

'I'll help you clear up if you want,' he said, 'then I'm going.'

'Going? Why? Are you still mad at me?' She pressed her lips together, holding back a desperate desire to cry. None of this should be happening. She'd screwed up everything. 'I'm so sorry. I didn't think you'd stolen the money. I knew you hadn't… It was when you suggested it, I panicked.'

He shrugged. 'It doesn't matter. It's not really that.'

'What's happened? Is it your mum? Ryan?' Much as she didn't want him to be hurting over them, she really wanted it to be that and not her. *Please, don't say it's me.*

'That's one part of it. One of many. Calum's just sacked me, that's another.'

'What? Why?'

'He overheard me mouthing off about him. I should have known better, but you know me, I've got a knack for ruining of everything.'

'No, Blair. You really don't.' She was the one with that talent. 'I could talk to Calum. He listened to me before.'

'No, don't. I don't want you to say anything to him. What's done is done. It was my own stupid fault.'

'You can't blame yourself.'

'I can. Because it was me. Anyway, I'm nearly done here and it's probably best if I… keep away.' He stared out the window, refusing to meet her eye.

'Blair, I really am sorry. I know you'd never steal anything or behave like that.'

'Who knows what I'd do,' he said. 'But that's not why I want to keep away.'

'Why then?'

'Because of you.'

If he'd thrust a cold knife into her chest, it wouldn't have hurt as much as those three words. Tears threatened but she held them back. They wouldn't get the better of her. 'You want to keep away from me?'

He nodded.

'Why?'

With a pained grin, he squinted at her, then looked away again. 'Because of the way I feel when you're around.

205

It's not right. We're friends. You're in the early stage of a relationship with Calum and I can't bear to watch it.' He rubbed at his forehead. 'Look, I better go now.'

He marched past her without a second glance, almost crashing into the door in his haste to get out. Rebekah's feet and legs had forgotten how to move. She was rooted to the spot. Her brain whirred over the things he'd said, settling on *the way I feel when you're around.* Did that mean he cared for her more than he thought he should? 'But that's how I feel too,' she whispered, holding her hand over her mouth. Was it so wrong if they both felt like that? Even if they were poles apart in their lifestyles?

By the time she made it outside, his van was gone. She jostled her way through the small remaining crowd of guests. Calum was perched on the wall, his long legs crossed in front of him, as he chatted with two men. Rebekah approached with as big a smile as she could muster but her heart was cold and empty. 'Calum, could you give me a hand with something, please?'

'Sure.' He jumped off the wall and saluted the two men on the way past.

'Why did you sack Blair?'

He rolled his eyes and sighed. 'Because I'm sick of him. I've tried to get on with him, I really have, but he hates me and I can't have someone like that working for me.'

'Can't you cut him some slack? He's going through a bad patch.'

Calum sucked in his lips. He waited for a measured pause before he spoke again. 'I don't want to make it sound like I'm badmouthing him just for the sake of it. I know you and he are friends and to most people, he's a nice guy. But part of the reason he has it in for me is jealousy. He hates the fact that I've made money. My family background is very similar to his; we weren't well off, but I made good.

I worked hard and invested. Blair's the opposite. I don't mean he doesn't work hard.' He threw up his hands as Rebekah opened her mouth to shout him down. 'I mean, he doesn't have money sense. You said he's in a bad patch, but that's just him. He's always into something dodgy. I've heard him talking to money lenders and all sorts who don't sound legit. And when he gets the money, what does he do with it? Blows it on a tattoo, has his hair done, buys a van? It's not how to invest. So, he's always in financial straits. He has been as long as I've known him. His brother is the same, only Blair's a lot smarter at covering it up.'

'I don't think that's right,' said Rebekah. 'But please, let him have the job back.'

'Not this time,' he said. 'I've already helped him out. This is once too often. And you know what, I don't want to say this because you're a smart, responsible woman who doesn't need me telling you what to do, but take care. Blair's intelligent enough in his own way. Watch he doesn't pull the wool over your eyes. He knows how to work the sleight of hand; while you're looking one way, he's slipping the money out the back door. Ryan was always the loud and obvious one, but it wouldn't surprise me if Blair's the same. They're cut from the same cloth after all.' Calum tapped his thigh and scanned around the garden.

Manic thuds pounded in Rebekah's ears. Surely that wasn't true. She'd met Ryan and Blair was nothing like him. Every atom in her heart wanted to trust and believe in him but her judgement was so suspect, how could she trust herself to get things right? What if he'd taken Mary's money planning to give it back and not realised it would be discovered so soon? 'Ugh,' she cried, launching the heels of her hands into her eyes. She couldn't bear it. It couldn't be true.

'Hey,' said Calum. She slowly uncovered her eyes. He swallowed and put his hands on Rebekah's shoulders. 'I... er...' He dropped his hands to her arms. 'I'm really bad at this kind of thing, but I mean it when I say, I'm glad we met. You've made me see the error of my ways. I don't think I'm penny-pinching, god knows, some weeks I hardly have a penny to my name, so much of it is poured back into the properties, but I was thoughtless with the rent. You helped me see that and do what was right.'

She gave a little shrug, which he seemed to take as a hint, and he backed off though she hadn't meant him to. 'I'm glad I was of some use.'

'You were. And I've been considering your housing project and maybe it's something we could work on. I'd like it if you stuck around for a bit.'

With a weak smile, she nodded. 'Thank you, Calum.'

'Good.' He rubbed his hands together. 'Should I help you clear up?'

'Yes, please.' Her heart weighed more than ten bags of flour as she cleared the garden. Without Blair, it was slow and dull work. Calum was efficient at drumming up help, if not very practical himself, but there was no conversation.

Rebekah surveyed the kitchen with her fingers on her forehead. So many dishes. She'd be washing all evening, even with the dishwasher running constantly. She needed Blair's rhymes and nonsense to help pass the time. She wanted a lot more from him but she couldn't bear to think about it.

She took a photo and sent it to her mother, the queen of entertaining. There hadn't been a lot of messages recently, not since she'd called to discuss Mary and the necklace. Cheryl wanted to visit herself but was too busy. Rebekah hadn't been able to discover with what.

ME: How do you like my attempt at a garden party? Hope you're well. I'm living the island dream!

Before starting on the dishes, she located Mary and helped her back to her cottage.

'I'm terribly worried about the money,' Mary said. 'I wish I could work it out. I beg your pardon, but for a moment I thought it might have been you.'

'Really?' Did everyone think that? Maybe she had a look of guilt she'd never be able to get rid of.

'Silly of me. But after the necklace.'

Rebekah's hand went to her bare neck. 'I'd still like you to have it back. I hate the idea of owning anything stolen.'

'No, no. It's so perfect for you. And it's not stolen anymore. It was mine and I gave it to you. I don't want it. I don't even want the money. I just want to know what happened to it. If someone needed it that much, they're welcome to it, but I'm worried it might happen again. I've never worried about anything like that before.'

'Hopefully it won't.' Rebekah swallowed a lump in her throat. The pain in her heart returned, crushing her. Where was Blair now? If he hadn't stolen the money, then who? She knew she wouldn't sleep a wink for worrying about it.

Chapter Twenty-Two

Blair

Blair couldn't go home. He slammed his foot down on the van and drove. Inside his head was a mess and nothing short of a brain transplant could change that. Misty rain hung about and the views were obscured by low clouds. Blair didn't care. He didn't want to see anything, he just wanted to be far away.

Partially by design, he ended up at Craignure. Now he'd got this far, he may as well go on. From here it wasn't too far to Autumn's house and he could do with a sister round about now. What if she was busy though? She and Richard were always so loved up, it felt cruel imposing himself on them. Call first? He hit the button on his dash, hoping she had her phone at the front window of her house, the only place she got good reception.

As he was on the verge of ending the call, she picked up.

'Hi, Blair. It took me a minute to work out what the sound was. I changed my ringtone.'

'Are you at home?' he asked.

'Yes.'

'Would you mind if I dropped by in half an hour or so?'

'Of course I wouldn't mind. Is everything ok?'

'Not really. I'll explain when I get there.'

He rocked up outside the beautiful modern house soon after. This was one of the most beautiful spots on the island. The house sat high on a promontory, looking out over the sea loch, Loch-na-Keal. Autumn opened the door, took one look at him and threw her arms around him. 'What's wrong? You look terrible.'

'I'm ok,' he said.

'No, Blair, you're clearly not. Tell me what's going on.'

'Is Richard here?'

'He's taken Peppy for a walk. Come in, have a seat and I'll get you a drink.'

He slumped into the wide grey sofa in the open-plan living room. Autumn bustled about in the kitchen area, boiling the kettle and bumping crockery on the worktop.

'Here we go.' She set a steaming mug in front of him and cradled her own. Her smile was as wide as ever and her turquoise blue eyes glittered with concern. Last year, he'd been the one helping her. Did he want to turn the tables? Would she really care? 'Tell me what's going on,' she said.

He sighed and ran his hand over his head, then picked up his mug and took a sip, even though he rarely touched tea. 'You know I've been working at the croft in Fionnphort?'

'Yes.'

'Well, the woman who lives in it – Rebekah.' He paused and took a deep breath. 'I like her.'

'Blair, you're so sweet.' Autumn put her hand on his knee and patted it.

'No, I mean I really like her.'

'I know what you mean,' she said. 'But what's the problem?'

'Loads of things. She's far too good for me for a start.'

'That's not true.'

'It is. But now she thinks I'm a thief.'

211

'Good god, why?' Autumn stared in disbelief.

'You haven't met Ryan yet, have you?'

She shook her head.

'When you do, you'll realise it's not such a big leap. My family aren't exactly squeaky clean.'

'Maybe, but we're not defined by our families. Richard said that to me last year when I was searching for Mum and it's true. You're not your parents or your brother. You're you. And lots of people love you for that. You're a really popular guy.' She rubbed his knee harder, as if trying to muster some enthusiasm. 'So, why does she think you're a thief?'

Blair explained about Mary's money, cringing at repeating Rebekah's accusation and hesitating before mentioning Brogan.

'Oh, poor Mary,' said Autumn. 'She's the sweetest lady in the world.'

'I know. But if it's Brogan... Well, it might not be, but what can I do?'

'You should ask him. When you messaged me the other day, you said you'd been playing football with him, so he must like you.'

'Maybe.'

'Then ask him.'

'Yeah, I'll try. Oh... and did I mention, I've been sacked?'

'What?'

'Yup. Sometimes I think there's no end to my idiocy.'

'Oh, Blair. What happened?'

He explained and let Autumn call Calum every name under the sun even though she'd never met him. When Richard returned, he shook hands with Blair. Blair always felt dwarfed by him despite being six foot himself. Autumn was like a midget next to him, but they still made the perfect couple. Him, tall, dark and reserved; her, short, freckly, and full of bubbles. She was tactful enough not to say anything about what had happened with Rebekah but she continued her unfettered abuse of Calum.

'You know that's Ron's son,' Richard said.

'What? Ron who looks after Peppy and skippers your boat,' said Autumn.

'The very same.'

'He doesn't sound like his dad,' said Autumn. 'Ron's a laugh.'

'Calum definitely isn't,' said Blair.

'Well, thankfully we don't all grow up like our parents,' said Richard.

Both Blair and Autumn agreed. Blair spent a good few minutes getting dog therapy by patting Peppy, the enormous deerhound, before the dog crashed on the carpet, taking up half the floor space.

'Stay for dinner,' Autumn said. Blair never refused a free meal and it meant he didn't get home until late. Exactly what he wanted because he knew he wouldn't sleep a wink.

*

The following morning, he parked his van in the Fionnphort village car park, round the back of the main street, close to the road he took to his caravan every day. From the car park, he tramped down a short hill to the main street through the village. He didn't want to see Rebekah. He couldn't face her, not when she thought he was dodgy. How could he blame her for thinking it? She'd met his family and dodgy went with the territory.

Mist hung over the still Sunday morning and it was too early for the buzz of tourists. The lane was empty except for a few sheep lying along the embankment. One of them let out a long rumbling bleat as Blair passed. He nipped onto Dee's doorstep and knocked, hoping she was awake after the partying of the day before.

Bleary-eyed and frowning, she opened it and peered around.

'Blair. What's up?'

'Hi. Sorry to bother you, but can I talk to Brogan?'

'Yeah, I'll see if he's up. Do you want to come in?'

'No. I'm going to the beach for a bit. Could you send him down to meet me? I've got a job for him.'

'Oh, great. I'll do that.'

Blair crossed the lane, jumped down the bank and trotted through the long grass to the edge of the shore. He found a flat boulder and sat on it. The wind played on his cheeks and the gulls cried in the distance. Blair picked at a tuft of grass. Would Brogan confess? Was it even him? Blair cringed at the possibility he'd leapt to the wrong conclusion and was about to accuse an innocent boy. The grass rustled and Blair looked around to see Brogan on his way down. The boy frowned as he approached.

'Mum said you wanted me to do a job.'

Blair tapped the boulder for Brogan to sit beside him. He rested his forearms on his thighs and stared forward at the sea racing in.

'What's the job?' Brogan dropped down beside him.

'It depends,' Blair said, still watching the foam spritzing against the rocks.

'On what?'

'Your answers.'

Brogan didn't speak but Blair glanced at him. 'Tell me about the bag you bought for your mum's birthday.'

Blair felt Brogan slumping. When he looked, the kid had his head in his hands.

'I wanted to get her something nice.'

'Why did you choose the bag?' asked Blair.

'We went on a trip over to Iona one day and she was going on about it. She even talked to the lady in the shop about it and asked if they ever put them in the sale. I knew she wanted it.'

'So you saved the pocket money you got from your dad to buy it? That was a great thing to do.' Blair drummed his thighs and looked at Brogan.

'What?' Brogan shrugged.

'Well, it's a great thing to do if it's true.' Nausea bubbled in Blair's gut. If he'd got this wrong, he would cause so much pain to so many people – not the first time he'd made a gross error of judgement.

'What do you mean?' said Brogan, hunching his shoulders.

'You tell me.' Blair sighed. 'I get how it feels to have no money but getting it dishonestly doesn't work.'

'You think I nicked it?' said Brogan.

'Did you?'

'No,' said Brogan, jumping to his feet and kicking the sand.

'You didn't take Mary's money?'

Brogan groaned. 'Ok. I did. I wish I hadn't.' He punched his forehead with both his fists. 'I was going to borrow it and pay her back, she's a nice old lady. My dad is lending me money, but it hasn't arrived yet. I didn't expect Mary to find it so soon. I'll borrow some from my school pals, then I can pay her back. I'll pay the boys back when Dad's money arrives.'

Blair blew out a low whistle. 'Oh, jeez, mate.' His insides churned. How many times had he felt like this? He'd never stolen money but he knew too well the horrid powerless sensation of having nothing and no way of getting it.

'I wish I hadn't done it. I feel sick. I wanted to get Mum something nice but I shouldn't have. Nice things aren't for us.'

'Look, I know how you feel. I really do. You remind me of myself. We never had anything when I was a kid. I made a mistake and we ended up in debt.' He got up and stood beside Brogan, putting his arm around the boy's shoulder. 'We need to get that money back.'

'I'm trying.'

'How much was it?'

'Sixty quid.'

'Ok. We need to do it without you borrowing it from all sorts. That's the slippery slope. Never spend money you don't have. I know that to my cost.'

'I'm looking for a job but I can't do anything. I thought that's what this was about.'

'I wish. I'm not in a place to offer you a job. I meant your job is to get that money back to Mary and to tell the truth.'

'Everyone will hate me.'

'Let's hope most people will understand. If you'd stolen the money and gone off and got a tattoo, then maybe not.'

'Is that what you did?'

'No. A pal of mine did it, but I still paid more than I could afford.'

'It's so cool, so are the dreads.'

'Yeah. I got them for free. My aunt's a hairdresser and she used me to practise on. I love them, but they're really heavy. Listen, I need to go. I'm working at Ardnish today but I've got a plan. You sit tight and I'll get back to you.'

'You're not going to nick money, are you?'

'Definitely not.'

They ran up the embankment. As they neared the top, a car passed by on the lane and Blair ducked. *Bloody Calum!* Calling around at this time on a Sunday morning. Not that Blair had grounds to complain. He'd known right from the start Rebekah was too good for him. Still, thinking about her with Calum was like someone had unleashed a tank of eels inside him.

'See you later, kiddo,' said Blair. 'I better be off.'

*

The mist had burned off by the time Blair reached Ardnish. A fresh wind came in off the blue sea, now topped with foamy white horses. Before he started working, he decided to nip in and say hi to Vicky and his dad. He tapped the steering wheel and shook his head. After spending so much time working, he'd neglected the people in his life.

Outside Gardener's Cottage, a black Freelander was parked in the rough courtyard area beside Mike's pickup. Richard's car. Blair smiled as he turned off the engine. That probably meant Autumn was there too.

The two-storey old stone house was constructed into the corner of a walled garden and had a quaint vibe with trailing plants growing up the side and around the front door. As Blair approached, he heard voices inside and realised the door was ajar. Maybe it was because he was thinking about Autumn that the male voices didn't register straight away, but as he got to the living room door, a loud cry and a clatter made him leap for the handle.

'What the hell?' Blair flung open the door.

A mug lay smashed on the wooden floor and several people huddled around a prone figure, struggling in their midst.

217

'Blair.' Mike looked up from the commotion, holding tight to a flailing arm.

Moving a few inches forward, Blair saw his brother's sandy hair. Ryan's face was scrunched up as he tried to get out of his dad's grip.

'What is going on?' said Blair. 'What's he doing here?'

'Let me go,' Ryan yelled and wrestled his arm free.

Mike let go and rubbed his forehead. Ryan dodged the others, put his head down, and made for the door. Blair stepped back and blocked it. They were the same height but Blair's shoulders were wide where Ryan was thin.

'Come on, Blair,' said Ryan, clenching his fists. 'I'm a free citizen, let me pass.'

'Tell me what's going on first.' Blair looked from Ryan to their father, to Vicky, and finally to Autumn, who was hiding in the crook of Richard's arm. 'Why the hell are you here?'

'Mike called this morning,' said Autumn. 'And asked if we could get him from the ferry.' She exchanged a look with Blair.

'I thought they'd get there quicker,' said Mike. 'I was helping a mate with his boat when I got Ryan's call.'

'Yeah,' said Ryan. 'But I'm not staying.'

'So, why are you here then?' said Blair. 'I don't get it.'

'He phoned from the ferry saying he wanted to meet Vicky and Autumn,' said Mike. 'But now we're hearing a different story.'

'Oh, yeah?' Blair folded his arms.

'Seriously?' Ryan flung his hands in the air. 'Why are you all against me?'

'We're not,' said Mike. 'That's why I'm trying to stop you from running off and doing something crazy.'

'Aw Christ!' Ryan whined.

'So, what's the real reason?' Blair asked.

'He owes someone money and they're after him,' said Mike.

'And I don't want any trouble,' said Vicky.

'And you're not my mum,' said Ryan.

'Don't be so rude,' said Blair, narrowing his eyes at Ryan. 'What are you going to do next? You've smashed a cup and made a scene, now what? Run away? Fake an asthma attack? It won't solve the problem. Running away from the dodgy money lenders won't save your neck. All it's doing is terrifying Mum and making you look stupid. Why don't you for once sit down, take a deep breath and approach this like an adult?'

Ryan raised his eyes to the ceiling and pulled a face.

'It would be a good idea,' said Mike. 'We've cut you a lot of slack but at twenty-three, you should grow up a bit.'

Blair gaped at his dad. That was the first time he'd ever heard him speak to Ryan like that. And it hammered something home – Ryan was twenty-three. Blair was three years older, but he'd felt like an adult since he was about twelve. 'Do you want to come for a drive with me?' said Blair. 'I'm working later, but I need to go and speak to Archie. Come with me and we can chat.'

Ryan grimaced, then peered over his shoulder at Mike.

'Do you want me to come?' asked Mike.

'No, Dad,' said Blair. 'It should just be us.'

'Come on then,' muttered Ryan. Blair moved out of the way and let him go.

'Watch him,' said Mike. 'I don't trust what he'll do.'

'Dad, you said it yourself, he's not a child. If he runs, let him. He'll end up crawling back anyway.'

Mike sighed and rubbed his chin. 'Ok.'

Blair gave Autumn and Richard a little wave. 'Sorry.'

'Take care,' said Autumn.

'It'll be fine.'

Ryan stood outside with his hands in his pockets. 'Are you going to lecture me too?'

'Nope,' said Blair, heading for the van.

'So what's this about then?'

'Whatever you want it to be about. I'm going to speak to Archie and you looked like you could do with getting out of there.'

'Well, they're all against me.'

'So you said.' Blair clicked his seatbelt and waited until Ryan did his. 'But maybe they just want to help you. As they've been doing since you were born.'

'How is it helping me saying they don't want me here?'

'Can't you understand why though? You lied that you wanted to come and see them, then turned up and said you wanted to hide from some thugs. You've left Mum at home with the risk of these guys turning up and she's freaking out that you've disappeared.'

'I'm not a kid.'

'Yeah, Ryan. That's true. But you can't pick and choose when you want to be a grown-up and when you don't.'

'I knew you'd lecture me.'

'It's not a lecture. It's the truth. If you want Mum and Dad to respect your decisions and choices, you have to show them you're capable of doing that all the time... Or at least most of the time. It's ok to make mistakes, but it's not ok to be reckless when it's hurting the people who love you.'

'Yeah, yeah, whatever,' muttered Ryan.

Blair drove through the estate, past the main house and down the track while Ryan huddled up by the window. Monarch's Lodge glinted white from its promontory enclosed by jagged cliffs; its garden rolled to the edge. Beyond the stone wall was a magnificent view of the sea below. Blair let it cleanse his mind as he pulled the van up at the front door. How could he ask for what he wanted? After saying his piece to Ryan, this was almost duplicitous. 'You wait here.' He unclipped his belt.

'Why? You got a girlfriend in there? You gonna give her one?'

'Just shut the fuck up.'

Before Blair opened the van door, Archie emerged from the house and set off in the opposite direction. Georgia hurried out behind and pushed her head under his arm.

'You're out of luck,' said Ryan. 'Her husband's home.'

Ignoring him, Blair jumped out. Archie turned at the sound of the gravel crunching under Blair's boots.

'Oh, morning, Blair,' he said. 'Do you need me to come up and see something?'

'Er… no… I…'

'Hello,' said Georgia with a broad grin.

'Hi.'

'Are you ok?' Georgia said.

'Listen, I need to ask a favour.'

'Sure, do you want to come in?' said Archie.

'What's up?' Georgia patted his arm as he stepped inside. 'You look a bit pale.'

They sat around the immaculately designed living area that Blair had spent time working on last Christmas. Georgia had decorated the interiors with her expert artist's eye. She'd promised him he'd always have work here if he needed it and he needed it now.

'I'm not working for Calum Matheson anymore. He let me go.'

'What happened?' Georgia asked.

'I said some stupid stuff about him and he overheard.'

'Eek,' said Georgia.

'But it means I'm free to do anything here, if you still need me or want me. I might be blacklisted already.'

'Don't be silly. You'll always have a job here,' said Archie. 'Unless you insult Georgia. You can say what you like about me. I'm sure it won't be anything I haven't heard before.'

'No way. I wouldn't say anything about either of you.' He smiled at Georgia and she chuckled.

'Well, then. You can start whenever you like,' said Archie.

'But not today,' said Georgia. 'I already told you, once you're full time, you're not doing weekends too. We'll get pulled up by employment law.'

Blair raised his eyebrows. 'Wow,' he said with a grin. 'When did you become an expert on that kind of thing?' Georgia was an amazing artist and photographer but notoriously scatty about everything else.

'She didn't,' said Archie. 'She made that up.'

Georgia threw out her hands. 'Worth a try though because really, Blair, you have to have some time to yourself.'

'Ok, I accept.'

'Great,' said Archie.

'I have another favour to ask.' He screwed up his face. 'But I hate doing it.'

'Ask away. You helped me above and beyond at Christmas,' said Archie.

'And me.' Georgia winked at him.

Blair's mouth twitched as he remembered the day he'd helped her set up a big surprise for Archie, when she'd blurted out that she'd fallen for him.

'So, we owe you.'

'Ok. I wonder if you'd advance me sixty quid. You can take it off my next wage.' Blair looked towards the window. Doing this made his skin crawl.

Archie frowned. 'Absolutely, I will, but…'

'Why?' said Georgia.

'It's a long story.'

'Are you in trouble?' Archie asked.

'It's not me. It's a kid I know.' Blair paused for a moment, considering the two of them. They were good people, they'd understand and not judge. With a deep breath, he explained about Brogan and the cash.

Georgia listened with her head cocked while Archie nodded.

'Tell you what,' said Archie, getting to his feet and pulling a leather wallet from his back pocket. 'Take this.' He pulled out three twenty-pound notes. 'Give it to the boy and tell him to confess. Put him on community service or whatever but consider his debt paid.'

'I can't,' said Blair. 'I want you to take it off my wages.'

'No,' said Archie. 'You can work extra hard if you want but you'll still get your wages. That money is to allow a hard-working nurse to keep a gift she deserves. Just make sure the boy understands.'

'Ok.' Blair looked at the money and sighed.

'You've always gone the extra mile for us. Even now you're doing this for someone else. I'm giving this to you as a friend, so you can use it to put things right,' said Archie.

Archie stood at the same time as Blair and clapped him on the shoulder.

'Don't be stuck and don't be a stranger,' said Georgia. 'You never ask for help, so this must be really important. But if you need help again, ask. You've been a good friend to us and we'll always be here for you.'

'Thank you,' said Blair.

Georgia hugged him and patted his back.

Blair stashed the cash in his pocket before he returned to the van, hoping this would do the trick. He wanted to believe Brogan was honest but he couldn't help hating the whole situation. The future was bleak for kids who made errors of judgement and didn't get the right support. Sitting in the passenger seat was a prime example.

'Listen, I'll drop you back at Dad's,' he said, starting the engine. 'I'm not going to lecture you or tell you what to do, but please, try to see the world from someone else's perspective, not just your own.'

'Yeah, yeah.'

'I mean it. And call Mum.'

Ryan closed his eyes and held his forehead. 'Ok.' He pulled out his phone.

Blair wasn't expecting miracles but it was a start.

Chapter Twenty-Three

Rebekah

Sitting in the garden room opposite Calum, Rebekah tapped her knee and sucked on her lip.

'Did you hear about Mary's money yesterday?' she said.

'No,' he replied.

'She had money stolen from a jar. I blamed it on Blair.'

'Hmpf.' Calum drummed on the arm of the sofa. 'And was it him?'

'Do you honestly think he would do something like that?' Some of his parting words were vague and ambiguous. *Who knows what I'd do.* What had he meant?

'I don't know, Rebekah.'

Rebekah stared out the window. Calum had called around to help finish the party clear-up but they'd barely got started. He was too preoccupied worrying about his Gruline property. On the table, her phone buzzed, and she reached for it. Her jaw fell slack as she read the text; the first one she'd had since sending the photo of the dirty dishes.

MOTHER: You'll make a party host yet! Guess what? Daddy and I are getting back together. We're flying to Kumasi on Friday. Just for a short holiday and for Daddy to put things in order, then we'll decide where to live. If you're still on Mull next month, we'd love to come over for a visit and meet the mysterious Mary.

'Are you ok?' asked Calum.

She looked up at him. 'I don't believe it; my parents are getting back together.'

'Are they divorced?'

She frowned and stood up. 'They were.' In all her chats with Calum, they'd never talked about her. She knew a few things about him but she'd never shared her stories. Blair, on the other hand… Yes, it all came back to Blair. If she left the island, it would still come back to Blair. There was unfinished business. Lots of it. Her heart ached, beating against her, begging her to let it out. What she really wanted was him. Just him. But did he want that? Unless she had the nerve to say something they'd be stuck in limbo forever. He'd hinted he had feelings for her. She had to believe it and try.

'Calum, would you mind leaving me for a bit? I'm really tired and I could do with some space.'

He got to his feet. 'Sure. You know, I get the impression you and I aren't going anywhere.' He lifted his palms. 'It's ok. I don't want to cut off your friendship but how about we leave it there?'

'Ok.' She nodded. 'I agree that's best too. I do like you… as a friend.'

'Yeah, that's cool.' He stood for a moment, then left with a brief wave.

Rebekah slouched into the seat and closed her eyes. Relief poured over her shoulders, but it was short lived. She'd dealt with Calum, but she felt heartless and cold. She'd dismissed him with nothing. Why? The little voice chimed in her head. *Because you want Blair.*

Maybe if she withdrew the money and slipped it back into Mary's jar, they could act as if it had never happened. They could go on as they were before. Though it would hardly be the same. Not if he really was dishonest. *He isn't!*

226

He'd always been the pinnacle of integrity and shown her nothing but respect… and love. Yes, love, exactly what she felt for him, a deep all-consuming love.

Suddenly resolved, she jumped up. One way or another, she was giving Mary her money. The Blair project was a whole other problem and, try as she might, she couldn't think of a solution. The only one that came into her mind was the one where she was holding him, he was kissing her, and they weren't just friends. They were so much more than that. That dream didn't seem to have a concrete road leading to it though. It was a hazy destination on the horizon she wasn't sure she could ever reach.

She grabbed her wallet and set off for the cash machine at the shop, but she'd barely stepped through the gate when she spied a group of people at Mary's door. Dee, Brogan and Blair. Panic grabbed her. Had Mary collapsed?

'Is everything ok?' She bounded towards them.

Dee's eyes were red and she rubbed at them.

'What's happened? Is Mary…?'

'She's ok,' said Blair.

'It's awful,' said Dee.

Brogan hung his head. The door opened and Mary peered around, her brow furrowing as she took in the assembled group. 'What's going on?'

A good question. Rebekah glanced at Blair and he vaguely looked back but gave nothing away.

'Can we come in?' said Dee.

'Yes, of course… Though there isn't much room.' Mary cast her eyes from person to person.

'I'll wait out here,' said Blair.

'But you should come in,' said Dee, 'it's thanks to you—'

'No, you go, but let Brogan explain. I'll hang about.'

Rebekah hovered uncertainly as Dee shut the door. 'What's happened?'

Blair pressed his lips together and crossed the lane. He jumped onto the embankment and slumped onto a tuft of grass. Rebekah followed and stood, towering above him.

'Are you going to tell me?'

He patted the grass beside him without looking up. She sat, feeling his heat the second she touched the ground; memories of that beautiful night under the stars played in her mind, how safe she'd felt. Why had she ever doubted him? She'd chosen badly before. Was it possible she'd found a good guy only to mark him as bad because she couldn't believe her own judgement? It wasn't him she needed to trust, it was herself. One bad judgement didn't mean everything she did was doomed and all men weren't Seth – especially this one; he was as far from Seth as you could get. Why was she overthinking it and letting paranoia get the better of her?

'Brogan took Mary's money,' he whispered. 'He wanted to get his mum something nice. He knew it wasn't right. He'd already tried to borrow some of it back from his dad to repay her and he wants to get a job.'

'Oh god.' Rebekah pressed her hands to her face.

'Yeah. It's all a bit crap.'

'So, is he confessing?'

'Yup. He's gone to confess and he's agreed on a plan with his mum where he'll work in Mary's garden and do some things around the house too, cleaning and stuff. Hopefully Mary'll be ok with that.'

'And the money?'

'I gave him the money.'

'But where did you—'

'Archie Crichton-Leith, the Ardnish Estate owner, gave it to me. He's a good friend.'

'I would have given it to you, Blair.'

He covered his face with his hands. 'But that makes me feel like shit. You suspected I stole it. How could I ask you after that?'

'I didn't really think that. This time last year, I was up for trial because a man I was dating and trusted framed me for defrauding the company I worked for. It all came back to me and I panicked that something like that was going to happen to me again. And when you asked if I suspected you, I didn't know what to say. I suspected Seth and didn't speak up.'

He dropped his hands and frowned. 'Why didn't you tell me this before?'

'Because I hate it. I'm always afraid people will think there's no smoke without fire. My confidence took a huge knock. I trusted Seth and he used me and played me. He very nearly had me locked up for his crimes.'

'But I would never do that.'

'I know. I wish I'd trusted my judgement but it hasn't always served me well.'

'Yeah, I get it. I just wanted to hold on to a tiny shred of my dignity and not have to ask for money from you. I've already had food, shelter, showers. I'm a total basket case. It's a frigging embarrassment.'

She touched his arm but he didn't look at her.

'Blair,' she said quietly. 'You might not have money, a house or whatever but you have the biggest heart of anyone I've ever met.'

'Do I?'

'Yes.'

'I'm everybody's friend.' He stared towards the sea; its gentle lilt washed up below, reminding Rebekah of the night they'd had their picnic.

She shuffled closer. 'Remember that night I asked you if I could kiss you?'

'Do you think I could ever forget?'

'Well, I have another request.'

He pulled back and raised a hand. 'I can't handle going down that road again.'

'You haven't heard the request yet.'

'Then shoot.' He met her eyes and his gaze blazed a path straight to her soul.

'I'd like you to kiss me again.'

'But I just said—'

She put her finger to his lips. 'Not as a friend. Kiss me from your heart, no rules, no holding back.'

'Why would I do that?'

'Because that's how I want to kiss you. I still want you to be my friend, but I want you to be a whole lot more too.'

'Are you serious?' His lips slowly curled up. 'Even though I'm a penniless wastrel?'

'My heart doesn't care about money.'

'Then come here.' He beckoned her closer and coiled his arm around her, pulling her onto his lap. She straddled him and looped her arms around his shoulders, gazing into his bright eyes. 'I've wanted to do this for months, ever since I saw you,' he said.

'So, what are you waiting for?' Her mouth slid over his and his lips were soft and warm. The gentle touch soothed the ache inside her and she relaxed against his strong chest, mesmerised by the circular rubbing of his broad palms on her back. Her heart beat fast, calling to her, pushing her closer. She wasn't ever going to stop kissing him. Even the distant click of a door and the sound of voices didn't stop them. Someone wolf-whistled and Blair shifted under her. She felt his lips curl up but he didn't stop. She pressed her forehead into his.

'Bekah Ama and Blair the bear, caught out kissing in the open air,' he said and Rebekah burst out laughing.

Chapter Twenty-Four

Blair

Blair started the van's engine and followed the car in front down the ramp towards the gaping jaw of the ferry.

'Dad actually believes Ryan's looking for a job on the island,' said Blair. 'If he gets one, that'll be a first. And how come the little shit is so lucky? I like Archie and I've sworn never to mouth off about him but I wish he wasn't so fucking generous. Ryan doesn't deserve anything.' Archie had given Ryan use of a tiny bothy while he sorted himself out. Blair was pleased Vicky had put her foot down and refused to let him stay with them. It was time he learned to stand on his own two feet; he was bloody lucky so many people were willing to help him.

'You never know,' said Rebekah. 'He's taken the first step.'

'Like us.' Blair smiled at her before bumping the van onto the ship and easing it into place. What Ryan was doing paled into insignificance. Blair had Rebekah and that was much more important. He reached out and put his hand on hers, cementing the connection, and she beamed at him.

'Are you sure your mum won't mind me coming?' Rebekah asked, unclipping her seatbelt.

'It's a bit late now if she does,' he replied. 'Unless you want to hang about on your own in Oban all day.'

'Not really. I want to be with you.'

'I'm happy to hear it, my lover, my friend, because without your company I go round the bend.'

'Oh, Blair.' Rebekah covered her face and laughed.

'Think of all the hours you have of this.'

'You're the gift that keeps on giving.' She looked at him and giggled; he gazed back, then leaned over and kissed her.

Rain and mist didn't prevent them from going outside on the deck. Blair wrapped his arms around Rebekah from behind, nuzzling down her wool collar to kiss her neck. 'Do you know what a novelty this is for me?'

'What? Going on the ferry?'

'No. Having a girlfriend. A real proper actual girlfriend.'

Rebekah laughed and her hair tickled his cheek. He buried himself in it.

He was too drugged up on love pheromones to worry much about the future. They could cross that bridge at some point. Right now, they were happy together. They'd spent their time together wisely, only taking their hands off each other long enough to visit various plots for sale on the island.

When his mum had called one evening to say she was moving out of her house, Blair had thought it some crazy reaction to Ryan leaving to live with his dad. But it might be the ideal solution. With all the threats and chaos of people hunting for Ryan, she'd taken up an offer from her sister to go and live with her.

'I just hope Mum's cleared up. The removal guys might take one look at her stuff and leg it.'

'We'll soon see, I guess,' said Rebekah.

'Well, my aunt Diane has a big garden, so it'll be better for Jet.'

They arrived at his mum's house to see the removal van outside, almost full. Blair felt an uneasy pang. His van had room for some bits and pieces but not a lot.

'Does your aunt have a big house?' asked Rebekah.

'Hmm. Not that big. Hopefully she'll have cleared her garage.'

Blair approached the door not sure if he wanted to see inside, but when his mum let him in, his eyes widened and he nodded his head. 'Hey, Mum. Well done, this is almost clear.'

Jet leaped on him and walloped his leg with his tail before moving onto Rebekah who was just outside the door.

'Jet, come in,' said Lynne, stopping as she reached the door. 'Oh, I didn't know you were here.'

'Yeah.' Blair rubbed his chin. 'We're, eh, together.'

'Oh, Blair.' Lynne raised her hand to her mouth.

'What's wrong?' he asked, afraid to hear the answer.

'Nothing.' She turned and hurried away towards the empty kitchen area.

Rebekah came inside as the two removal men needed in. Blair frowned at her. 'Go to your mum,' she said. 'She looked upset.'

With a heavy sigh, Blair stepped into the kitchen. 'What is it, Mum?'

She turned to look at him, her eyes red and tears welling along the lower lids. 'I just want it to be ok for you.'

'It will be. Well, I obviously can't see the future, but we're ok just now.'

Lynne nodded. 'I'm so glad. I hope this is it. I hope you can settle and have a proper life.'

'Haven't I had a proper life so far?'

She shook her head. 'I'm sorry, I put so much on you. I know what a burden I've been.'

'No, Mum, don't say that.' He closed the gap between them and put his arms around her.

'I've been a terrible mum. But you were always such a good boy.' She shook in his embrace. 'You were the sweetest child; you used to cuddle me when I was sad. You'd rub my back with your wee hand and say, "cuddles never stop and neither does love". It breaks my heart to think about it now.'

'Why?'

'Because they did stop. And it was my fault. Ryan was hard work, the opposite of you. I was worn out running after him, then when your dad hit the bottle – money was tight and he did nothing around the house – I needed you to help me. I forgot about the cuddles and all the nice stuff.'

'You did what you had to do. I knew you loved me. I just didn't always understand why you loved Ryan, but that was selfish.'

'I love you both. But Ryan always needed so much attention, he took up all my time, and I neglected you. I'm so sorry. I hope things work out for you with Rebekah because you deserve to be happy. You really do. You've been the family rock for a long time and it's time for you to get something back.'

Blair held her for a few moments longer, remembering only vaguely those days when he'd been little and carefree, when Lynne had been the mum who took him to the beach to look for shells before Ryan was big enough to find his voice and his attitude.

'Let's finish up here,' he said. 'Everything will work out fine.'

He didn't know that. In fact, nothing was certain. Rebekah was wandering around the small grass area with Jet when he came out. 'Are you ok?' she asked.

'Yeah, it's just my mum.'

'I heard, sorry. It's a small house. Is she all right?' She put her hand on his arm. 'She's so proud of you.'

'Yeah.' Blair ran his hand over his hair. It was a lot to take in. 'I need to ask you something before we do anything else.'

'Anything.'

'I don't feel we can go on like this without some kind of idea of where it's going. So... Where is it going? Where are we going?'

She leaned on his shoulder. 'I'm not sure.'

'We do have a future, don't we?' Blair slipped his arms around her. He'd never tire of the joy that soared through his heart when she was beside him.

'I hope so. I want us to. If you do.'

'Of course I do, but my life is complicated at the best of times. You've had a big adventurous life while I've been dragging my heels trying to get by.' Jet nuzzled into his hand for a pat, apparently annoyed at Blair giving all the attention to Rebekah.

'My life hasn't been that adventurous. It's been hard work most of the time.'

'Yeah, but you've been to university, you've had an important career. What are you doing about that? Don't you want to go back?'

'Isn't what we're planning to do here important enough?' she asked.

'It is for me,' said Blair. 'But is this enough for you? It can't compare with an international aid organisation and life in a big city.'

'How would you know?' Her eyes bored into his, her pupils wide and glossy.

'I wouldn't and that's the point. I've never been anywhere. I've only left Scotland once.'

'Does it matter?'

'Yes. You've been in big business, all over the world.'

'And look what happened to me. The thought of going back terrifies me. I can't go through it again. That's really why I grabbed the chance to go to Fionnphort. I needed to escape. The kind of life I had before was full of stress, watching my back and constant worrying that I was making the right choices.'

'And what you have here is better than that?'

'Infinitely. Because it's not what I have. It's what *we* have. Here, I can do what I love and if I can do it with someone I love, then what could be better?'

Blair tilted his head and smiled. 'That sounds perfect.' He pulled her in for a hug. 'I just hope I'll be enough for you.'

'If anything, you're too good for me.' She inched back and looked at him.

'Maybe we're just right then.'

Rebekah smiled. 'Exactly. This is my chance to walk away, but I'm not going anywhere. I miss Ghana, yes, but I want to try a different life on an island, starting my own charity, however small, and being with you.'

Blair let out a deep breath and rubbed his forehead.

'If it's money you're worried about, then please don't.'

'I won't scrounge off you or have you keep me.'

She smirked. 'No? You'd make a very cuddly pet.'

'Haha.' He crushed her in his arms. 'Bears don't make good pets.'

'Once you're working steadily, we'll sort things out. Why don't you set up a monthly payment to your mum, if that makes you feel better? Tell her that's what she's getting from you and no more. Let her help herself.'

He nodded. 'Ok. But once she's with Diane, hopefully, things will get better. Diane doesn't take any nonsense.'

'Fab,' said Rebekah, then she poked him in the chest. 'And you also need to stop blaming yourself for a mistake you made years ago. You've done more than enough to atone for that. It's time to cut loose.'

'Yes, boss.' He rolled his eyes. 'I can see you're going to be a tougher taskmaster than Calum.'

'You have no idea.'

For a while they cuddled up, watching the removal men put the last pieces in. Blair savoured the soft touch of Rebekah's forehead on his cheek. 'I should get Mum. She's probably still emotional.'

'Because she cares about you.'

'And because she's leaving the house, though she's not even been here a year. She gets attached to things, that's why she's such a hoarder.'

'Time to go,' said Lynne from behind.

Blair turned around as she locked up and they piled into the van. Jet was safely snuggled up in a cage while the three humans squashed along the front seats.

'Well, this is cosy,' said Lynne to Rebekah. 'Hopefully you and I are going to get on, otherwise, it'll make for an awkward journey.'

Blair resigned himself to his mum breaking the ice by telling Rebekah every embarrassing story from his childhood. Diane's house was in Lochgilphead, about an hour south of Oban on a very bendy road. After the stories, they listened to the radio for a bit before pulling up to Diane's bungalow. She was similar in height and looks to her sister, but her hair was shocking red in an angular cut with sharp edges tinged with pure white.

'That's some hairstyle,' Rebekah whispered to Blair as the sisters embraced.

'She's a hairdresser,' he replied. 'She's the one who did my dreads.'

Diane looked up at that moment. 'Blair!' She stretched her arms wide to hug him. 'I see you're looking after your hair. Good boy. And you're his girlfriend?' She turned to Rebekah.

'Rebekah. Pleased to meet you,' she said.

Diane shook her hand and smiled before eyeballing Blair. 'You're punching, young man, definitely punching.'

As Blair rolled open the garage door, ready for the removal men, Rebekah pulled him aside. 'What did she mean by punching?'

Blair grinned. 'That I'm punching above my weight; i.e. you're far too attractive for me.'

Rebekah shook her head. 'What nonsense.'

After Lynne was settled in, Blair and Rebekah took a late lunch. Seeing his mum this relaxed eased any remaining tension in his chest.

When it was time to go, Lynne pulled him in for a hug. 'You're such a wonderful son. I don't deserve someone as good as you. What you've done for this family is more than I can ever say. I love you so much. I wish I'd been there for you instead of you having to be there for me.'

Blair swallowed a lump in his throat and fought back tears. 'No probs, Mum.' He patted her back and held her tight. 'Cuddles never stop, remember.'

'Thank you, son.'

Blair rubbed his eyes dry in the van, as Rebekah said her goodbyes and jumped in beside him. She leaned on his upper arm and squeezed it as he pulled off. 'You really are great.'

*

By the time they arrived back on Mull, they were both yawning. The long drive to Fionnphort seemed to crawl by. Blair yearned to get back and curl up beside his love.

They tumbled out of the van and hightailed it through the driving rain into the croft. Blair started the fire and Rebekah set the kettle to boil. Finally, they were together huddled on the sofa in nightclothes and a blanket with a mug of cocoa each and a blaze tickling their toes.

'Once the winter kicks in, you might regret your decision to stay here,' said Blair.

'Then why don't we take a holiday,' said Rebekah, resting on Blair's shoulder.

'Because I can't afford it,' he said, placing his mug on the end table.

'Well, that's ok, you can pay me back in cooking and other services.' She deposited her mug and drew closer. 'And if we go to Kumasi, we can stay at my father's house, so we won't need accommodation.'

'I'd love to but I—'

'I just said—'

He kissed her to stop her talking, then got carried away devouring her lips. His hands slipped around her waist and he rolled her backwards onto the sofa. She sighed as she moulded into him. He undid the tie on her silky robe and let it fall open, revealing her gorgeous brown skin covered only by a deep crimson, satin nightdress that set his insides alight. 'I was going to say I don't have a passport.'

'Oh, well, we can easily fix that.' She tugged at his pyjama t-shirt and he hauled it over his head. Her smile and the desire in her eyes made him groan.

He dipped in and resumed kissing her. With his thumbs, he gently pushed down her thin straps, placing his lips on the soft skin below her collarbone. She let out a gasp that was music to his ears. 'I'll go anywhere with you, anytime,' he murmured, showering her with love until she was putty in his arms. 'If you're homesick or bored, I promise, I'll travel to the ends of the earth with you. Wherever you go, I go too.'

'Me too,' she whispered, arching into him. 'I've found my missing piece right here.'

Epilogue

Rebekah

Smoke from the barbecue curled around, filling the air with smouldering fumes and the smell of onions.

Rebekah had almost reached her six months on the island and she was staying for good. To celebrate, she was throwing a housewarming party.

'When better to have a barbecue than the beginning of October?' Georgia Rose laughed as Blair introduced her to Rebekah. 'Scottish weather is so hit or miss you can pretty much have them any time here.'

Rebekah shook her hand, feeling an instant warmth from her broad smile and open expression.

'And this is Archie Crichton-Leith,' said Blair with a smirk. 'Sorry, I still can't say your name and be serious.'

'Tell me about it,' said Archie. 'Nice to meet you, Rebekah. Blair's filled me in on a lot of your ideas and I think they're great. We're working on a similar project at Ardnish. We're planning on doing up cottages to provide affordable accommodation for locals.'

'That's fabulous,' said Rebekah.

'Well, we currently rent out the mansion house as a holiday castle but I want to keep the estate cottages for islanders. There's too big a trend for incomers; it's pushing islanders out and losing us valuable people who are forced to live off-island.'

'Archie has it all sussed,' said Georgia.

'Georgia does all the hard work.' He patted her on the back. 'But if you're starting a housing trust, I'd be happy to work alongside you.'

'Yes, that would be fab. We need to have a proper meeting. I'll get something pencilled in.'

Rebekah mingled, watching as Brogan helped out on the barbecue with Blair. They both jumped back as one of the burgers caught fire. 'That's worthy of Rebekah, that one.' Blair looked up and winked.

'Cheeky!' she said.

'You'll never guess what,' said Brogan.

'Best put me out of my misery then,' said Blair. 'What?'

'Troy Copeland is on the island.'

'What? Your favourite footballer?'

'Yes,' said Brogan. 'You know he's still injured, right? Well, I saw this mega fancy Porsche in Tobermory one day; it had blacked-out windows on the sides, but I looked in the front and I saw him. He was in the passenger's seat with his cap pulled down, but I totally know it was him.'

'Wow,' said Blair. 'Maybe he's having a holiday to recover.'

'Maybe. I want to find out where he's staying.'

Rebekah shook her head and turned to Dee. 'Is Brogan ok?'

'Back to himself again,' said Dee. 'He's learned his lesson. I hope he has anyway.'

'Mary's coming along later though she says she's not fond of burgers.' Rebekah laughed but her expression dulled as she looked towards the gate.

'Here comes my best friend,' muttered Dee. 'Though I can't complain, he came to my birthday party and refunded me a month's rent. He must be ill.'

'Oh god.' Rebekah barely heard Dee's words, she was too busy looking at Calum. Why was he here? She hadn't invited him and now he'd turned up. What would he think about being excluded?

He strolled towards her with his hands in his pockets.

'Hi,' she said. 'I, er…'

'I wasn't going to come,' said Calum. 'But when I got Blair's message, I thought it best to make friends. It's a small island when people fall out. I know that better than anyone.'

'Blair's message?'

'He invited me and apologised… Well, I know what it's like to put your foot in it, so, we're all good.'

'Right. And you've heard about us… being together.'

He nodded and gave a little shrug. 'All's fair.'

'You're ok about it?'

'Why wouldn't I be?'

She examined him, hoping to read something from his eyes but his expression was as unreadable as ever.

'Looks like a good do,' he said. 'And how are you, Dee?'

'Oh, ticking along,' she said.

'Good.' He ambled towards the barbecue, struck up a conversation with Blair and they both smiled and joked.

'I don't get him at all,' said Dee. 'Most of the time he's a grumpy arsehole. Then he rocks up here nice as pie, laughing and joking.'

'Me neither,' said Rebekah. And she was done trying to figure him out. She liked him as a business colleague and friend, but he would never touch her heart the way Blair did.

When the food was ready, Rebekah collected Mary and brought her along for her lunch – burger free. Mary took a bench seat and laughed with Autumn and Richard as smoke billowed high from the barbecue. 'I'm calling it the bear-becue,' said Rebekah. 'Blair's my teddy bear.'

Blair beat his chest. 'Ok, wrong animal, but hey.' He chuckled and flipped another burger.

'Aw,' said Autumn. 'You two are so cute. I'm so glad he's found you.'

'It's marvellous,' said Mary. 'And this is a lovely party. All my favourite people in one place.' She patted Autumn's arm and beamed at Rebekah. 'I seem to have collected an unexpected family. All you little gems hidden away and now you've turned up, it's wonderful.'

'I'm so glad you think so.' Rebekah leaned over and kissed Mary's forehead. She spotted Blair heading towards the house. 'Excuse me a sec, I need to tell Blair something.'

She caught up with him, grabbed his hand and pulled him to the back of the house. 'Jeez,' he said, pushing her up against the wall. 'This is a bit risky.'

'Oh, stop it.' She prodded his chest, grinning as he kissed her neck. 'Why did you invite Calum?'

Blair pulled back and shrugged. 'To gloat.'

'Are you serious?'

He laughed and leaned his forehead against hers. 'A bit. But I thought it was best if we made friends. He hasn't said anything bad to you, has he?'

'No. I'm just surprised.'

'I didn't tell you because I knew you'd object. But if everything's cool, then you have two choices.'

'What are you talking about?'

'Either kiss me or get back out there.'

'Maybe we could do both,' she said, sliding her arm around his neck and moving in.

*

245

October had rolled in with a mixed batch of weather but on the day Peter and Cheryl were due to arrive, the sun put in a welcome appearance.

'I've got used to the weather here,' Rebekah said, 'but I suspect it'll be too cold for Mother and definitely for Daddy. I hope they've got warm clothes.'

The croft was completed and looked as good as new. With their differences set aside, Calum was happy to let Rebekah use it as long as she wanted. Ideally, she wanted to purchase it from him but she didn't think he'd allow that. So she contented herself with renting it. Blair had ditched his caravan and moved in. The past couple of months had been a beautiful whirlwind. Blair was a stud in the bedroom and an angel in the kitchen – the perfect combo. With his sleeves rolled up, he kneaded a pizza dough into shape. Rebekah kicked off her shoes, lounged back and watched.

She'd put in an offer for a plot; the first step in her affordable homes project. Through the excitement of waiting for her parents to arrive, she checked her phone every few seconds, not only for news of their whereabouts but for any communications from the estate agents about the sale.

'Have you heard from your mum and dad yet?' Blair asked, chucking a lump of dough into a bowl and covering it with a tea towel.

'They're on the island,' she said. 'But they're probably travelling down the glen where there's no reception.'

'I wonder how Mary feels about all this. It must have been strange enough finding out you were Elsie's granddaughter. What will she make of your mum?'

'I don't know. I hope she's ok.' Rebekah fiddled with her nails and gazed into the dancing flames in the fireplace.

Long ago, had a little girl sat in a bare-walled croft doing the same? What a strange world it must have been for her grandmother, perched on a little wooden stool on the earthen floor. Mary had described in detail how primitive life on the islands had been for many, right up until the war and for some, even after. Conditions had gradually improved for crofters after several acts of parliament, but it was too late for Elsie. She had chosen to see the worst in the situation and kept it a secret for seventy years.

Half an hour later, a car crunched up the lane. Rebekah leapt to the window and peered out. 'They're here.'

Her mother was barely out of the car when Rebekah jumped on her.

'Oh, darling,' her mother said. 'What a welcome.'

'I'm just so happy you're here, both of you.' She ran around and her father wrestled her into a bear hug.

'Yes, it's all worked out for the good,' said Peter, smiling broadly at Cheryl. 'Now, introduce this young man.'

Blair raised his hand as he stood by the gate and Rebekah beckoned him forward. 'So, this is Blair, my partner.' It had taken her thirty-one years but here she was introducing a man to her parents. Finally, she had one she was sure was a keeper. 'Blair, this is my father, Peter, also known as Kobi, Yeboah.'

'And which do you prefer?' asked Blair, shaking his hand.

'Peter is fine, young man.'

'Pleased to meet you, Peter.'

'And this is my mother, Cheryl Quinn.'

Cheryl whispered, 'He's very handsome,' as she whisked past Rebekah and took Blair's hand. 'I'm charmed. You look almost too young for Rebekah.'

Rebekah coughed into her palm; a five-year age gap wasn't too bad. And if it was… Well, tough! Because she was keeping him.

'I think I am,' said Blair.

Cheryl raised her eyebrows. 'Maybe don't tell me. I'm already a bit traumatised by these roads. I thought some of the ones in Ghana were bad.'

'Come, come,' said Peter. 'You can be any age as long as you treat my daughter with the respect she deserves.'

'I will,' said Blair.

'He already does,' said Rebekah.

Cheryl smiled at Rebekah as the men walked ahead. 'Obviously, I don't know him yet, but I love him already. He's gorgeous. I adore his hair. I never thought you'd go for anyone quite so…'

Rebekah waited. 'So what?'

'Rugged, I guess. He's a real hunk. I saw you more as a *man in a suit* type of girl.'

'I tried that and didn't have much success.'

Cheryl took her arm. 'This one has success written all over him.'

The fire crackled and Rebekah tossed off her shoes and warmed her feet as she, Blair and her parents sat around the snug living area, passing the afternoon in pleasant chat. Blair's easy manner had him talking to her parents like he'd always known them.

As the light faded, Blair dragged himself off the floor where he'd been sitting near the hearth and made his way to the kitchen area. He kept chatting as he rolled out the pizzas and put them on to bake. Rebekah put her head to the side and smiled. She could watch this all evening.

'Ok, grab a plate,' he said. 'We'll do this buffet style. The dining table is a bit small for four.'

Cheryl gaped at the food, holding her hand to her chest, then soared around the kitchen island with her arms wide, grabbed Blair and planted a huge kiss on his cheek.

'What was that for?' Blair grinned wide-eyed, halfway through rolling a cutter across the huge pizza.

'Because I was dreading mealtimes. Rebekah is a darling daughter and so clever at lots of things but her cooking is absolutely dire.'

Rebekah threw up her arms. 'I can't deny it. Blair has already seen some of my worst episodes.'

'You're getting better though,' he said. 'You haven't burnt anything in at least a week and I haven't scraped cake mix off the walls for a while.'

They all laughed. The talking lasted into the evening and only when the sun had fully set and Cheryl was yawning, did they decide to call it a day.

Rebekah didn't mind that it was only eight-thirty; she was happy to cuddle up to Blair whenever she could. The bed was cool when she got in, just the way she liked it – Blair warmed her better than any blanket.

'I'm a bit nervous about tomorrow,' she said, rolling into his arms the second he was under the covers.

'It'll be ok,' he said, holding her close. His voice was like a warm balm, soothing away her fears. 'It might be emotional but it's important. Mary thought she had no family left. Now she's discovered you and your mum.'

'I hope we don't disappoint her.'

'You haven't. She likes you, she always has. She's a kind person; she sees the best in people. She adopted Autumn about five seconds after she turned up at her door last year. She forgave Brogan and I suspect she's forgiven your grandmother.'

'I know, she's so sweet.' She'd not only forgiven Brogan; she'd asked him why he hadn't asked for the money. If she'd known why he wanted it, she'd have given it to him and told him to put both their names on the card. 'I guess thirteen year olds act more on hormones and instincts than rational thoughts.'

'They do. And sometimes adults do too.' Blair tumbled her onto the pillow and kissed her softly.

*

The following day, Cheryl and Peter were dressed up like they were going to a formal gathering.

'You know Mary's a humble woman, right? She doesn't have any pretensions or airs and graces. In fact, that's why Grandmother didn't like it here. She thought it was beneath her,' said Rebekah.

'We only dressed like this out of respect,' said Cheryl. 'We owe her that much.'

'She won't mind how you're dressed,' said Blair. 'She sees past things like that.'

'She sounds very wise,' said Peter.

'I guess if you live that long, you learn what's important,' said Blair.

Peter smiled. 'And you're wise yourself, for such a young man.' He clapped him on the shoulders.

'How young do you think I am?'

'I really don't want to know.' said Cheryl, 'I'm nervous enough already.'

Blair lifted his eyebrows and raised his palms at Rebekah, silently asking her what she'd told them. She winked back.

Just before ten, they set off along the lane to Mary's croft. Rebekah knocked and stepped back to wait. Mary's fluffy head looked around the door. 'In you come, I've been waiting.'

With only three armchairs in the living room, Blair and Peter took the wooden chairs from the table by the window and set them close to the circle of armchairs by the fire. Rebekah chewed on her lip, and her leg twitched slightly.

Mary sat on her usual seat beside her little mahogany occasional table, set with a tray containing her essentials: her magazine, a pen, paper, the TV guide and remote control. After the introductions, she rested back in her chair. 'This has been an interesting few months. I remember telling Blair here not so long ago that I was the last of my family. Now I find out I have relatives when I least expected it.'

'Mary, I hope you believe us,' said Rebekah. 'If I was in your position, I'd be sceptical. I wouldn't like you to think we're trying to con you. You know we don't want anything from you.'

'I believe you,' said Mary. 'I saw the shock when I told you about Elsie. And I know you don't want anything from me.' She touched a little brooch on her chest. 'I've always wondered who I should leave the house to. I suppose one day I won't be here anymore.'

'Don't say that,' said Rebekah.

'It's true. And now I've met you, it makes things clearer.'

'I don't want you to leave it to us,' said Rebekah. 'We don't deserve it.'

'I wouldn't say that. You're a good, kind girl.' Her smile filled the room, lightening Rebekah's heart. 'But what I was actually wondering was if I could leave it to your charity? I'd like it to go back to the island.'

Rebekah put her hand to her mouth to hold back a sudden wave of tears. 'Oh, Mary, that's such a wonderful thing to do. Once we're up and running, if you want to do that, I'd be so grateful. And someone on the island will benefit.'

Mary nodded, still smoothing the little brooch with her fingertips. Rebekah glanced at Blair. The corners of his mouth turned up and he winked. 'Mary, you're a treasure.'

'Oh, nonsense. You're such a charmer. But I'm relieved to have sorted the house.' Her gaze roamed over Cheryl. 'You look very like Elsie. I can see the likeness in your eyes.'

Cheryl blinked and smiled nervously. 'I know my mother wasn't pleasant to you, but I brought some photos. I understand if you don't want to see them but I wondered... Maybe if you were curious.'

'Oh, I am. And I found one for you.' She opened up her magazine and pulled out a small brown and white picture and passed it to Rebekah who held it between her and her mother. 'That's us outside the croft. It was pulled down to build this place.'

Rebekah looked closely and knew it was the same girl in the photograph with the handwritten note that had seemed like the start to a mystery story. Maybe it had been just that and Rebekah had solved it. Elsie and Mull hadn't been compatible. Just as Elsie hadn't thought Cheryl was compatible with Peter or Ghana. For someone who'd been a rock in Rebekah's formative years, something in her grandmother's mind had been crooked. For years, Cheryl had given up her husband to assuage her mother. Now both she and Rebekah were happy with their partners. All the pieces had finally fallen into place.

Blair reached out and grasped Rebekah's fingers as Cheryl shifted over to kneel by Mary's chair and show her the pictures.

'This is great, isn't it?' he whispered. 'It's like some kind of healing session.'

Rebekah nodded.

They stayed with Mary all morning, until she looked ready for a nap. 'I'll bring some lunch along if you like,' said Blair before they left.

'You're an angel,' she said, then took Rebekah's hand. 'And so are you. You turned up unexpectedly, you've taken our community to heart and you're working wonders for us.'

'Not really.'

'Yes, really,' said Blair and Mary together. They all laughed. As they walked back down the lane, Rebekah's phone rumbled.

'Oh my god,' she squealed. 'I got it.' With a shaky hand, she turned the phone to Blair, showing him an email. 'I got the land. We can build the first house.'

Blair threw his arms around her. 'I love you,' he said.

Happy tears leaked from the corners of her eyes. 'Oh, Blair. I love you too. And I love this island and I love what we're planning to do here.'

'Me too. You're the best thing that's ever happened to me.'

She held him as tight as she could

'Is everything all right?' asked Peter from ahead.

'Everything's perfect,' answered Rebekah. 'Just perfect.'

The End

Share the Love!

If you enjoyed reading this book, then please share your reviews online.

Leaving reviews is a perfect way to support authors and helps books reach more readers.

So please review and share!

Let me know what you think.

About the author

I'm a writer, mummy, wife and chocolate eater (in any order you care to choose). I live in highland Perthshire in a little house close to the woods where I often see red squirrels, deer and other such tremendously Scottish wildlife... Though not normally haggises or even men in kilts!

It's my absolute pleasure to be able to bring the Scottish Island Escapes series to you and I hope you love reading the stories as much as I enjoy writing them. Writing is an escapist joy for me and I adore disappearing into my imagination and returning with a new story to tell.

If you want to keep up with what's coming next or learn more about any of the books or the series, then be sure to visit my website. I look forward to seeing you there.

www.margaretamatt.com

Acknowledgements

Thanks goes to my adorable husband for supporting my dreams and putting up with my writing talk 24/7. Also to my son, whose interest in my writing always makes me smile. It's precious to know I've passed the bug to him – he's currently writing his own fantasy novel and instruction books on how to build Lego!

Throughout the writing process, I have gleaned help from many sources and met some fabulous people. I'd like to give a special mention to Stéphanie Ronckier, my beta reader extraordinaire. Stéphanie's continued support with my writing is invaluable and I love the fact that I need someone French to correct my grammar! Stéphanie, you rock. To my fellow authors, Evie Alexander and Lyndsey Gallagher – you girls are the best! I love it that you always have my back and are there to help when I need you.

Also, a huge thanks to my editor, Aimee Walker, at Aimee Walker Editorial Services for her excellent work on my novels and for answering all my mad questions. Thank you so much, Aimee!

A Special Mention

A huge thank you to my friend, Lyn Williamson, who was instrumental in bringing this book about. Lyn has helped me from the beginning of my writing career, always encouraging me and supporting me with her wise words. I thought she might like to invent a character for one of the books, my idea being that it would be a minor character I could slot into a story, but no, Lyn came back with the fully-fledged character of Rebekah, waiting for a story of her own!

Lyn's life in Ghana provided a backdrop to Rebekah's past and childhood.

I really hope I've done your creation justice in this book, Lyn! And thank you so much!

More Books by Margaret Amatt

Scottish Island Escapes

Season 1
A Winter Haven
A Spring Retreat
A Summer Sanctuary
An Autumn Hideaway
A Christmas Bluff
Season 2
A Flight of Fancy
A Hidden Gem
A Striking Result
A Perfect Discovery
A Festive Surprise

Free Hugs & Old-Fashioned Kisses

Do you ever get one of those days when you just fancy snuggling up? Then this captivating short story is for you!

And what's more, it's free when you sign up to my newsletter.

Meet Livvi, a girl who just needs a hug. And Jakob, a guy who doesn't go about hugging random strangers. But what if he makes an exception, just this once?

Make yourself a hot chocolate, sign up to my newsletter and enjoy!

A short story only available to newsletter subscribers.

Sign up at
www.margaretamatt.com

A Winter Haven

She was the one that got away. Now she's back.

Career-driven Robyn Sherratt returns to her childhood home on the Scottish Isle of Mull, hoping to build bridges with her estranged family. She discovers her mother struggling to run the family hotel. When an old flame turns up, memories come back to bite, nibbling into Robyn's fragile heart.

Carl Hansen, known as The Fixer, abandoned city life for peace and tranquillity. Swapping his office for a log cabin, he mends people's broken treasures. He can fix anything, except himself. When forced to work on hotel renovations with Robyn, the girl he lost twelve years ago, his quiet life is sent spinning.

Carl would like nothing more than to piece together the shattered shards of Robyn's heart. But can she trust him? What can a broken man like him offer a successful woman like her?

A Spring Retreat

She's gritty, he's determined. Who will back down first?

When spirited islander Beth McGregor learns of plans to build a road through the family farm, she sets out to stop it. But she's thrown off course by the charming and handsome project manager. Sparks fly, sending Beth into a spiral of confusion. Guys are fine as friends. Nothing else.

Murray Henderson has finally found a place to retreat from the past with what seems like a straightforward job. But he hasn't reckoned on the stubbornness of the locals, especially the hot-headed and attractive Beth.

As they battle together over the proposed road, attraction blooms. Murray strives to discover the real Beth; what secrets lie behind the tough façade? Can a regular farm girl like her measure up to Murray's impeccable standards, and perhaps find something she didn't know she was looking for?

A Summer Sanctuary

She's about to discover the one place he wants to keep secret

Five years ago, Island girl Kirsten McGregor broke the company rules. Now, she has the keys to the Hidden Mull tour bus and is ready to take on the task of running the business. But another tour has arrived. The competition is bad enough but when she recognises the rival tour operator, her plans are upended.

Former jet pilot Fraser Bell has made his share of mistakes. What better place to hide and regroup than the place he grew to love as a boy? With great enthusiasm, he launches into his new tour business, until old-flame Kirsten shows up and sends his world plummeting.

Kirsten may know all the island's secrets, but what she can't work out is Fraser. With tension simmering, Kirsten and Fraser's attraction increases. What if they both made a mistake before? Is one of them about to make an even bigger one now?

An Autumn Hideaway

She went looking for someone, but it wasn't him.

After a string of disappointments for chirpy city girl Autumn, discovering her notoriously unstable mother has run off again is the last straw. When Autumn learns her mother's last known whereabouts was a remote Scottish Island, she makes the rash decision to go searching for her.

Taciturn islander Richard has his reasons for choosing the remote Isle of Mull as home. He's on a deadline and doesn't need any complications or company. But everything changes after a chance encounter with Autumn.

Autumn chips away at Richard's reserve until his carefully constructed walls start to crumble. But Autumn's just a passing visitor and Richard has no plans to leave. Will they realise, before it's too late, that what they've been searching for isn't necessarily what's missing?

A Christmas Bluff

She's about to trespass all over his Christmas.

Artist and photographer Georgia Rose has spent two carefree years on the Isle of Mull and is looking forward to a quiet Christmas... Until she discovers her family is about to descend upon her, along with her past.

Aloof aristocrat Archie Crichton-Leith has let out his island mansion to a large party from the mainland. They're expecting a castle for Christmas, not an outdated old pile, and he's in trouble.

When Georgia turns up with an irresistible smile and an offer he can't refuse, he's wary, but he needs her help.

As Georgia weaves her festive charms around the house, they start to work on Archie too. And the spell extends both ways. But falling in love was never part of the deal. Can the magic outlast Christmas when he's been conned before and she has a secret that could ruin everything?

A Flight of Fancy

She's masquerading as her twin, pretending to be his

girlfriend, while really just being herself.

After years of being cooped up by her movie star family, Taylor Rousse is desperate to escape. Having a Hollywood actress as a twin is about all Taylor can say for herself, but when she's let down by her sister for the umpteenth time, she decides now is the time for action.

Pilot Magnus Hansen is heading back to his family home on the Isle of Mull for his brother's wedding and he's not looking forward to showing up single. The eldest of three brothers shouldn't be the last married – no matter how often he tells himself he's not the marrying type.

On his way, Magnus crashes into a former fling. She's a Hollywood star looking for an escape and they strike a deal: he's her ticket to a week of peace; she's his new date. Except Taylor isn't who he thinks she is. When she and Magnus start to fall for each other, their double deception threatens to blow up in their faces and shatter everything that might have been.

A Hidden Gem

She has a secret past. He has an uncertain future.

Together, can they unlock them both?

After being framed for embezzlement by her ex, career-driven Rebekah needs a break to nurse her broken heart and wounded soul. When her grandmother dies, leaving her a precious necklace and a mysterious note, she sets out to unravel a family secret that's been hidden for over sixty years.

Blair's lived all his life on the Isle of Mull. He's everybody's friend – with or without the benefits – but at night he goes home alone. When Rebekah arrives, he's instantly attracted to her, but she's way out of his league. He needs to keep a stopper on his feelings or risk losing her friendship.

As Rebekah's quest continues, she's rocked by unexpected feelings for her new friend. Can she trust her heart as much as she trusts Blair? And can he be more than just a friend? Perhaps the truth isn't the only thing waiting to be found.

A Striking Result

She's about to tackle everything he's trying to hide.

When unlucky-in-love Carys McTeague is offered the job of caring for an injured footballer, she goes for it even though it's far removed from the world she's used to.

Scottish football hero Troy Copeland is at the centre of a media storm after a serious accident left him with career-threatening injuries and his fiancée dumped him for a teammate. With a little persuasion from Carys, he flees to the remote Isle of Mull to escape and recuperate.

On Mull, Carys reconnects with someone unexpected from her past and starts to fall in love with the island – and Troy. But nothing lasts forever. Carys has been abandoned more than once and as soon as Troy's recovered, he'll leave like everyone else.

Troy's smitten by Carys but has a career to preserve. Will he realise he's been chasing the wrong goal before he loses the love of his life?

A Perfect Discovery

To find love, they need to dig deep.

Kind-hearted archaeologist Rhona Lamond returns home to the Isle of Mull after her precious research is stolen, feeling lost and frustrated. When an island project comes up, it tugs at Rhona's soul and she's desperate to take it on. But there's a major problem.

Property developer Calum Matheson has a longstanding feud with the Lamond family. After a plot of land he owns is discovered to be a site of historical importance, his plans are thrown into disarray and building work put on hold.

Calum doesn't think things can get any worse, until archaeologist Rhona turns up. Not only is she a Lamond, but she's all grown up, and even stubbornly unromantic Calum can't fail to notice her – or the effect she has on him.

Their attraction ignites but how can they overcome years of hate between their families? Both must decide what's more important, family or love.

A Festive Surprise

She can't abide Christmas. He's not sure what it's all about. Together they're in for a festive surprise.

Ambitious software developer Holly may have a festive name but the connection ends there. She despises the holiday season and decides to flee to the remote island of Mull in a bid to escape from it.

Syrian refugee Farid has made a new home in Scotland but he's lonely. Understanding Nessie and Irn Bru is one thing, but when glittery reindeer and tinsel hit the shelves, he's completely bemused. Determined to understand a new culture, he asks his new neighbour to educate him on all things Christmas.

When Holly reluctantly agrees, he realises there's more to her hatred of mince pies and mulled wine than meets the eye. Farid makes it his mission to inject some joy into Hollys' life but falling for her is an unexpected gift that was never on his list.

As their attraction sparkles, can Christmas work its magic on Holly and Farid, or will their spark fizzle out with the end of December

9 781914 575860